SEA DEVIL

BOOK ONE

A DELILAH DUFFY MYSTERY

JESSICA SHERRY

Published by Jessica Sherry

www.jessicasherry.com

Copyright © 2015 Jessica Sherry

2nd Edition

ISBN: 978-0-9962941-0-2

Mystery

To Joe, the hero of my story

Acknowledgements

*Thanks to Joe, Ethan, and Abby for calling
me a writer, even when I couldn't.*

*Thanks to my mom and dad, who took me to church to find God
and to the beach to get to know him better.*

Chapter One

TURTLES

IGHWAY TWELVE STRETCHED in front of me, dotted with tourist traffic. Though not a tourist, technically, I'd made two touristy mistakes so far: traveling to Tipee Island on a Saturday morning in June along with hordes of vacationers and leaving the top down on my Jeep Wrangler so I'd be beachy-cool. The sun was planting its kisses in interesting places, burning the backs of my ears, the bridge of my nose, and even my cleavage—what little there was.

My name's Delilah Duffy, and making mistakes is kind of my thing. Not just the dumb, bumbling Clark Griswold or Amelia Bedelia variety either. But mistakes that shake your whole world. I needed a place where my mistakes wouldn't catch up with me, a place to start over. Course, sitting still in traffic, my journey stalled in frustration.

I inhaled the salty air, and gave Willie, my golden Lab, a playful rub on his head. We'd been racing through tiny North Carolina villages and beachy meccas for over an hour only to stop dead in traffic less than a mile from the prize—Tipee Island. To our left, a wall of sand blocked the ocean, a white sheet over a masterpiece. To the right, a shield of thickets, ironed down by the ocean's winds, hid the Cape Fear. The island treasures were being kept from us.

Willie groaned and flashed me his begging eyes. His paw nudged my arm. He had to go.

Sand flew back in my face as Willie bounded up the dune.

"Hold on, Willie." Willie couldn't wait. He pulled me to the top and quickly marked his territory among the sea oats.

A sign declared the beach a sanctuary for nesting sea turtles: loggerheads, leatherbacks, and green turtles are a few of the endangered turtles that nest there. At night, female turtles trek up the beach, dig their holes, and bury over one hundred eggs each. Then they skedaddle back to the sea. Even the turtles are tourists here.

Unlike the turtles and the traffic, tourism wasn't for me. I'd turned in the keys to my one-bedroom apartment and teaching career to become an islander and bookstore manager—a brave new world to replace the one I'd ruined. Failing here'd be devastating. It'd mean moving back home with my parents and finding yet another career, the third in a short time. I loved teaching but couldn't go back to it again. Besides, I'd no idea what else I'd do, except work at *Ruby Tuesday* because I'm a sucker for a good salad bar.

Short wooden fences marked off the underground turtle nests. Willie started digging. I tugged him away. He accepted the admonishment, sniffed the air, and took off on a new mission. I gave him the leeway he needed as he did his other business.

The ocean called to me like an old friend, but I don't swim. When I was six years old, I nearly drowned. I tripped into a tarp-covered pool at a friend's house, sinking into the water while tangled in the plastic. Sometimes, I still feel myself choking, wanting air but not finding it. That day, my friend's dad brought me back to life, but I lost two other things: my adventurous spirit, and my mother's permission to go to friends' houses.

Still, Dad insisted on teaching me how to swim. Born and raised on Tipee Island, he couldn't stand his daughter being anything less than a great swimmer. My accident only convinced him more. I was seven when I suffered months of his torturous lessons, making it the worst summer of my life.

I swam again the summer I was sixteen—the best summer of my life. I spent two glorious months with my grandparents, shadowing my Aunt Candy. I wanted to be just like her—beautiful, smart, sophisticated. Six years older, she took me to parties, forced me to wear my first bikini, let me try my first beer, and gave me the confidence to go after what I wanted. I swam once the entire visit for the attention of a gorgeous boy. It'd been like a baptism.

The appeal of swimming isn't lost on me, but submerging into what you can't see is frightening, like walking into a strange black room. Anything could be in there, waiting, lurking. The poet Dylan Thomas wrote, *"Do not go gentle into that good night"* about death. He could've meant dark water, too. Tidal wave nightmares, a double serving of water and darkness, swallowing me up have haunted me for years, exasperating my fears. My stomach mimicked the rough chop of the waves just thinking about it.

Willie barked in my direction. I reached out to give him some reassuring pets.

"Ma'am?" a voice said behind me.

I jumped and let out a wimpy scream.

My heart pounded to see a police officer on the dune with me. His sunglasses reflected my surprised face, like a fun house mirror. I wished I'd worn more make-up.

"Everything alright, ma'am?"

"Of course. Sharing a little ocean moment with Willie, that's all. Nothing wrong with that, right?"

"No, but you have two other problems." He pointed to the road below us. Traffic moved. Car horns blared. Angry faces shot up at me. My Jeep blocked a whole line of hot-tempered tourists.

"Oh, no!" I started my descent back down the hill, but the officer stopped me.

"Hold on. I said two problems. You have to clean up your dog's mess."

"Seriously?"

"Yes, ma'am."

"I'm holding up traffic. Isn't the poop the lesser of two evils here?"

"Move your vehicle onto the shoulder." He took Willie's leash from my hand. "Then come back to clean up the mess and retrieve your animal."

I flushed with embarrassment and frustration. No time to argue. I huffed and skirted down the hillside. Halfway down, I tumbled, skidding the rest of the way on my bottom. Sand ended up in some uncomfortable places. I tried shaking it out while passing by the flashing Dodge Charger. Another policeman laughed and shook his head as I scooted by.

I edged the Jeep onto the sandy shoulder. I got back out and waited to cross the street as the traffic moved past me. They honked their horns and gave me plenty of stink-eyes but wouldn't let me cross back over. I couldn't blame them for holding me up when I'd done the same to them. Amused, the second officer finally stepped out, stopping the angry wave of traffic with one authoritative hand, so I could cross and climb the sand mountain again.

"One problem solved. Now on to number two." The officer holding Willie's leash grinned. I huffed, my hands finding my hips like my mother does when she's lecturing me, which is fairly often considering I'm twenty-nine.

"I have nothing to clean up the number two with. Can't I just bury it? He had to go. There was nothing I could do."

"The law states that pet owners must collect and dispose of waste properly to avoid citation." He peered at me over the rim of his sunglasses.

Crystal blue eyes, so light they're almost not even blue. A sudden wave of recognition hit me.

My mouth dried up. Still, I managed, "How m-much is the citation?"

He smiled. "Fifty dollars."

I knew him. He was the gorgeous boy. His name tag confirmed it. *S. Teague.* Thirteen years ago, I'd spent a summer pining after Sam Teague, and years healing from his rejection. The urge to kick him in the shins and take off running popped into my mind almost simultaneously with the wish to jump into his arms and let him carry me off to, well, wherever he wanted. I needed a serious mental makeover. Instead, I closed my eyes, thinking *please don't remember me... please don't remember me.*

He said, "A plastic bag would work. Do you have one?"

"No. My whole life is in that Jeep, and believe me, I weeded out everything disposable."

"I have one, unless you prefer the citation?"

I rolled my eyes and shook my head. He handed me the leash and returned to his police car. Willie panted, smiling up at me as if we'd made a new friend.

"You're a sorry judge of character, Willie."

When Teague returned with the bag, I snatched it out of his hand and did my duty. "Gosh, things must be pretty boring on Tipee Island for you guys to bother with small-time offenders like Willie and me."

"It's no bother. Worth it to say hello to an old friend. It's good to see you, Delilah."

I didn't know what to say, but stood there staring at him, mouth agape and eyebrows pinched.

He pulled off his sunglasses. "You, um, haven't forgotten me. Have you?"

I wanted to say, *"Yes, I've totally forgotten you."* Or play it cool and tell him he looked vaguely familiar, like I'd seen him on a wanted poster somewhere. But I couldn't do either of those things.

In nervous situations, my mouth usually gushes like a geyser. I can't shut up. But something about him stunned me silent. He'd changed over the years. Grown taller, broader, more handsome. His blond hair was trimmed short, not the shaggy surfer look I remembered. Still, the smile was the same. I smiled back.

I cleared my throat. "Course, I remember. You gave me my only crash course in surfing. That's not easy to forget."

"You aren't either. I'm glad you're back, though it'll be an uphill battle for you."

My heart skidded. "What do you mean?"

"Facing off against your aunts and the whole town. Reopening Beach Read won't be easy." I gave him a puzzled look, confused why he knew my plans and that there was some kind of perceived controversy about them. "Don't worry. As long as you go in charging, even uphill battles can be won." He smiled encouragingly.

"You've lost me. I don't know what—"

"Yo, Teague," his partner called. "We're up!"

Teague took a step down the dune but stopped and extended his hand. "Need help down?"

The scratchy grains of sand in my underwear urged me to accept. I wanted it to feel awkward, taking his hand, but strangely, it didn't. I reminded myself that as a police officer, this kind of thing—getting cats out of trees; helping young ladies and their dogs down sand dunes—was his job. That's why it felt so normal.

Safely at the bottom, I snatched my hand away. "Thanks."

He dashed to the passenger side of the police car. "Where're we headed?"

"111 Starfish," his partner answered.

"Wait! That's where I'm going. That's the store."

"Meet you there." Teague ducked into the passenger seat and the Charger raced away as if it were the only car on the road.

Willie and I jumped into the Jeep. I fumbled with the keys.

"Looks like the battle's started without us, Willie. Better start charging." I peeled off the shoulder, earning a well-deserved honk from the tourist I cut off. I clenched and unclenched the steering wheel.

"*Welcome to Tipee Island! We tipee our hats to ya'll!*" read the sign as I entered town. I huffed. Traffic. Teague. Tacky puns. Plus, whatever police situation awaited me—if it wasn't all over and done with by the time I arrived, slow tourists. Maybe the female turtles had the right idea.

Chapter Two
STARFISH

BEACH READ BOOKS, Gifts and More capped off a short strip of stores like an exclamation point, and likewise, it was the center of a commotion. I jerked the Jeep into the side lot behind Aunt Candy's convertible, eyeing what looked like dark-colored streamers hanging limply from the store's blue and white awning.

Only they weren't streamers.

Dead snakes. Their bodies drooped over the sidewalk and blood drizzled onto the concrete in polka dots. Snakes littered the light fixtures, even the doorknob. Dozens of gross snake bodies spanning types and sizes.

It looked like a demon's welcome home party. Medusa and her snaky hair, Voldemort's evil pet, and the devil in the Garden of Eden all came to mind, along with words from Tolkien's *The Lord of the Rings.*

"*There is some new devilry here, devised for our welcome,*" I recited softly.

"So, you know about the curse?" Teague's partner Officer Williams asked.

"Actually, I was quoting Tolkien. What curse?"

No one answered, spellbound by dead snakes. Some snakes were in later stages of decay with bones emerging from their slimy bodies. Hanging upside down, one snake's skull poked through its head. A rotten death smell joined the sea breezes, turning my stomach.

"Found it like this," Candy said. "You're late, by the way."

"Sorry, I had a poop issue."

"Your stomach again?"

"Not me. Willie. This is so creepy and weird. Why would anyone do this?"

Williams said, "Used to hang dead snakes from trees to bring rain."

Teague shook his head. "I'll call it in. We'll need pictures."

Williams pushed back the growing crowd and sectioned off the sidewalk with yellow crime scene tape. Teague made calls into his walkie-talkie and filled out paperwork on a clipboard. I stood with Candy, feeling helpless, creeped out and downright homesick, for no home in particular.

Candy texted away as fast as her tangerine fingernails would let her. My shoulders slumped. The warm welcome I'd hoped for— and needed—vanished in her apathy along with the quiet, new start I'd envisioned.

The street sign at the corner of Starfish Drive turned my attention away from the snake circus. Starfish are hearty sea critters that don't give up easily, even when torn to pieces. If starfish could regenerate themselves from nearly nothing, so could I. Right?

Beyond the vandalism and the covered-up windows, I saw the store I remembered. The plywood covering the display windows detracted from its charm, as did the *For Sale or Lease* sign. But the store's sign made me smile. Perched above the blue and white awning, it was in the shape of a frothy blue wave and read: *Beach Read Books, Gifts, and More.*

I'd fallen in love with two things the summer I was sixteen—the gorgeous boy, turned gorgeous but bothersome cop, and books. Only one love was short-lived.

The first time I'd come in to Beach Read that summer, Great Aunt Laura, with her gorgeous red hair and beautifully freckled skin, told me I'd blossomed, and reminded her of Tennyson's *Lady of Shalott.* I'd had no idea what she was talking about then. Later, I guessed it was because of my pale skin, long, wavy brown hair, and that I'd been sequestered in a tower all my life—my mother's a tad overprotective. It was as true then as it was today—*I am half sick of shadows,* like the poem says.

Great Aunt Laura shoved books at me like they were bricks of gold. *Wuthering Heights* was the first one. No wonder I fell in love that summer, and no wonder it ended badly.

Teague asked, "Any idea why someone might—"

"People are sickos," Candy said.

"It's the curse." In his fifties, Officer Williams had an air of authority about him. Bald up top, he wore a gray goatee that stood out like a zebra stripe against his dark skin.

"Are you kidding?" I huffed.

"Nope." He shook his head. "Place has been a tobacco shop, clothing store, dollar store. All bankrupt before Laura Duffy turned it into a bookstore. Course we know what happened to her."

"Aunt Laura died of cancer." It hurt to say the words even though it'd happened over ten years ago.

"I know," Williams said, as if I'd made his point for him. I rolled my eyes. "Place's been empty ever since for a reason and now this. Looks like snakes slithered up from hell."

The crowd agreed with Officer Williams. An old lady gasped. A mother gathered her two young children closer. A grown man visibly shivered. I sighed.

"This was probably the action of bored, albeit morbid, teenagers, not the result of any curse, Officer Williams. But come to think of it, the curse of the abandoned bookstore... I think I saw that on an episode of *Scooby-Doo* once."

Teague chuckled, but I amused no one else.

Candy tapped her heel against the concrete. "He's not kiddin', Delilah. Why do you think it's sat empty for so long? I heard there's a band of pirates buried underneath here. That's why this place is so unlucky."

Williams nodded. "That'd make sense."

"Ooh, pirates," a woman from the crowd cooed. A young boy clapped excitedly.

"Nonsense!" My stomach churned.

Candy rolled her eyes. "Well, you may not believe it, Delilah, but everyone else on the island does."

"Everyone?" I surveyed the crowd. They were awestruck.

"Not everyone." Teague glanced up from his clipboard. His uphill battle remark rang in my ears.

"Everyone." Candy flicked her long blond hair. "Clark'll love this for the paper. The police photographer, Billy Mott, also works for Clark, you know." Candy giggled. I cringed. My uncle, Clark Duffy, owned and edited *The Tipee Island Gazette*.

When I decided to reopen the bookstore, my father—a business owner himself—had boatloads of advice. He said, "*Bean,*" because that's what he calls me. When I was a toddler, I stuck green beans up my nose and had to be taken to the emergency room to get them removed. Ever since, he's called me Bean. "*Bean, when you run a business, you have to know what customers need and want, even when they don't.*"

"Wait!" I called out. The officers looked up. "Is it too late to call you guys off?"

"What do you mean?" Teague asked.

"I don't want to press any charges. I don't want the

photographer here. Can you tell him not to come?"

Candy flashed me a bothered look. "What the hell are you doing?"

"Perception is everything," I said. "If this is in the newspaper, then people'll think this stupid curse thing is true. Won't be good for business."

Teague stopped writing, but said, "It's not about business. It's about crime."

"Look, no damage has been done. Vandalism is only a misdemeanor. It's not like someone'll get in any real trouble over this, anyway."

With hands on her hips, Candy asked, "How d'you know that?"

I shrugged. "Working with teenagers for seven years."

Williams folded his bulky arms over his chest. "What about cruelty to animals?"

I ducked under the police tape and eased over to the dead snake museum, pointing to their carcasses. "These snakes weren't killed for this. That black snake looks like road kill the way it's flattened out in the midsection. Those two copperheads have been dead for several days. And, look at that water moccasin. It's got a fish stuck in its mouth. Is that a catfish?"

Everyone looked, but no one responded.

"Well, it choked on the catfish, stupid snake. It bit off more than it could chew." I held up a pointed finger. "That's a tobacco idiom. Comes from putting too much tobacco in your mouth at once." With a sigh, I went on, "Now that my nerd-dom is firmly established, these snakes died of natural causes and were collected for my welcome present. Besides, is your department prepared to do necropsies on these snakes just to pin a cruelty to animals charge on someone?"

Teague chuckled. "Ah, no. Probably not."

A flash lit up my face. Billy Mott'd slipped into the mix of people, apparently keen to get some candid shots of me with the snakes.

"Sorry, Delilah," Teague said. "We have to file a report, just in case."

"In case of what?"

"In case it happens again."

Again? My shoulders slumped. I still couldn't believe it'd happened a first time.

"Officer Teague!" A young blond pushed her way through the crowd and snapped her fingers when she didn't get Teague's attention.

Williams scratched his head. "Oh, Lord."

"Oh, my lands!" She eyed the snakes with a hand to her heart. "What's going on? I was headin' to work and saw all the commotion. Are you alright?"

"Mandy, everything's fine." Teague met her at the caution tape.

Candy leaned toward me. "That's Mandy Davis. She's a waitress at The Crab Shack and a Pilates instructor. That girl can bend like a paperclip. They've been datin' for a while."

"So? I don't care." Really, I didn't even though Mandy was annoyingly pretty and perky, like a cheerleader. "I've got to stop this freak show and get these snakes down. Can you help, Candy?"

Candy rolled her eyes and clickety-clacked her heels across the sidewalk. She got something from her car, clopped back over, and handed me a set of keys. "I'm outta here. Got things to do. Besides, I'll be a monkey's uncle before I'm settin' one pretty toe in that place. Probably infested with pythons."

I shook my head. "Highly unlikely. Pythons aren't indigenous to North Carolina."

Candy cast me a stony glare. Then she shook her head, making all her gold, beach-themed jewelry jingle. Her refusal to help wasn't a surprise. Candy wasn't the type to get dirty, ever. Her tangerine dress, matching mani-pedi, and perfectly pieced hair were all testimony to that. "Be at Mom's for dinner, though. She's expectin' you."

Candy peeled out in her convertible. My shoulders sagged. The snake hazing had marred our reunion, though we really hadn't been close since we were teenagers. The beach, music, boys, parties—Candy'd been the perfect summer hostess in those days.

Teague interrupted my daydream with a heavy-duty trash bag and latex gloves.

"Mott's done. You're free to discard the remains. Williams and I can stay until we get a call."

With a sigh, I said, "Thanks."

Teague held out his hand, like he'd done on the dune. I took it. I'm an idiot.

"The keys?" A smile eased over his face. "If you'd like me to check inside the building."

"Course." Face flushing, I snatched my hand away and gave him the keys. "I wasn't thinking or maybe I was thinking too much. Maybe this whole thing's a mistake. I'm flustered, grossed out, and it's a big day for me, you know. I'm sorry." I clamped my lips shut.

"It's okay, Delilah."

I let out a puffy-cheeked sigh as he headed to the front door. Officer Williams opted for crowd control, saying something about not wanting to get involved with curses.

I stared up at the disgusting display. The slimy bodies reeked and oozed. Their skins peeled away from their bones, almost melting under the hot June sun. I pulled the gloves on and got under the first black snake, hanging four feet down from the metal bar of the awning. I clumsily held the bag under the body one-handed and grabbed onto the snake with the other. With a gentle pull, the snake came down. The crowd gasped. The snake brushed my neck. I screamed. Officer Williams laughed.

Still, the snake landed safely in the trash bag. The crowd clapped. I curtsied.

"Only about twenty more to go." Williams chuckled.

"Thanks for all your protection and service, Officer Williams."

"No problem."

Teague came up behind me, forcing me to jump—again. My bag slapped against the concrete, and I almost used my gloved hand to brush the hair away from my eyes. Almost.

Teague smirked. "You okay? I didn't mean to—"

"How's the inside?" I asked.

"Fine. A mess, but it's not vandalized."

"Okay. Messes, I can handle."

"I didn't see any snakes. I'll check the third floor. The entrance to the apartment is around back, right?"

"Yes," I said. Teague rounded the building while I returned to my clean-up work.

The fourth snake tumbled grossly into the trash bag, slapping into the other snake bodies, when Teague returned.

"Come with me," he said. My stomach knotted.

"Oh, no." I left my death bag and pulled off the soiled gloves. "What now?"

Williams stayed behind to ensure that no one bothered anything, as if anyone would. I followed Teague around the right side of the building.

"What's your plan for the upstairs?" Teague asked.

"Uncle Joe said that I could live there while I'm trying to get the business going. Free furnished apartment."

"Really? He said that?"

My feet stopped. "Not more snakes?"

"No, no snakes."

I raised my eyebrows. We turned the back corner where we stopped at the foot of the wooden stairs that led to the apartment. Behind the staircase sat a long green dumpster that reeked of beer and rotten seafood.

I followed him up the steps with tired feet and a heavy heart.

The stairs led all the way to the flat roof, but we stopped at the purple paneled door with two panes of glass. To the right was a small broken window. Teague opened the door, which creaked like it belonged in a haunted house. He led the way inside.

"The door wasn't secured," Teague said as I looked around. "Looks like you've had a squatter."

The open apartment was broken up by four columns. The exposed beams on the ceiling were littered with nests. The walls were chipped and dirty brick. The cabinets in the tiny kitchen hung unevenly from their hinges. Their cubbyholes had become animal dwellings decorated with feces, leftover animal bits, and feathers. To the left was a single door. I reached for the handle.

Teague grabbed my hand. "Ah, wouldn't do that if I were you. It's the bathroom." I pulled my hand away. "It'll have to be gutted."

A second door to the left was also closed. I pointed to it. "What's that?"

"Closet. It's empty, except for spider webs."

The only furniture was a cot in the corner, but it'd been thrashed to cotton bits, as if Freddy Kruger'd been trapped inside and sliced his way out. Empty soda cans and other trash covered the floor.

"I can't live here."

"It's not so bad," Teague said. "Just needs some work. You should call Damon Carver."

I nodded. Aunt Candy's husband Damon was a general contractor and, after Great Uncle Joe, the owner of the building, next on my list to call.

The room was hot and smelled like death and dumpster. I felt faint thinking I'd made another huge mistake.

"I need some air," I said finally.

I followed Teague out of the apartment, but instead of heading downstairs with him, I went up the next flight to the roof.

Hundreds of times, Great Aunt Laura and I'd retreated to the roof when business was slow. Thankfully, it was just as I remembered. The best ocean view was in the far right corner. I leaned against the brick ledge and let the ocean breezes dance around me and through my hair. The glittering expanse seemed as endless as the possibilities this ocean town could provide for me, snakes and squatters aside. Still, the heaviness on my shoulders didn't relent. My mother's objections that I'd heard over and over for weeks swirled in my ears with the winds. *This foolhardy plan to reopen Beach Read is just running away from your problems, like you always do. Instead of hiding in a book, you're hiding in a bookstore. It'll never work.* I let out a soul-weary sigh. Was she right?

Loud voices shattered my pity-party. Across the street at Beach Realty, a young man argued with a professional-looking woman in the parking lot.

"Please, hear me out," the man said. In his early twenties, the guy's broad shoulders reminded me of a football player. He shoved a paper at her, but she refused to take it. She shook her head and put a hand on her hip.

"There's nothin' I can do!"

She left him there, defeated. I knew the feeling. I circled the roof and found the stairs again, ready to return to my disgusting duty. By the time I reached the snake scene, the young man had joined the small crowd.

I ducked under the yellow tape.

"How was the roof?" Teague handed me a fresh pair of gloves. In my absence, he'd disposed of a handful of reptiles for me. The job appeared less overwhelming.

"As I expected. The only thing so far—"

"Teague, we got business," Williams called from the car. "415."

Teague snapped off his gloves. "Gotta go."

"Thanks for your help."

"You're welcome. Oh, and Delilah—In case no one else says it, welcome back."

He rushed to the Charger. After a gentle smile which I couldn't help but return, he disappeared.

From the sidelines, the defeated young man I'd seen from the rooftop slipped under the tape. "Want some help?"

"It's super gross."

"I don't mind." He took the bag out of my hands and held it open for me.

"Thanks. I'm Delilah Duffy."

"Darryl Chambers." He wore a yellow neon t-shirt with Via's printed on the pocket.

"What's Via's?"

"Via's Sports Bar and Gentleman's Club."

I didn't think much about his answer, only I wanted to keep talking for the distraction. With each squishy touch on the snake bodies, my stomach churned uneasily. "Oh. Do you work there?"

"For now," he said. "I'm a bouncer. Get paid to beat up idiots."

I pulled another snake into the bag. He caught it easily. Less than a dozen to go. With the cops gone, the crowd dwindled. Perhaps they'd finally realized there were much better things to see at the beach than a bunch of dead, decaying snakes and a frazzled wannabe bookstore manager.

"Via's is right over there." He pointed down the alley. "We're neighbors. Well, more like butt buddies. We share that dumpster."

Our two businesses backed up against each other, separated by a narrow alleyway and sparse, unkempt shrubbery.

"Wait! Hold the phone! Did you say it was a gentleman's club?"

"Yeah, a strip joint." He chuckled, as if he'd been waiting for my reaction.

"Oh, my gosh. There's a strip club right across the alley from Aunt Laura's store?"

"You're having a bad day, aren't you?" Darryl asked.

"Kinda." I yanked another snake into the bag.

"When I was a kid, my brother and I used to find baby snakes in the marshes and keep 'em as pets. Never worked out, though. Momma didn't like it. We'd try to make pets outta anything—bugs, mice, lizards. That your dog in the Jeep over there?"

I nodded. "That's Willie. I named him after William Shakespeare."

"Best defense against criminals is a good watchdog. Lucky you got 'em."

I glanced up at the dangling snakes and nodded.

Another snake dropped in the bag, shifting its weight. It fell to the ground with a squishy thud. We both leaned over to pick it up, bopping our foreheads together.

I laughed, rubbing my noggin with my arm. Darryl did the same.

"Sorry 'bout that," he said. "I gotta hard head."

"No harder than mine." I smiled.

A green pickup truck pulled up to the curb, and the automatic window on the passenger side went down.

"Darryl, let's go!" A blond woman with a bob haircut sat primly in the driver's seat. She cast a curt look in our direction.

"My mom." Darryl shrugged.

"Thanks for your help." He left me holding the bag.

I finished the snake work, trying to control my gag reflex, and tossed their bodies in the dumpster without ceremony.

Willie bounded out of the Jeep, sniffed the alley and marked his territory. I pulled him along to the front sidewalk.

"We have work to do, Willie."

We stared up at the three-story brick building. The brown and red bricks peeked through the chipped white paint like odd freckles. The blue paint framing the upper windows looked like broken veins. Still, the weathered look wasn't so bad.

The glass front door flanked by picture windows begged for brilliant book displays. I couldn't wait to replace the *For Sale or*

Lease sign with the one I'd made—the *Countdown to the Grand Reopening of Beach Read* sign. I'd snagged some thick cardboard in bright pink neon from the dollar store, pasted the words in chunky die-cut letters, and affixed a hook onto a black square to hang the numbers.

For now, the sale sign looked rather depressing.

The door jingled open, making me smile at the montage of sweet memories stirred, along with the dust. Specks drizzled down like snow as we walked under the chimes. Tall and dramatic, the store was a beautiful mess. Dark wood floors reached out to walls lined with matching shelves—floor to ceiling, two floors up. A rusty spiral staircase stood in the back corner and led up to the interior balcony. Four square columns marked each corner, mimicking the loft apartment upstairs, and led the eyes up to the ceiling. The air was a mix of dust, mildew, and decay. Everything needed a thorough cleaning, but despite the cracks in the wood and parts that needed sanding and new stain, I didn't care. Like the paint on the outside, the worn look suited the place.

I could still see Great Aunt Laura's red hair bobbing through the store as she hunted for some new adventure for me.

"Tell me what happened on your date," she'd prodded the day after I'd gone to the beach with Sam Teague. We'd curled up on the cushy beanbags in the corner, and I spilled everything—Sam teaching me to surf; our picnic lunch; hunting for shells; dancing in the waves.

"Whatever our souls are made of, his and mine are the same," I'd told her, like in *Wuthering Heights*. What a mistake that had been!

I circled the store, climbed the staircase, and leaned over the balcony. We used to fly paper airplanes off this ledge, taking bets on where they might land. One got caught in the light fixture. Aunt Laura'd left it there until Great Uncle Joe insisted it was a fire hazard.

My eyes drifted from the light to the countertop below it—a

heavy, dark wood mammoth covered in dust. I looked closer. My mouth fell open. Words'd been etched into the dust on the top. *It'll be great*—a message from Teague. A short smile edged up on my lips.

Such a romantic, Laura's eyes had welled with happy tears to hear me talk about Sam. I didn't have the heart to tell her what'd happened while we were dishing at the store. Sam Teague'd dropped by Grandma Betty's house and given Aunt Candy a message for me.

"He's just not interested in you. He wouldn't say why and believe me, I asked. He said it was a nice day, but that's all it was."

I ran my fingers along the dusty railings, sending particles flying.

Back downstairs, I turned to the rear of the store. A short hall led to an office, bathroom with a small shower, and a storage closet. Dusty boxes filled the corners. The hall ended with an emergency exit that led to the back alley.

"What do you think, Willie?" I returned to the counter. He sniffed the floor. "It *will* be great. It's a beautiful mess, but we'll get it cleaned up."

By my seventeenth birthday, Laura'd closed the store. The following summer, she was bedridden. Her red hair looked like fire against the white pillows.

Her first question to me was, *"What're you reading?"* The second, no less important question, was, *"How's your Heathcliff?"*

I answered with a simple, *"Fine."*

She shook her head weakly. *"Don't give up."*

She died a week later, lying in bed with her husband holding her hand.

She knew it hadn't worked out between Sam and me. Love at sixteen rarely does. Still, her telling me not to give up could carry over to Beach Read. I could be the one handing over books like bricks of gold.

Emily Dickinson's poetry came to mind. "I dwell in possibility," I told Willie.

Chapter Three

FAMILY

SUMMERS AT MY grandparents' oceanfront dream home meant freedom and adventure. We spent our days at the beach, sunning and playing with waves—or in my case, watching others play in the waves. Sometimes left alone, I traipsed around the island as I pleased, finding perfect reading spots where I'd lose myself for hours.

Looking up at the house, I longed for the warm welcome I'd missed so far.

Grandma Betty greeted me wearing a wide smile and a rooster apron. She has a thing for roosters. Grandma Betty even looks a little hen-like: tall, pear-shaped, with a long neck and a beak-like nose. She has short, spiky gray hair, kind eyes, and a smile that makes everyone feel welcome.

"You're a sight for sore eyes." She embraced me. Willie barked hello and walked in the house like he owned the place. "How you been, girl?"

Opting for simplicity, I gave a weak, "Okay." She led me

through the dining room to the back of the house. The kitchen smelled heavily of onion and garlic.

"Shrimp and grits," she announced proudly.

"You made my favorite? That's so sweet, Grandma." Down the hall, the house opened up to a living room with a wall of windows looking out to the ocean.

The Duffy clan's lighthearted chatter halted abruptly—very unlike them. They stared at me like I was Hester Prynne donning her bright, red letter *A*. Why the cold reception?

"Everyone, welcome Delilah." Grandma Betty put her hands on my shoulders. "She's had a long trip. Some good Southern hospitality's in order."

Uncle Clark hopped over the coffee table for a hug and whispered, "Now you know how Daniel must've felt in that den." He chuckled and backed away. I cast him an odd look, as Grandpa Charlie reached out and grabbed me.

"Good to see you, Bean! Traffic okay?"

"Mostly uneventful," I said.

My three aunts, Candy, Clara, and Charlotte stood near the window looking like Roman goddesses with their flowing sundresses and blond locks. Especially decked out, Clara and Charlotte wore hats and shoes of Charlotte's design from their store, Top to Bottom: A Hat and Shoe Boutique, Beach Read's neighbor.

Peter Saintly, Clara's husband, offered me a drink from the bar. I asked for water with lemon. Mamma Rose sat regally in the rocking chair in the corner. Her sheet-white hair was curled tightly, as if she'd just gone to the salon. She gave me a warm smile and waved me over. Eighty-nine years young, as she likes to say, Mamma Rose is my great-grandmother on my father's side. As I crossed the room, I said hello to everyone: Rachel and Raina, Clara's eighteen-year-old twin daughters, Damon Carver, Candy's husband, and their girls, Neisha and Nikita, who played cards on the coffee table. Willie followed along behind me and did his part to lighten the mood.

"Heard you had a rough induction party this afternoon," Clark said, following me. "Any comment?"

"No," I said sternly.

Ever persistent, Clark said, "Must've been freaky."

Grandpa Charlie asked what he meant, and Uncle Clark happily reported the story of the snake prank.

"You know, there's only one snake farm in a fifty-mile radius," Clark said. "It's in Shawsburg, owned by a guy named Freddy Weaver. He sells them as pets, to zoos and aquariums, even markets their skins."

I scoffed. "Gross."

"There's a market for snakeskin shoes, boots, purses. Isn't that right, Charlotte?" He bellowed the question across the room, and Charlotte turned her back on him. He laughed.

"What are you—" I started to ask, but Grandma Betty called everyone to dinner. The Duffy clan shuffled to the dining room. Mamma Rose invited me to sit next to her. Raina took my other side.

"What a lovely necklace, Raina." I eyed the silver piece dangling outside her t-shirt. "It's unique."

Her hand went up to it, and she smiled. "Thanks, it was—a friend made it."

"Any plans for the summer, Raina?" I asked as we got settled.

"Um, well I'm volunteering at church, Vacation Bible School and workin' at the Piggly Wiggly. Maybe some with my mom—"

"Raina will get ready for UNC, Delilah," Clara cut in loudly, "majorin' in business—"

"And art," Raina said.

Not to be left out, Rachel cleared her throat. "I'm making tons of money this summer. I'm workin' at the Sweet Treat sellin' lemon ices on the beach, and babysittin' and workin' for mamma on the side." She smiled widely and had she been standing, I think she would have curtsied.

Grandma Betty placed the main platters on the table. Grandpa Charlie said the blessing. Clinks of dishes danced across the room as plates passed along.

"So, I spoke to your mamma the other day." Aunt Clara sat diagonally across from me, but her voice carried to the entire table. "She has a job lined up for you at her school."

"I know. I'm not interested."

Charlotte said, "Be nice working with your mamma, don't you think?"

Most Duffys had soft southern accents that could make almost anything sound pleasant. Except for me working side-by-side with my mother, that is.

"Are you kiddin' me? Delilah'd hate that! I saw them talkin' about mammas like yours on *Oprah* one time. They call 'em helicopter parents. Isn't that ingenious?" Grandma Betty lifted her fork and twirled it around. "Helicopter parents because they hover 'round all the time."

"Mamma, I'm only suggestin' Delilah put some serious thought into this foolish little venture," Clara said. "Teachin' is what she knows. She doesn't know a danged thing about runnin' a business."

"Neither did you, as I recall," Mamma Rose said.

"I'm not going back to teaching," I said in the sternest voice I could muster without sounding angry. "That part of my life is over."

"Well, surely there's somethin' else you can do with a degree in books or whatever." Charlotte perked up. "What about writin' for the paper?"

All eyes turned to Uncle Clark. He smirked. "Or you could teach her how to make hats, Charlotte."

"No one has to teach me to do anything. I'm reopening Beach

Read. Might seem risky, but I'm willing to take my chances."

"Right." Clara shook her head. "You've got nothing to lose, since you've lost everything already."

"Who cares about the rest of us?" Charlotte tossed her napkin on the table.

Clark cast his sisters a disapproving stare. "Don't include all of us in this. We aren't all against you, Delilah."

"Why would any of you be against me?"

"Uncle Joe didn't tell you?" Candy sounded surprised.

Frustrated, I said, "Tell me what?"

Clara started to speak, but Clark cut her off. "My sisters had their sights set on Beach Read first. You pulled the rug right out from under them."

My mouth dropped open. "I had no idea. Uncle Joe never said—"

"Of course, he didn't," Clark said. "Keeping it a bookstore is better than flipping it into a shoe and hat mega-mall."

Clara gasped. "Mega-mall? How dare you! I'd never have a mega-mall of any sort."

"We were goin' to expand. Our store is famous. We're in demand. I was goin' to have my own design studio." Charlotte pouted.

"Then you had your little, well, whatever got you fired, and now all our plans are in the toilet." Clara huffed.

Mouth agape, I tried piecing this news together, so I could figure out what to say, but Candy spoke up first.

"It's not exactly set in stone yet. She's gotta earn it to keep it. Uncle Joe gave a stipulation."

"This whole thing's givin' me heartburn." Grandma Betty took a long swig of water.

"Delilah has two months to turn a profit," Candy said. "If she can't show Joe that Beach Read can make money by the end of August, then he'll sell to Clara and Charlotte."

Clara and Charlotte screamed, giggled, and gave each other high fives. I sank in my chair, mind spinning. Two months! That was no time at all!

"Will the repairs to the building be included in my deficit?" I asked, but Candy gushed with her sisters over the good news.

"What repairs?" Damon Carver asked from Candy's other side.

"The easier question is what I don't have to fix." I couldn't help the defeated tone in my voice, though Damon promised to help.

I zoned out. Conversation went on around the table while another wave of my mistakes washed over me. My aunts were right: I knew nothing about running a business. A profit in two months seemed impossible.

"Wait one cotton-pickin' minute," Grandma Betty called out suddenly. "I don't like what's going on here. Not one bit, and this is my house."

"Amen to that." Grandpa Charlie heaped another serving of greens onto his plate.

Betty said, "Clara and Charlotte, you've had years to buy Beach Read from Joe and haven't done it, so you've peed in your own pool. And, Candy, why didn't you tell Delilah about these stipulations before she came all this—"

"I only just gotta hold of the contract myself, Mamma," Candy said. "Came *FedEx* yesterday afternoon. Uncle Joe should've told her."

I nodded. "Joe never said a thing about stipulations or that anyone else wanted the building."

"Joe probably didn't want to scare you off," Clark said.

"No matter how you got here, you're here," Grandma Betty went on, "and I expect ya'll to be supportive and help Delilah do her best, 'cause we're family—"

"Excuse me, but no." Clara wagged her pink fingernail. "Business is business. Top to Bottom's the lighthouse that brings customers to this town. We've got seniority and a whole community that benefits when we grow. So, Delilah, your failure means our success. The advertising in Clark's newspaper goes up. Candy gets a juicy commission. Every business on the boardwalk gets a piece of the pie. We all win. Besides, a musty bookstore's about as useful as ants atta picnic these days."

Candy said, "And Mamma, the term cotton-pickin' is offensive."

Damon laughed. "It's fine, Candy." Though Damon was African American, and Candy wasn't, she usually got offended on his behalf, even when he didn't notice the offense.

I excused myself and disappeared into the bathroom.

Chapter Four

GHOST CRABS

GHOST CRABS SKIRTED by my feet, driving Willie crazy. He barked and chased them as they scuttled across the sand. All for nothing. They were much too fast for him.

"I'm hoping for a ghost crab kind of life, Willie. They don't bother anyone, and no one really bothers them." I smirked. "Well, except for overly playful dogs but that's not so bad."

We'd been walking the beach for almost an hour. I had a mostly finished warm beer in my hand, and a spare bottle shoved in my pocket. After returning to Beach Read only to feel more discouraged, Willie and I had to get away. Thankfully, there are no shortages of escapes on Tipee Island.

The ocean breezes pulled my hair away from my face like hands running through it. The Tipee Island Fishing Pier jutted out into the darkness of the Atlantic ahead—the marker for home. On the other side, over the boardwalk and across Atlantic Avenue, sat Starfish Drive.

Willie tired of the ghost crabs and raced to the pier. I jogged to catch up, but he made it to the other side and found something else to play with. Sam Teague, this time in shorts and a t-shirt, stroked Willie's fur and wrestled him to the sand, much to Willie's delight.

"You know he has to be on a leash, right?" Teague asked, looking up at me. "$35 citation."

"But, you're off duty. Please don't—"

"And Ms. Duffy, drinking on the beach?" He stood up, a smile drifting over his face. "That's another citation."

I raised an eyebrow. "I have another one." I pulled the unopened bottle from the pocket of my sundress. "Could be yours."

"Bribing an officer?"

"Accepting?"

He took the bottle and twisted it open. I clinked my bottle with his and swallowed what was left.

"So, following me?" I tossed my empty bottle in a nearby trashcan with a loud clank.

"I live over there." He pointed to the stretch of cottages behind us. "I saw you walking earlier, so I wanted to catch up with you when you came back."

"To get me for the leash thing?"

"No. It's Aunt Bev's canasta night. A bunch of old ladies are playing a mean game of cards in Bev's kitchen. Whenever I walk in, they whistle and hoot. Aunt Bev calls me a distraction. So, when I saw you out here, I thought I'd see how you were doing, if only to get me out of the house."

I chuckled. "That's right. Aunt Bev and Uncle Ken. I remember that you lived with them growing up."

"Yes, I moved back home last year." The slight hesitation in his voice made me think it embarrassed him.

"Well, I'm about two steps away from living with my parents, so I can't judge. How are they?"

"Um, Bev's great. Winning at cards, I think." He cleared his throat. "Ken died two years ago."

I stopped walking as if I couldn't think and move at the same time. "I'm so sorry."

Teague's face pinched in odd surprise before smiling again. "It's okay. He died doing what he loved—tinkering in his garage. Heart attack."

I nodded, feeling inexplicably sad. I'd never met Ken, only knew about him through the one day I spent with Sam on the beach. Still, hearing about his death combined with missing Great Aunt Laura almost made me tear up.

Teague offered me his beer. "Where are you staying tonight?"

I took a sip. "In the store."

"I'm impressed."

I shrugged. "I have an air mattress."

"Can't your relatives put you up?"

"Some offered," I said, "but, I didn't want to start off this adventure being afraid. Beach Read's my new home, no matter how dirty it is. Besides, I've got Willie, beer, and boxes of books. What more do I need? Do you think it's a mistake?"

"Not at all, unless our vandal strikes again, but he probably won't."

We walked down the beach, catching glimpses of ghost crabs in the pier lights. Willie tagged along, lagging behind us like a chaperone.

"You aren't afraid, are you?" he asked after a minute. "That curse thing is just talk—"

I waved my hand dismissively. "Oh, I know. I'm *slightly* creeped out." I laughed, and sang, "Snakes, spiders, and rats… oh, my," to the tune of *Lions, tigers, and bears*, but it didn't sound anything like *The Wizard of Oz*. Still, he chuckled politely.

He handed me the beer again. "I don't mean this the way it'll sound, but I could stay with you, for company." I crinkled my eyebrows together. "It's not a come-on, Delilah. The first night's the hardest in a new place, especially the way you found it. We were friends, once. I'd hate to think so much has changed since then."

I took another swig of the beer, unsure what to say. The word 'friends' snapped at me like a crab's claw. Spending one day together didn't make us friends, and the word sounded like a sad consolation prize. Labeling us as 'friends' felt inaccurate—because we weren't—and short-changed—because I'd once hoped for more than that. But I wasn't about to argue semantics.

He shook his head. "I'm sorry. Dumb idea to offer."

Finally, I grinned and motioned back toward his house. "I'd hate to disappoint the ladies."

He grinned. "They'll manage. There are embarrassing pictures of me all over the house."

"I know this is just your way of getting to the rest of my six-pack," I went on, "but I'm sure Willie and I will be fine. The offer is appreciated, though. Who knows? If tonight goes badly—"

"Let me see your phone," he said. I pulled my phone from deep inside my pocket and handed it to him. "Wow, what are you doing with this ancient phone?"

"It's cheap, and I can't stand complicated phones." I kicked at the sand.

"Creaks when you open it. It's an old person's phone."

I gave him a playful punch on his arm. "Don't tease me!"

"Yes, ma'am." A kind and sweet smile crossed his face as he programmed his number. "If you have trouble, call me. Anytime." He handed it back. I nodded, though I doubted I would—either have trouble or call him if I did.

Maybe it was the beer—I'm a lightweight—or the company, but my mind completely jumbled, fluctuating oddly between the events of the day, what lay ahead and Teague's soft cologne. Sharing a beer with Sam Teague felt surreal, and strangely natural.

"Do you know Freddy Weaver?" I asked.

"The snake guy. Yeah, I already talked to him. Denies any knowledge of the incident. But, Captain Tanner, who operates the *North Carolina*, the morning ferry, confirmed that Weaver was a passenger before dawn this morning."

"Uncle Clark made a remark at dinner about snakeskin shoes and purses. He directed it to Aunt Charlotte, but I can't imagine that she'd do something like this."

"Your aunts definitely want the building and that means they want you out of it."

"Yeah, they made that clear at dinner." I shook my head. "You know, I was a flower girl at Aunt Clara's wedding. Wore my first and only hoop skirt." I chuckled, thinking about how many times I'd spun around in the gorgeous pink and white dress. "Aunt Charlotte used to let me play dress-up in her sewing room, taught me how to tie a proper bow, and the difference between satin, silk, and lace. Hard to believe they'd be so—"

"Ruthless?"

"Yes, ruthless."

Teague's eyes darted over to me, and he tilted his head. "It could've been someone else. Clara's turned much of the town against you. She's a politician as much as she's a businesswoman."

"Yes, she has that... *vaulting ambition, which o'erleaps itself.*"

"*Hamlet?*"

"*Macbeth.*"

Teague grinned.

"I'd no idea that reopening the bookstore would upset so many people. I can't believe Uncle Joe didn't tell me."

"If he had, would you've come?"

I smiled. "No."

"Maybe that's why he didn't. That has to count for something."

"It does, but he's not here. I don't know if I can fight this fight."

"What are your other options?" he asked.

I shrugged. I really didn't have any, though *Ruby Tuesday* was sounding better and better all the time. I couldn't explain to Teague that despite my education and seven years of experience, I couldn't return to teaching. Instead, I made light of the question.

"Think the poop police have an opening?"

"We don't hire habitual offenders. On that note, you wouldn't be qualified for traffic control or our technology department either, I'm afraid."

"I'm just mounting up strikes against me," I laughed.

"You show promise, though." He pointed to the beer. "You're prepared and excellent at dead snake removal."

"You got most of them."

"Eh, give yourself a little credit. Most people would've run for the hills."

"There's still a chance I might."

"You don't strike me as a runner."

In the darkness, I rolled my eyes because that's exactly what I was.

He handed me the beer again. "If dead snakes and ruthless relatives didn't scare you off, then I'd say you got this. Everything'll be fine."

A crab scurried across my left foot, tickling my skin. I took a deep breath. For the first time that day, the shadow of my past lifted off my shoulders.

Chapter Five

RACING

I STARED BLANKLY at my *Countdown to the Grand Reopening of Beach Read* sign, feeling like a baby sea turtle. They emerge from their eggs and race to the sea, hoping they won't get picked off by the vicious preying birds. How many days did I realistically need to get Beach Read's doors open? What number would tell the good people of Tipee that I meant business without dooming myself to fail?

For once, I'd charged my phone. I grabbed it from the cord and found Great Uncle Joe's number.

"Bean Sprout! What's shakin'?" he asked in his raspy voice. "How's the ol' place?"

"It's seen better days." Gently, I reported the conditions.

"Candy's responsible for takin' care of the place. That really frosts my cookies. She's so hell-bent on becoming top seller at Beach Realty, she's let family stuff slip to the wayside. Anyway, I'll cover the repairs."

"Thanks, Uncle Joe, that'll help. I didn't mean to cause so

much trouble. I wish you had told me about Clara and Charlotte and the stipulations."

"So, you could back out? When it rains, it pours, Bean. There's some other nut job wantin' it, too. Anyway, I'm puttin' them both off, 'cause I know Laura'd want me to. You were like a daughter to her."

"She meant the world to me, too."

"Profit doesn't have to be much. Keep your expenses low, and you'll do fine."

I took a deep breath, my heart thudding. "Yes, I will."

"Time's a'wastin'. Get Damon over there to get the work started and tell 'em to send me the bill."

I thanked him again and got off the phone. Staring at the neon sign once more, I picked a six from the pile. The grand reopening would be Saturday. The race had begun.

The day slipped by in cleaning and organizing. Before I knew it, the light disappeared from the windows—I'd removed the plywood covering the windows outside and replaced them with my blue bedsheets for some privacy inside. Going an entire day without facing anyone felt refreshing.

But my alone time didn't last.

Damon and his crew started work upstairs Monday morning, the dumpster out back ending up being very convenient for the construction crew. All morning, the thuds and bangs of trash being tossed from the stairs drove Willie bonkers. I leashed him, and we went for a long walk.

We padded along the boardwalk, stopping to look over the gates at Jubilee Park. The Ferris wheel circled, the Tilt-a-Whirl spun, and the air was alive with giggles and laughter. I smiled.

"Saw Sam Teague for the first time here, Willie, in the fun house." I scanned the grounds and didn't see the colorful building I remembered. In its place, there was a roaring go-cart track.

I pulled Willie's leash and continued toward the beach. "Why am I thinking about him at all?" Willie panted.

Aunt Clara waited outside the door of Beach Read. She wore a leopard print dress, matching shoes, and a fedora-like hat with a lacy veil. She appeared to be on the prowl.

She huffed when she saw me. "There you are. I see that you've started work on the place. Five days?" She motioned toward my awesome sign.

"Yep."

"We'll see. You're wasting their time and Joe's money." She sighed, pointing to the work trucks parked along the side of the building. "But, what do you care, right?"

A hand went to my hip. Willie moaned and tugged at the leash. "What do you want?"

She reached in her typewriter-sized purse for a stack of papers. "Only to give you this. Call it a store-warming present."

I glanced down at the stapled stack—a long list of signatures. "What's this?"

"A petition. These people have vowed not to patronize your store to support Top to Bottom."

I flipped the pages. Back and front, the names went on and on. "How many are here?"

"Seven-hundred and thirty-two. Woulda been more, but we only kept it out for a few days."

I eyed the header on the first page. "You wrote *A petition to support Top to Bottom's expansion and against an experimental business*. Did you tell people it was a bookstore?"

Aunt Clara tilted her head. "If they asked."

"Come on, Willie. Let's go."

"Wait!" Clara stepped closer. "Stop this whole thing and I'll give you some start-up money to get ya goin' someplace else. Plenty of beautiful beaches 'round here."

"I don't want your money or another beach."

Clara smiled. "Look at this place, Delilah." She put her arm around my shoulders. "It's an eyesore. A hot mess! I can turn it into somethin' beautiful. We could do it together. You could come work for me at the store. I'll give you the start-up money, too, to get you settled. How does $10,000 sound?"

I cringed. I eyed the store's chipped paint and dirty windows. Hard work wouldn't even scratch the surface; it would take years of devotion to get it back to its former glory. Still, there was no relic of the dead more precious to me than this one.

"The answer is no."

"You'll regret it, when you end up crawling back home to Mommy and Daddy, jobless, hopeless—"

"But not heartless, at least."

Clara left, but she wasn't my only visitor that day or the only one trying to make me do something I didn't want to do. Clark came by later.

"I'm running a story about you." Uncle Clark looked like Clark Kent—nerdy and handsome. I hoped there was a superhero beneath his glasses, button-downs, and khakis, because owning the paper gave him great power and responsibility.

"About the store, I hope."

Clark leaned against Beach Read's counter. "We need to talk about why you left teaching."

"I burned out."

"Clara's telling everyone you were fired. People want to know why."

I tossed my cleaning rag on the counter and folded my arms. "People just want gossip."

"But what's the truth? Clara's working diligently to get answers."

I shook my head and clamped my lips together.

Clark leaned across the counter again. "I spoke to Jonathan Dekker. Your high school's assistant principal had a lot to say."

My heart thudded. I felt hot. I didn't answer but cocked my

head and gave him an angry stare. It used to be that such a look would silence my students. It didn't work with Clark.

Clark leaned closer. "He's the mysterious boyfriend you've had for the last year or so? Thought it was strange that you never brought him home to meet us. I thought you'd gotten your panties in a bunch over something stupid like Candy did with Damon."

Because of his race, Candy had kept her relationship with Damon a secret for over a year, she was so worried about how they'd react. I hadn't kept Jonathan a secret by choice; he'd never wanted to meet my family, not that I wanted to tell Clark that.

"Delilah, did you get fired for sleeping with the boss?" His voice was soft, as if a lower volume made the accusation softer, too. My lungs felt like they were collapsing. Anyone talking to Jonathan made me feel sick.

"It wasn't like that. And it's no one's business."

Clark scrutinized my face like he had a magnifying glass. "Then, it must've been something else. Something worse? Delilah, what did you do?"

"I won't talk about it." I slammed my hand on the counter and fled out the front door. Instead of giving Clark a chance to pry the information out of me, I raced around the side of the building, eager to get to the Jeep and feel the wind against my face.

Loud voices brought my mission to a dead stop.

"What the hell are you talkin' about?"

I peered around the corner to see two men in an angry conversation behind Beach Read. One was Darryl Chambers. The other man was more Jell-O than muscle, five inches shorter, and had sloping shoulders.

"You don't know what you're doing," the shorter man said. "You're screwing up everything!"

"I'm taking control of my life. You should do the same before you get in trouble, or worse. Before it's too late."

"Isn't it already too late?"

Darryl shook his head. "You should sign up, too. We could do it together."

"That ain't for me, and you know it."

"Then, I don't know, but you gotta stop with this bullshit."

"Since when did you get all high and mighty?" The shorter man's voice climbed again. "You're the one who started it in the first place!"

"It was a mistake!"

"Too late! You can't back out now. I'll make sure of it."

"If you care about me at all, Ronnie, then you'll make this as easy as possible," Darryl said. "I've always done my best for you."

"Right, where would I be without you?" Ronnie asked sarcastically. "Good ol' Darryl, always looking out for his little brother. Well, I don't need you! You do this, then you don't have a brother no more."

Ronnie shoved Darryl weakly and headed back to the strip club parking lot. Darryl didn't follow. An image of two little boys catching snakes in the marshes popped into my mind. I felt sad for him.

Darryl slammed his fist into the side of the dumpster. The noise thundered, startling me into a scream. I turned to run back to the store but bumbled into Uncle Clark instead.

"There you are. We aren't done—"

"Shh!" I told him, but Darryl Chambers'd already come around the corner. His hand bled around the knuckles.

"Are you okay, Mr. Chambers?" Clark asked.

"Fine." Darryl walked on toward Via's.

"Why you'd want to live and work behind a strip club is beyond me," Clark remarked once Darryl was out of earshot. "Let's get a drink."

"Right, so you can get me drunk and then grill me about my past to beef up your story?"

Clark chuckled. "Don't be an idiot." He slipped his arm around my shoulders. "I wouldn't need to get you drunk for that."

Somehow, I believed him.

Chapter Six

HONESTY

CLARK INSISTED THAT I freshen up before going to the restaurant because he wouldn't be seen with someone who looked like a "cleaning lady." The Crab Shack, at the corner of Starfish Drive and Atlantic Avenue, boasted ocean views, a comfortable dining area, and gourmet fare.

Mandy was our waitress—Teague's cheerleader girlfriend. She was depressingly beautiful.

Clark eyed me curiously. I hated when he did that.

"Don't like the waitress?" he asked after she headed off.

I gave him an irritated look. "She's fine."

Clark chuckled. "You need to work on your poker face, especially since you've got secrets to keep."

I huffed. "Why are you so interested in my secrets, really?"

"A concerned citizen suggested that it would be in the community's best interests for me to investigate the reason you left teaching."

"A concerned citizen, huh?"

"Clara may be devious, but she has a point. If a sexual predator moved into one of our neighborhoods, I'd run a story. What's the difference?"

"I'm not a sexual predator!"

As I said that, Mandy brought our drinks. I sat back in my seat. With a distasteful expression on her face, she set the drinks down, and Clark waved her away.

"Right, but you did something bad enough to get fired from a teaching job—not an easy thing to do after seven years. I'm confident it wasn't about the Dekker relationship."

"So, Jonathan didn't tell you anything?"

This time, Clark leaned back. "Only that for the last two weeks of school, you were on leave. They brought you before the school board in a closed session. Dekker claims your contract wasn't renewed for administrative reasons."

I smiled. "You don't know much."

"If I print what little I know and leave the public to come up with their own theories, you might as well be a sexual predator. That's what they'll say. Beautiful young teacher, unmarried, lonely, around all those athletic young men—"

"That's enough! That's not what happened. I'd never do that!"

"I know you wouldn't, but it's terrible, isn't it? The way people think."

I took a deep breath and shook my head. "I don't care what they think."

"Lunch with Jonathan Dekker is all I need. He didn't give away the prize, granted, but he's not exactly a shut door. He told me on the phone that you two were—" Clark stopped to look down at his notebook. "Ah, friends with benefits."

I cringed. My stomach turned.

"Classy, huh, Delilah?"

"You're not getting the story from me, so do what you have to, Uncle. I lost a job I loved, and I must live with that, but I'm moving on with my life. At least, I'm trying. You want to keep me under the shadow of my mistakes. That's not fair. I've already paid dearly for those. The whole thing's like a noose dangling by my head, and you're ready to shove me into it."

With each word, my voice grew sterner. My heart thudded with anxiety at the thought of Clark spilling my life on the pages of the newspaper. I closed my eyes and took a breath while twisting the linen napkin in my lap.

Clark's face softened. "It's that important to you to keep it quiet?"

"My life here will be over if it comes out."

Uncle Clark broke into a wide grin. He raised his hands and clapped. "Glad you inherited the Duffy family determination. You'll need it. Waitress!"

Mandy sauntered over as instructed, grinning. My shoulders sagged.

"Get Mike over here. We need real drinks."

Again, she bounced away.

Clark chuckled, watching my expressions. "You really don't like her, do you? What's up with that?"

I twisted my napkin again. "She's really pretty, huh?"

"Gorgeous, if you like Barbie dolls."

"Who doesn't like Barbie dolls?"

"Good point. Why the interest—"

"Quit changing the subject. What're you going to print, Clark?"

"The story coming out tomorrow is about the snake prank. My photographer, Billy, said that's what you called it."

I nodded. "That's all it was."

"You're wrong about the prank part. It was a warning. Let me introduce you to Mike."

A handsome thirty-something man smiled as he approached our table, very George Clooney-ish. He had soft, curly brown locks and matching eyes that seemed thoughtful. He extended his hand and held mine in his for more seconds than needed, which was surprising since I smelled like furniture polish and dust.

"Mike, this is my niece, Delilah. Delilah, this is Mike Ancellotti. He owns the joint."

"Pleasure to meet you, Delilah. I hope you're enjoying the island."

Clark shook his head. "Delilah's not a tourist. She's taking over my uncle's shop on the corner."

"Ah, so she's the troublemaker, huh?" Mike laughed. "I hope you're keeping it a bookstore. This island really needs a bookstore."

My heart almost leapt out of my chest. "Yes, I am."

"When's the grand reopening?"

"Saturday."

Mike's grin expanded. "I'll be your best customer. Mandy tells me you need drinks. Let me make you something special."

He left the table and headed back to the bar. I smiled. "Oh, my, he's like butter."

Clark laughed. "Butter?"

"Sorry, I didn't mean to—"

"He's single. A ladies' man, I hear, but otherwise a decent catch. You want me to set you up?"

"No!"

"Okay, okay," he said. "Everyone needs… butter, though. Just remember that."

I shook my head quickly. "No time for butter."

"Well, I wouldn't get too comfortable with Clara on the hunt for secrets," Clark said. "Truth'll come out. Always does."

"Why can't it just be left alone? Whose business is it anyway?"

Clark leaned in. "You're right, but you've stepped into a circus here and everyone's waiting for the big show. Besides, you really want to carry that burden? It must feel like lead on your shoulders. Are you Atlas? Might be a relief to drop it."

"Drop it? Yes, that would be a relief. Let's do that."

Mike Ancellotti delivered the most beautiful drink I'd ever seen—a myriad of mixed blues, dark at the bottom to sky blue at the top. With my own ocean in my hands, my goals seemed reachable again.

"My special recipe," Mike said. "I'm calling it the Delilah."

"Yikes!" Clark rolled his eyes.

Chapter Seven

SIGNS

SEA FOLK ARE superstitious people, constantly on the lookout for signs. They take their albatrosses—can't kill them; they hold the spirits of dead sailors—and women—bad luck on a ship—along with a slew of other handed-down beliefs seriously. Dolphins swimming with the ship is a fortunate sign. Sharks swimming behind is not—duh. Birds flying in various groupings or directions can mean good or bad fortune. Almost everything means something.

My bad signs were growing. A serious string of unearned stink eyes from Clara-supporters followed the dead snakes. Plus, tidal wave and snake nightmares tormented me every night. Last night I woke up soaked with sweat. It took me several scary moments to realize I hadn't been dragged out to sea.

Wednesday morning burned hot and bright. I changed the sign in the window. Three days until the grand reopening.

I spent the morning at The Cotton Exchange, a half-mile of warehouses and dirt lots filled with vendors. On the island's center, near the slit where the Intracoastal Waterway (ICW) reaches up into the guts of the island, The Cotton Exchange is *the* place for bargain hunters.

Lenny Jackson, who looked like a tattooed Mr. Clean, operated a table of housewares and knickknacks. He wore a t-shirt from Via's Sports Bar and Gentleman's Club, just like Darryl Chambers had.

I pointed to his shirt. "You're a bouncer?"

"Prevention Specialist." He gave me a smoky chuckle. "I prevent bad things from happenin'."

"We're neighbors," I said. "I'm opening up the bookstore behind Via's."

"That's good to hear. Empty buildings are breedin' grounds for trouble. Glad it's finally being put to use."

Lenny talked me into two lamps, a chandelier, a Mr. Coffee, and a set of six Charlie Brown mugs. It took two trips back and forth to the Jeep to deposit my new wares. When I was done, I saw Darryl's brother talking with Lenny. I wouldn't have thought much of it except that Lenny put his hand on his shoulder, squeezed tightly, and then pushed him away—a move that began as fatherly and ended meanly.

The Cotton Exchange provided me with a Jeep full of used furniture for the apartment. For the store, I purchased a child's chalkboard easel and a few beanbags. My bounty lifted my mood.

That changed upon my return to Beach Read. A strange woman stood by the store's front windows, staring.

I parked quickly.

The woman smiled as I joined her on the sidewalk. She was in her fifties, wearing a jean dress. Her bob haircut and perfect make-up made her skin look like porcelain. She introduced herself as Mavis Chambers—Darryl Chambers' mother—before pointing out my storefront windows.

They'd been covered with newspaper clippings, the headlines

underlined in red marker.

Duffy vs. Duffy: New Proprietorship Halts Expansion Plans; Top to Bottom rises to the Top: Starlet Places Order for Original Hat; First Lady of North Carolina Visits Top to Bottom: A Hat and Shoe Boutique; Beat the C Days at Top to Bottom: Cancer Benefit; Local Businesses See 6% Average Sales Increase; Top to Bottom Brings Off-Season Shoppers to Tipee; Duffy Sisters Host Christmas Eve Benefit for State Park; Clara Duffy-Saintly Honored as Businesswoman of the Year...

Over fifty such articles plastered the windows. A cluster of them covered up my countdown sign completely.

"What is this?" My heartbeat raced double time, and my stomach churned.

"That's what I was gonna ask you." Mavis Chambers smiled. "I was walking by and thought it was weird. Who do you think did it and why?"

"Could've been anyone. This town hasn't been very welcoming." I took a long look around the street to find it barren. Toward the beach, I spied a few oblivious tourists, but no one out of place. A shiver passed through me.

Mavis walked up to the article taped at eye-level on the door. "Or even kind. Gosh."

Scrawled across the top, *"GO HOME!"* stood out in red marker. The article underneath wasn't from a local paper, but from a Durham suburb where I'd taught. *High School Teacher Questioned by School Board*. Barely two inches long, the article didn't say much, including my name. Still, that someone'd threatened me with my past, twice in two days, felt invigoratingly irritating.

"Someone's being a bully," Mavis said, putting her hand on my arm gently. Her fingers felt like ice. "You should take 'em all down."

"I'd like to, but not yet." I smiled at Mavis and shook my head.

She shrugged. "Good luck, honey," she said before heading

down the street.

I whipped out my phone, huffed, and hunted through my programmed numbers. When Teague answered, I sighed, turning back to the articles.

"So, when I call you, is it the same as calling the police or am I just calling you?" I asked.

"What happened?"

"It's not as bad as the snakes, not police-worthy. But I remembered what you said about it happening again and thought I should tell someone."

"I'll be right there," Teague said.

I flipped the phone shut. Three gulls yapped overhead and flew toward the shore. Fortunately, I'm not superstitious because that's a warning of death.

Teague drove a green Toyota truck and wore plain clothes, putting me at ease.

"You're right. Not as bad as the snakes." Upon closer inspection, he pointed to the Durham article. "What about this one?"

"That's nothing." I snatched it down, wishing I'd done it sooner.

"Delilah, is it about you?"

"It doesn't matter."

"Yes, it does." He rolled his eyes at my stubbornness. "Can I see it, please?" I shook my head. "I'm trying to help you, you know. You called me."

I shoved the tiny article into his hand. He straightened out the wrinkles.

"*High School Teacher Questioned by School Board.*" He scanned over it quickly. "This is our best clue to figuring out who did this. Who knows about your situation in Durham?"

"I've told no one."

"No one?"

"They've made assumptions, I'm sure, but I haven't talked about it. I mean, everyone knows that's where I'm from, that I worked there, but not why I left. Clark tried to find out, but got nowhere, even after a few drinks."

"Clark could've easily tracked down this article."

"Yes, but Clark wouldn't do this. Besides, the drama helps his paper."

"Maybe he's creating drama, not just reporting it." Teague took a picture of the scene with his phone and collected the articles into a folder. I helped, happy to get them off the window.

Teague glanced at me while we worked. "You know, everyone makes mistakes. Whatever happened in Durham, you could tell me."

"No, I can't. It may not seem like a big deal to you, but I don't want one more person thinking less of me. I lost friends and my sort-of fiancé over this. I don't want to lose anything else."

"I'm not them, Delilah."

I grunted. "What makes you different?"

Teague shrugged his broad shoulders. "I know you. Whatever you did, I'm sure you did it for the right reasons because that's just who you are. Honestly, it wouldn't matter to me at all except knowing might help us now and talking might give you some peace."

He finished what he said with a short smile, while I stared at him, stupefied. He removed the last of the articles and set the file in his truck.

Finally, he said, "How about a break? Let's take Willie for a walk."

After our perfect beach day and Teague's devastating rejection when we were teenagers, I'd spent the rest of summer cloistered in my room in Wilmington. His message had reduced me to tears I'm ashamed of now. In Candy's room, I cried for three days before Dad finally came to get me. At home, I wasn't much better, as if

Teague'd opened a painful door that I couldn't shut. Depression had reached up through my bedposts and wrapped her icy fingers around me. It took forever for me to feel normal again.

The same person who'd caused my teenage hell now held Willie's leash as we made our way down Starfish Drive toward the beach. Neither of us said much. Tipee'd been an unkind place, so far. Teague'd made it better. It troubled me how that could be possible.

We rounded the corner of Starfish and Atlantic toward the beach. Passing by the windows of The Crab Shack, my mixed-up feelings retreated.

"Sammy! Sammy!" Mandy Davis rushed out of the restaurant and bubbled over to Teague's right side, placing her arm around his waist. "I was hopin' to run into you."

"Mandy, this is Delilah Duffy. Delilah, this is Mandy Davis."

I grinned widely and shook her soft, petite hand. "We met at the restaurant."

"Right." She barely looked at me and hung onto Teague's shoulder like her balance depended on it. She was tall, like him. Tan and beautiful, like him. I slouched. "Are we on for tonight?"

"No, I—"

"Honeypot, you promised!"

I grabbed the leash out of Teague's hand. "I'll let you two talk it out. See you later."

She waved me goodbye and pulled Teague toward the restaurant. Willie and I dashed away. We crossed the street and fled to the pier. Instead of walking, I found a shaded spot underneath and leaned against one of the dryer pilings. Willie jumped around anxiously. Despite Teague's previous warnings, I let him off his leash.

"Don't go far, Willie." He raced to the surf.

The Tipee Island Fishing Pier stretches into the Atlantic almost a thousand feet and hovers above the beach around twenty-five feet. One of only a handful of structures to dare infringe on the ocean's space, the waves pound into it like target practice.

Sitting beneath the pier, leaning my back against the tall, thick piling, I felt targeted, too. I pulled my knees up to my chest and rested my head. Annoying tears popped into my eyes. Three days until opening and again I felt defeated.

"Hey, you okay?" Teague came around the corner of the piling.

I wiped my eyes quickly. "Fine."

He sat across from me, against a neighboring piling, so close that if I'd stretched out, my feet would've been in his lap. Strangely, I imagined he'd only smile and let me, if I were brave enough to try. I shook off the idea, deciding it would definitely fall into my ever-growing mistake category.

"I hope I didn't get you into any trouble back there," I said.

"Why would you?"

"With Mandy, honeypot. She's very beautiful."

Teague raised an eyebrow. "She knows that."

"I hear she's into the whole Pilates thing. I tried Pilates once. Hurt for four days. I decided that if my body was meant to bend that way, it wouldn't feel so bad afterwards. I heard Mandy's as flexible as a paperclip—"

Teague chuckled. "You know an awful lot about her."

"Candy mentioned it. I didn't ask. She volunteered." I stopped talking long enough to take a breath. "To clarify, I wasn't asking about her or her relationship to you. Candy just said it, as if I'd want to know, which I didn't."

Teague laughed at me. "I get it."

"I want to be clear."

"Actually, the more you talk, the more unclear you are."

I sighed.

Teague nodded, a knowing grin on his face. "You're a nervous talker. I remember that."

I cast him a confused expression. "What?"

"You talk a lot when you get nervous. It's a thing you do."

I tilted my head at him. "Showing off your observation skills, Officer Teague?"

"Has nothing to do with being a cop," he said. "I remember that from our day on the beach. When we were practicing how to pop up on the board, you were so worried about doing the wrong thing that you told me about your mom fighting your English teacher over a B on a paper that should've been an A. You told me about your best friend. What was her name? Lisa? Anyway, she liked this guy who was wrong for her because he watched wrestling on TV, and you felt that was equivalent to a male soap opera. You told me *many* things."

"Oh, my gosh." I buried my face in my hands.

"When I picked you up, you told Candy goodbye half a dozen times and narrated our way to the car. You even said, 'I can't believe he's opening the door for me'."

My face flushed. My palms sweat, making the sand stick. "I'm so embarrassed—"

"Don't be. I loved it."

I dusted the sand off my hands. "I can't believe you remember all that."

"I remember everything about that day."

I got caught up in his eyes and how sincere he seemed. Still, the ache that followed that perfect day returned, grasping a hold of my chest like a vise. I looked down at the sand. That day hadn't been as perfect as I'd thought, especially with my motor-mouth.

Teague said, "She's not my girlfriend, if you're wondering."

"Why is everyone so eager to give me information? I wasn't wondering, actually. I'd be fine with it, even if you were married by now. That'd be acceptable, and none of my business. Mandy seems a very willing candidate, Teague. She called you honeypot, which is an odd endearment. Is that a *Winnie the Pooh* reference? Anyway, if she isn't your girlfriend, she'd sure like to be."

He laughed. "There you go again."

"Please, stop pointing it out."

"Okay." He leaned closer. "I helped Mandy's little brother and made the mistake of accepting a dinner invitation—once. Ever since, she makes it seem like we're dating, especially around other people. We're not."

The breeze kicked up. Willie bounded back over to us, soaking wet from his ocean bath. He shook out his fur right between us.

I swiped the water off my arms. "Willie!"

"That's what happens when you let him off—"

I put my hand up. "Let Willie have his fun."

Our feet moved a little slower on the way back. Teague held Willie's leash and kept his other hand in his pocket. My arms hung loosely at my sides, occasionally brushing his, especially when people passed, forcing us closer together. Noticing those insignificant interactions made me feel like that sixteen-year-old girl again, diving headfirst into trouble. Teague had other things on his mind, though.

"I'm concerned about these warnings," he said. "You should consider some security."

"Security?"

"Cameras, an alarm system—"

"I can't afford that. I've got two months to show a profit or I'm out. Besides, nothing's happened to me—"

"Yet."

"Nothing will," I said. "Someone's trying to scare me. That's all."

"Yeah, but it's not working. Things could escalate. At least, move in with your grandparents, until things settle down."

I huffed. "If I do that, then they'll think their antics are working. I don't want to give them the satisfaction."

"You could instigate more trouble. Not a smart idea."

"Well, most of my ideas turn out to be bad ones. Why stop the trend? Don't worry. I'll lock the doors up tight. I've got Willie. I've got your number. I'll be fine."

Chapter Eight

BINGO!

ON WEDNESDAY EVENING, Grandma Betty and Mamma Rose insisted I attend Seaside Baptist's bingo night, promising that I'd meet potential customers and mingle with an 'in' crowd. A string of multi-colored golf carts in the gravel parking lot told me I'd bring down the average age of the group. Gray heads filled the fellowship hall. A handful of them had donned oxygen tanks. Half of them sat in scooters or wheelchairs. This was the 'in' crowd?

Huffing, I spotted three exceptions to the gray-haired rule. Reverend Bill Richards, around forty, ran the show in a bright Bermuda shirt and shorts. His blond hair fell over his eyes and reminded me a little of a halo. A chubby red-haired man around my age dutifully escorted his mother. Grandma Betty informed me that he was Neil Greene, Park Ranger.

Finally, there was Sam Teague. Sitting across from Grandma Betty and Mamma Rose, he wore his uniform and a broad smile. I wasn't sure whether to feel bothered or relieved to see him.

"There you are!" Grandma Betty tapped the seat next to her.

"We're about to start."

"Samuel was just tellin' us about the lovely day you two spent at the beach when you were teenagers," Mamma Rose said. "I didn't realize you were friends."

Grandma Betty handed me two bingo boards. I nodded, and said, "Yes."

"Delilah, this is my aunt, Beverly." Teague turned to the woman sitting next to him. I shook her extended hand. Her dark hair contrasted with Teague's, but they had the same wide, personable smile that made me want to jump into conversation.

A gruff-looking man interrupted, pointing at me. "I read about you in the paper. You're the fox in the henhouse."

"Excuse me?"

He edged in beside Teague and smiled. A front tooth was missing, but that didn't discourage him. "Fox is right. You sure are foxy! That there was a funny picture of ya in the paper with dem snakes."

He nudged Teague, prompting him to introduce us. "Ray Crackle, this is Delilah Duffy," Crackle shook my hand across the table.

"Delilah ain't a fox in nobody's henhouse," Grandma Betty said. "We're real proud of what she's doing—most of us, anyway."

"Ain't no difference to me," Crackle said. "I'm a fisherman. Ain't got no use for women's shoes or books. But I sure like it when two she-devils go at it." He shook his head. "Used to be that they had mud wrestling down there at Via's, but I guess it was too darn durty for 'em. Shame."

My chin dropped, but nothing came out.

Mavis Chambers, sitting down across from Crackle, said, "You ain't supposed to say every little stupid thought in your head, Ray."

"Mavis, them damned boys of yours were a'pissin' on my roses again," Crackle said, finger pointed. "My Hybrid Teas went all limp and wilty."

Mavis scoffed. "My boys did no such thing."

"As sure as I'm sittin' here, they did. Next time, I'm callin' the police on those little bastards."

Teague rolled his eyes. Crackle settled down.

"It's nice to see you again," I told Mavis. "I'm Delilah Duffy. I don't think I ever told you my name."

"That's alright. I know all about you." Mavis shook hands with me daintily and arranged her set of boards and blotters across her section of the table. "If I had enough capital to invest, I'd open my own business, too."

"What type of business, Mavis?" Grandma Betty asked.

"Dolls. Buy, sell, trade. I do that already online, thanks to Ronnie. But, I'd love working every day in a room full of beautiful, perfect little dolls." Her eyes lit up, and her smile grew.

"You're a nut case," Ray Crackle said. "Who'd buy that crap?"

Mavis took a steady breath. "I wouldn't expect you to understand." She turned to me. "This is exactly why I prefer my inanimate family."

Shocked, my gaping mouth edged into a weak smile. Teague smirked across the table.

Bingo went badly. For a game that required no skill except paying attention, I was terrible. By intermission, the experienced gamers looked at my two boards, shaking their heads in disbelief.

"You're bad luck," Ray Crackle said, changing seats. "You're bringing down the whole table!"

My stomach felt uneasy and a dull pain teased my temples.

Returning to the fellowship hall after the bathroom, I passed Mavis Chambers on her phone.

"Everything ready?" She had one finger pressed into her exposed ear, though the only noises in the hall were my muted footsteps and the rattle and hum of the AC unit. "Yes, I have a Corrine. Mint condition. She's a peach!" she relayed to the caller. I pictured her inanimate family, her dolls, and a shiver slipped through me.

Bingo's second half didn't get any better.

Teague's hand crossed over to my boards. "You missed B12 and O63. Bingo's not your game?"

"Can't focus." My headache beat against the inside of my skull. "I need some air." I handed Grandma Betty my boards and left the table, much to the surprise—maybe relief—of all the die-hard bingo players.

Seaside Baptist isn't oceanfront, but the teasing breezes reached me, anyway. I stood outside the building, breathing it in and basking in the bright moon.

The door clanked open a moment later. Teague joined me. "You okay?"

The ocean breezes mixed with his smell, something like coconut and cocoa butter. I took a deep breath. "Headache."

Teague pointed to a nearby bench underneath an enormous magnolia tree. "Let's sit."

I leaned back against the wood rails of the bench, resting my neck and staring into the night sky through the thick magnolia leaves. A deep breath later, I closed my eyes.

"I can help with that headache. Do you trust me?" Teague asked.

I chuckled at the question, and spat out a definite, "No."

He laughed at not receiving the answer he expected. "Just relax. I'm going to—"

He stopped talking. The tips of his fingers pressed against my temples. I tensed up.

"You don't need to do that. I'll be fine if I can just rest my eyes. With all that's been going on, I'm a little overwhelmed, and with the crowded bingo room and the noise and those dreadful lights in there, that old person smell, and all the dust I'm kicking up at the store, it must be getting to my sinuses. I just—"

"Stop talking."

61

Again, I obeyed. The gentle pressure of his hands took over. Slowly, the tension slipped away like I'd settled into a warm bath.

"Want to hear a story?" Teague asked. I glanced up at him, and he grinned.

"Does it have a happy ending?"

"Not sure yet, but I'm betting it will." His fingers were strong against my skin, but soft at the same time. I couldn't believe he was touching me, that he wanted to. Was this in his job description? Cats out of trees, ladies down dunes, and headache relief?

"Before I came back to Tipee, I worked in Nags Head. One night, we responded to a robbery in progress at a 7-11. A gunman stole money and cigarettes. As I pulled up, a green Ford Taurus sped out of the parking lot, nearly taking out a pedestrian. I pursued him. He was bold, desperate, driving up on the sidewalks, running red lights. Anyway, he made a clever turn and dropped out of sight. I came to an intersection and had to decide which way to go."

"How did you choose?"

"It's instinct to turn right," he said. "Easier, quicker. In a high-stress situation, I guessed a perp would act on instinct. I turned right."

"Did you find him?"

"I spotted a green Ford Taurus," he went on, his fingers never losing their gentle rhythm. "He was driving normally, like he was trying to blend in. I pulled him over without incident. He was this very nervous, young black kid, said he was a college student. Anyway, we detained him, searched the car. Found a bag of pot, but no gun, money, or stolen cigarettes."

"So, was he the robber?"

"Nope, I got the wrong guy."

"That's an easy mistake. At least you got him for the drugs."

"Mistake is right. The kid turned out to be the mayor's son, home from college. Not knowing that, I booked him for the drugs, and brought him in for questioning as a suspect in the robbery. I figured he'd ditched the goods when I lost sight of him. The mayor found out, went ballistic. The media caught wind of the story. Instead of it being a mistaken identity case leading to a drug bust, they called it racial profiling leading to false arrest. I got fired."

My eyes popped open. "Oh, no!"

He breathed out heavily. "Tipee was the only department that would take me then, mostly because I knew people. At the time, I thought I'd fallen into a shit pit I couldn't claw my way out of it."

"Shit pit. How poetic. Did it get better once you were here?"

"Not for a while. The department was torn about me. The ones who knew me from way back teased me relentlessly. The ones who didn't know me, like my partner Williams, assumed the stories were true. Took a while for my friends to get bored and for the rest to become friends."

"Can't imagine anyone thinking you're a racist."

"People'll believe anything. How's your head?"

"Better." I smiled. "Thank you."

Teague stopped my head massage and sat down next to me. "Anytime."

"So, what're you trying to tell me with all this, Teague? I'm sure that's not a story you share just for the hell of it."

He laughed. "You're right. I don't. I guess the point is that there's a bright side to screwing up. If that hadn't happened, I'd still be there. That would've been a bigger mistake. There were many things about my life that needed to change, but I wouldn't have done anything without being forced to. My mistakes gave me nudges about my life."

"Nudges?"

"Yeah, nudges. I needed them. Mistakes can lead to blessings, eventually."

A smirk crossed my face. "I still don't want to make any more of them."

"You do better than you give yourself credit for. You're opening in three days, despite everything. You should be proud."

I smiled. I couldn't help it. "You're awfully sweet to me."

"Weird, huh?"

The phone in his pocket beeped and buzzed. He stepped away to take the call.

He returned with, "It's work. I have to go. Better get Aunt Bev."

"I can take her home."

"You don't mind?"

"It's the least I can do since you cured my headache." I grinned. "Go. I'll take care of her." He squeezed my arm gently and walked away. A few steps later, he turned.

"Delilah, may I take you to breakfast in the morning? Eight?"

I wanted to say no, but somehow, I said, "Yes."

Chapter Nine

OCTOPUS

THE FEMALE OCTOPUS only mates once in her life, and that's because the one time kills her. After a single romantic interlude, she spends a month of fasting while taking care of her unhatched eggs. But, it's not starvation that gets her in the end. Her body is genetically programmed to kick the bucket after her eggs hatch. She's simply done.

A positive person might look upon this scientific fact as rather romantic. Having lived life and enjoyed a beautiful encounter, the female knows that nothing could come close to surpassing it, so she dies.

I am not a positive person.

She waits until the absolute last moment of her precious life to give in to the genetic need to reproduce and is so disappointed with the whole thing that she dies out of despair. Disappointment and dating go together.

Thursday morning. Two days until the grand reopening of Beach Read. Instead of preparing, I was waiting. It was 8:43.

I'd woken early, so I'd have enough time to go to Grandma Betty's house for a real shower. The shower at the store—a narrow box with dim lighting—is okay, but it's hard to shave my legs. I arrived at her house around six. Took a long, hot shower, dressed, had coffee, and got back to the store by 7:30.

I should've stayed in bed.

My phone rang at 8:45. I answered with an exceptionally chipper, "Hello?"

"I'm sorry," Teague said. "We're on a call, and I've gotten—well, I'm running late—"

"Late for what?"

"Breakfast."

"Oh, that's right. It'd slipped my mind," I said. "I have so much work to do, it's probably best if we forget the whole thing." I got off the phone with him quickly.

At ten, Beach Read received a huge shipment of books I'd ordered. Boxes filled up the floor. It thrilled me to have something new to occupy my thoughts. Aunt Laura had left me with a decent supply, but I'd enjoyed choosing a slew of new titles.

Aunt Laura had also left behind an ancient yellow pricing gun and several spools of stickered tape. Once I figured out how to use it, I priced each book with careful consideration, slapping the neon sticker across the ISBN on the back.

Tapping at the door sent Willie into a fit of barks and made me jump. I yanked the door open, hitting the chimes into a tangent.

Teague smiled warmly. Eyeing the pricing gun in my hand, he said, "Don't shoot." I rolled my eyes and moved out of the way so he could come in.

"You look busy." He glanced around at my boxes. "Is that why you haven't answered my last two phone calls?" I looked at him, perplexed. My phone sat on the counter. I picked it up and showed him it was dead. "Ah. Thought you might be mad at me."

I plugged the phone into the charger. He leaned against the

counter. "I should have known better—making a date for breakfast. Never know what might happen. I hoped it might be a slow night, and I wanted to see you as soon as I could. That was the soonest."

I continued working on my books, unfazed. "Turned out to be a good thing. When I saw the UPS guy, I had too much to do anyway, so I'm glad you stood me up. Gave me time to come to my senses. What were you saying last night about mistakes turning into blessings?"

He chuckled. "Oh, so you *are* mad. I'd be offended if I weren't so touched."

I stood with my back against a stack of boxes. Teague stepped closer.

"I'm sorry," he said softly, "truly." His eyes pulled me in and kept me prisoner in that spot. "You ever been in one of those situations? All night I watched the clock, hoping the minutes would go by quicker. Then, a half-hour from the finish line, we got a call. Then I wanted the clock to stand still, so I wouldn't disappoint you. Reminded me of high school, waiting for the bell to ring, so I could get to the beach. I haven't had a night that long in ages." His fingers brushed my arm. "Forgive me?"

My breath caught in my throat, but I huffed and ducked away. "I don't have time for this. I have about ten boxes of books to price and organize. Once that's done, I have to create an inventory, which'll be a trick since I don't have a computer. Learn the register, get set up at the bank, get enough money for the till, how to do credit cards... I have a ton of stuff I need to do, is the gist of what I'm saying."

He smiled, knowingly. I knew he was thinking about my nervous talking again.

"Let me help." He grabbed the pricing gun out of my hand. "I can handle this thing." He pulled the trigger, sending a sticker out of the chamber, which he then set on my nose. I rolled my eyes but couldn't help the inevitable smile that escaped, anyway. "I'd pay $10.95 for you." He laughed. I snatched the price tag away, balled it up between my fingers, and tossed it at him.

I cocked my head. "You'd be more of a distraction than a help."

"Come on. Let's go to brunch or lunch. Whatever you want. I'm all yours."

I let another smile slip, scrutinizing his tempting invitation. "That's a scary thought."

The mail spilled through the front door's slot. I headed for it, thankful for the distraction. A familiar envelope caught my eye. I ripped it open.

"Everything okay?" Teague asked. I didn't answer.

Inside the business-size envelope was a small blue sticky note. The top read *From the Desk of Jonathan Dekker* and the handwritten part read *Miss me?* My shoulders fell.

Clark must have told him where I was.

"What is it?" Teague headed over, but I balled up the note and the envelope before he could get there. I held them tightly in my hand.

"Nothing."

"No, really. Tell me. What's wrong?"

I gave him a smile. "Nothing's wrong. Just an enormous bill that I wasn't expecting. You know what, though? I really think you should go—"

"I don't believe you," he said. "A bill?"

"Yes, a bill."

"You ball up all your bills like that? Let me see it." He held out his hand.

"No, it's none of your business. You should go. You need sleep, and I need—"

"What do you need?"

I hesitated. About a dozen smart ass answers popped into my mind, but his concerned face disarmed me. It would've been enough that he had piercing, soulful eyes that made me feel like the only woman in the world when he looked at me, but combining those eyes with his strong face, broad shoulders, beautiful blond hair, and soft lips that curved into the kindest of smiles…

Well, it hardly seemed like God was playing fair.

I looked at the floor. The innate quality about me, the part that says *I-need-someone*, told me to drop everything and go eat with him. *Just give in.* The louder part reminded me of the dead female octopi, the balled-up note in my hand, the long wait this morning, and the misery thirteen years ago—that was never far from my thoughts.

"I need to be alone."

Moments later, Teague left.

Chapter Ten

CALM

WORK ON THE apartment moved fast; Damon and his crew
neared completion. The store was as ready as I could get it.
So, on Friday morning, I hit up the Piggly Wiggly for orange juice,
fruit, muffins, and bagels. I carried the bags into the store and set
up a mini-buffet on the counter. Then, I ran into Darryl Chambers
behind the building.

"Good morning, Ms. Duffy." He smiled, his green eyes almost
sparkling in the sunshine. His hand was bandaged from his recent
fight with the dumpster. "Sorry I scared you the other day. Me and
my brother are like oil and water sometimes. You know what that's
like. You've got a crazy family, too."

"I do. Call me Delilah. You're working on Damon's crew,
aren't you?"

He shrugged. "Yeah, it's my main job lately. Quit Via's."

"No more beating up bad guys?"

"I'm sure I'll still do a little of that." He grinned. "I'm goin'
finish that light fixture before your grand openin', Ms. Duffy. I

mean, Delilah."

"Thanks. I have breakfast for everyone in the store."

"I'll tell the others. It thrilled me when Damon said we were working on your apartment. I feel like I already know you."

Another worker got his attention and called him over. A few minutes later, the store bustled with construction workers digging into the food I'd set up.

Aside from the chandelier I bought from The Cotton Exchange—the light fixture didn't get done after all—the store looked great. All I needed now was customers. So, instead of spending Friday night obsessing about last-minute details, I did something very uncharacteristic of me. Willie and I hit the boardwalk for Tipee Island's first evening of fireworks for the season and accepted Grandma Betty's offer to spend the night in a real bed. Ah!

The boardwalk and fishing pier overflowed with crowds. Willie and I melded into the folds. Everyone was there. We had a long chat with Uncle Clark, and short hellos later with Aunt Clara and Uncle Peter. I spied Rachel hanging out with a group of her young friends near the beach. Then later, I noticed Raina sitting on the pier, alone. I was about to see if she wanted company when Willie and I were distracted.

Mike Ancellotti tapped me on the shoulder, turning me around. "I'm glad you came out, especially on the eve of your grand opening."

"Everything's ready, I'm happy to say."

"Who's this?" Mike leaned down to give Willie some attention. Willie licked his face. Mike laughed.

"Willie. He's happy to meet you."

"I love dogs. I had three growing up. None now, though."

"My dad insisted on Willie. Said if I couldn't land a husband, I had to have a dog, as a matter of safety." We started walking together.

"That's very protective of him."

"Yes, my folks are like that."

Mike nodded. We started walking the length of the pier together, edging through the growing crowd. He slipped his hand around my waist to guide me around the mass of people. Surprised by the touch, I nearly tripped over a wayward board. Mike led me to what he called the 'primo spot' at the end of the pier, left corner. A bench ran the length of the end. Years ago, this'd been one of my favorite reading nooks.

The fireworks boomed at 9:30. The brilliant lights smashed into the sky and lit up our faces. I glanced over at Mike to find him looking at me.

"Beautiful," Mike said.

"They are…"

"I wasn't talking about the fireworks."

"Oh." I looked toward the black ocean, splattered with mirrored lights, and tried to compose a response that wouldn't come. Should I be flattered or bothered? I couldn't tell.

"I'm sorry," he said after a moment. "I've embarrassed you."

"Nope, not embarrassed," I said, though I couldn't hide my flushed face under the bright lights. "Thank you for saying that, and, um, likewise, you're very—" *Don't say butter. Don't say anything about butter.* "—um, appealing, too. I mean, you shouldn't judge a book by its cover, but it's impossible not to. You, um, have a nice cover."

Mike laughed while I clamped my lips shut, determined not to let my nervous talking go any further.

Fifteen minutes and many awkward words later, we headed toward the street, along with the rest of the crowd.

We neared the end of the planks, and he stopped. He ran his hand through his hair, sending his light array of curls falling around his head. "I'll come by the store tomorrow."

"Okay."

"And Tuesday night, to take you out to dinner."

"What?"

"I'm asking you out," Mike said, smirking.

The idea struck me funny, like he had to be joking. "Why would you want to do that?"

He laughed. "How it works is that you see someone you like, talk to them, find out you want to spend more time with them, and that's when the date comes in—a set aside time to meet and enjoy each other. Surely, you've had these before?"

I blushed. "Yes."

"Anyone serious right now?"

"No."

"Then, why not?"

"I don't know. I'm still reeling from the compliment you gave me earlier. It's a lot to take in. Plus, I'm sure I'll be swamped with the store—"

"All the more reason to get away. From one business owner to another, you'll need a break."

My mind spun, one half arranging excuses and the other half shooting them down. Mike smiled hopefully. He had kind, dark eyes and a playful smile. Still, the word *mistake* echoed in my mind. I considered Teague. Mike might be a fun distraction.

"You'll have a good time, promise," he added after many moments of silence. "I know a great restaurant. There's music and this cool atmosphere. You'll love it. Please, say yes."

With a deep breath, I said, "Okay."

"Excellent. It was a tough call, but you made the right choice." We both laughed, and I started feeling less like an idiot.

After a long goodbye, he headed across Atlantic Avenue toward The Crab Shack. I strolled leisurely with Willie toward my Jeep, parked near the pier in anticipation of heading to Grandma Betty's.

"He thinks I'm beautiful, Willie." Willie didn't seem impressed.

I sighed dreamily, looked up, and found Sam Teague standing

by his police car. Willie rushed over, yanking the leash out of my hands. Officer Williams was busy writing a parking ticket for a vehicle nearby. He gave me a short nod as I walked over.

"Enjoy the fireworks?" Teague asked, petting Willie.

"Lovely."

"I see you've met Ancellotti."

I couldn't help but grin. "My Uncle Clark introduced us. He named a drink after me."

"Fall for that bit, did you?"

"I guess. He asked me out."

"What did you say?"

With a raised eyebrow, I said, "Yes."

"I thought you weren't going to make any more mistakes."

"Why don't you go solve a crime or something?"

He grimaced. "That looked pretty criminal to me."

On the way to Grandma Betty's, with the top down to be beachy-cool, I listened to the radio. The local station was the only one that came in well.

"You're listening to Milo and Baby Chris, Tipee Talk Radio, and we're talking about the latest victim of the Granny Bandits—Corrine Masterson," Milo said. "According to inside sources, the bandits broke into her Tradewinds home Wednesday evening between nine and ten while Mrs. Masterson attended Seaside Baptist's Bingo night. Stole jewelry, an undisclosed amount of cash, her television set, a silver tea service, a Roomba. They even took her alarm clock and coffee maker. A Mr. Coffee."

"Now that's just criminal!"

I grinned. Criminal behavior seemed to be going around.

Chapter Eleven

GRAVEYARDS

A MISTY HUE settled across the island during the night, surprising me when I walked out onto Grandma Betty's front porch just after dawn on Saturday morning. The rooster thermometer on the deck read eighty-four degrees. The early fog would soon burn off in a blazing sun.

Still, it looked creepy over the ocean. Driving down Atlantic Avenue, I thought of The Graveyard of the Atlantic, off the North Carolina coast, where thousands of shipwrecks litter the ocean floor. I buried my uneasiness, thinking about the grand opening instead.

Willie growled as we neared the front door to Beach Read. My *Countdown to the Grand Reopening* sign, boasting its huge number one, was stained with mysterious red splotches.

"What's that, Willie?" I leaned closer to the window. The spots weren't on the sign, but on the glass. I backed up. They dotted the entire window. A light shone from inside the store.

Willie growled again.

I fumbled for my keys and scurried to the doorknob. The used chandelier that I'd bought from Lenny at The Cotton Exchange dangled high above the counter. Its cheap crystals glimmered, most of them. Some were stained red.

I unlocked the door, my hands shaking. Willie pushed in first.

"Willie!" He rushed in barking, his paws sinking into a pool of blood.

A body lay in the middle of the bookstore.

I raced over. Darryl Chambers lay motionless on his side, blood soaked around his midsection. Trembling, I felt his wrist. Cold and still. An object fell from his hand into mine—a painted sand dollar.

The metallic smell in the air, the sticky blood on my fingers, the reality that Darryl was hurt—was dead—made me feel sick, scared, and horrified all at once. Willie barked and growled, mimicking my turmoil.

"Come on, Willie!" Grabbing the tuft of fur at his neck, I pulled. The ladder from my storage closet leaned precariously against the nearest column. I turned toward the counter, dragging Willie away, and saw a message written on the wall.

I let go of Willie.

GO HOME!

Scrawled out in blood behind the counter, the words made me gasp. Pushing the sand dollar into my pocket, I pulled out my phone. Frantically, I flipped the phone open, smearing blood all over it, and fumbled ridiculously before hearing a ring on the other end.

"I didn't… I meant 9-1-1. I m-messed up—"

"What's wrong?" Teague asked.

"Sam, he's dead. There's a dead body. I-I should've listened to you—"

"It's okay." Teague's voice stayed steady and calm. "I'll be there in a minute. Are you safe?" The siren erupted through the phone.

I scanned the room. Nothing moved, except for Willie. "I think so."

"Stay on the phone with me." To someone else, he said, "10-54," followed by my address. "Delilah, are you inside the store?"

"Yes."

"Go outside. Wait for me at the curb."

My hands hardly working, I leashed Willie and pulled him outside. He left bloody paw prints from the door to the light post, where I looped his leash. I collapsed on the curb.

"Delilah, are you still with me?" I answered in a half whimper.

The Dodge Charger screamed around Atlantic Avenue, fishtailing as it curved. It screeched to a halt five feet from my legs. The two men raced out. Williams went inside the store.

Teague knelt down in front of me. "Are you alright?" His concern brought tears to my eyes, but I couldn't form words. "Is this your blood?" He touched my hands, turning them over in his. I shook my head.

His blue eyes squinted, measuring me up. "You're okay. I'll be right back."

Three more cars arrived. Teague and Williams marked off the building and sidewalk with crime scene tape. Teague moved me into the passenger seat of the Charger, door open. I let my legs hang outside the car. Willie settled by my feet.

"You'll be more comfortable here," he said. "It'll be awhile—"

"I'm so sorry," I blurted out, tears streaming. "This is my fault. I had no idea—"

"Delilah, this isn't your fault." Teague leaned down, one hand petting Willie's fur and the other resting on my knee.

"That message was for me. Darryl must've come back to fix the light, and then someone did this."

"You can't hold yourself responsible for the derangement of others." Teague handed me a handkerchief from his pocket. A dark blue *ST* was embroidered on the corner. "Everything'll be okay."

I nodded, blotting my eyes. He smiled reassuringly and went

back to his work.

I calmed down, refocusing on the business of murder unfolding around me. Unlike TV, there wasn't a great commotion, minus the initial sirens. The whole of it was rather peaceful and respectful. Everyone did their part, writing notes and gathering up objects into bags.

But, as the morning wore on, businesses stirred. Early bird tourists came out of their holes for first dibs on primo spots on the beach. As the attention grew, Williams and Teague shifted from inside to out, discouraging looky-loos and questions. The men inside, now joined by Billy Mott, hurried their pace. A doctor arrived, followed by an ambulance.

I rested my head against the cushioned seat. My eyes caught an array of pictures gracing the visor over the driver's seat. Officer Williams had placed pictures of his wife and two daughters there, smiling widely.

I pushed Teague's visor down. No pictures. My eyes almost went right over an object hanging from the mirror. I looked closer and pulled it down. At first, it didn't seem like anything more than a tattered collection of strings, dirty and frayed, braided together into a loose circle. I held it in my hand, ran my fingers along the length of it, and the memory returned.

"*You're about to lose your ankle bracelet,*" he'd said, pointing to the loose knot.

"*I got it at one of those touristy shops on the boardwalk,*" I'd told him. "*Candy said I needed some decoration. She tried to talk me into a bellybutton ring. I bought this.*"

He'd shaken his head. "*You don't need any decoration, but I like it.*"

I'd pulled it from my ankle. It was soaked with all the surfing we'd done, but I liked the mix of blues twisted together. "*Give me your arm.*"

I tied it to his wrist.

"You're giving it to me?"

"Yes, so you never forget me."

A shadow closed in on the car, so I hurriedly put the bracelet back on Teague's visor.

"Ms. Duffy?" The man wore Dockers khakis and a thin button-down mustard colored shirt. His mustache made him look like he belonged in the 70s. "I'm Detective Harlan Lewis. Let's move to the alley, so we can talk."

He led Willie and me around the corner of the building to the gravel lot near the Jeep, away from most of the prying eyes on Starfish Drive.

"Is this blood?" He pointed to my hands.

"Oh, sorry. I touched the body. I got it on my shorts, too." He immediately called for one of his associates to take samples from my clothing and hands.

"Why did you touch the body?"

"Pulse. I was looking for a pulse. I mean, I knew he was dead, but thought maybe. I mean, if I were lying there, I'd want the first person to find me to check for a pulse, just in case. It could've been faint, you know. There could've been a chance."

He nodded. Sweat beaded up around my temples. I felt inexplicably nervous. Something about Lewis' straight back and burrowing eyes made me want to shrink away from him. He was rigid and emotionless.

"Is that your vehicle, Ms. Duffy?" He pointed to the Jeep. I nodded. "We'd like to search it."

"Why? The Jeep was with me—"

"The perpetrator could've slipped out the back after you parked."

A shiver scurried down my back. "Sure, go ahead."

Detective Lewis called Teague over to search the Jeep. Teague pulled a pair of latex gloves from his utility belt and opened the driver's side door.

"What time did you arrive this morning, ma'am?" Lewis asked.

"6:30. I spent the night at my grandparents' house."

"Where do you live?" Lewis asked.

"Here, at the store, since last Saturday. The upstairs apartment is under construction."

"Did you know the victim?"

"Not really. He was working on the upstairs apartment. He must've changed that light fixture. The chandelier wasn't up yesterday when I left."

"What time was that?" Lewis scribbled notes in his leather tablet. Behind him, Teague opened up the glove compartment and rummaged through it.

"Um, about eight."

"Did you return to the building for any reason after eight?"

"No."

"Did you go directly to your grandparents'?"

My defenses rumbled inside of me. "No, I went to the boardwalk, hung out there for the fireworks. I got to their house around ten."

"Anyone see you?"

"Lots of people saw me." Nervous acids popped inside me, forcing too many words. "Spoke to Uncle Clark about running an ad in the paper, too expensive. Got a very high-browed hello from Aunt Clara. Saw my grandparents there. Spent most of my time with Mike Ancellotti. He said I was beautiful. Even asked me out, though I'm not so sure that was a good idea—saying yes to the date. Teague saw me there." Both men stared at me. I took a deep breath. "You know, I'm not so sure I—"

"Did you hear any noises or notice anything strange when you arrived this morning?"

With a small flashlight, Teague peered under the seats. I winced thinking how long it had been since I'd cleaned the Jeep.

"Blood on the window. The light was on," I said. "Willie

growled."

"How did you find the door when you arrived?"

"It was locked. That's strange, isn't it? The killer must've left by the back door, right?"

Lewis shifted his weight from one foot to the other. "Unless the killer had a key. Does anyone have a key aside from yourself?"

"My great-uncle, Joe Duffy. He owns the building. Probably Candy Carver."

"Aside from touching the body and letting your dog run through the blood pool, did you disturb anything else in the room?" he asked. My eyes squinted.

"I didn't let Willie run around willy-nilly. And I didn't mean that to be a pun. Ugh! I didn't expect a dead body in my store. He got in the door before I did, and it was shocking." I huffed. "I touched the door to unlock it. That's it. Once I knew for sure he was dead, I called Teague and waited outside."

I clamped my lips together tight.

Lewis closed his notebook. "Okay, Ms. Duffy. That's all I need right now. The building will be off limits for at least a few days or longer—"

"*What?*"

"To preserve the integrity of the crime scene. Standard procedure."

Teague circled behind the Jeep to open the back.

I fisted my bloody hands. "Holy Moses! This sucks. I mean, I'm very sorry about what's happened here, and I'm all about cooperating, but damn! I've got to get this store open. Oh, God, it can get any worse."

"Lewis," Teague said over his shoulder. I looked up from my hissy fit to see that he was holding a gun by his gloved fingertips. "It was jammed behind the tire."

Chapter Twelve

TSUNAMIS

"**M**Y TIRE?" MY heart pounded double-time. "That's not mine!"

"Ms. Duffy, you must come down to the station for further questioning," Lewis said, his beady eyes perking up. "Is that a Beretta?"

Detective Lewis edged over to Teague and admired the weapon. Another associate bagged the evidence. I leaned against the brick wall, trying to steady my heartbeats. Deep breaths. Stay calm.

"I'll take Willie over to Betty's house," Teague said, gently taking the leash from my hands. "You'll be fine. Just tell the truth. You'll be out of there before dinner."

"Is he arresting me?"

"No, he's asking questions. He has nothing to hold you on."

A tear slipped down my face. I swiped it away. A tsunami of fear fell over me. Clammy and shaking, I felt faint.

The other officers fiddled with the gun like a new toy. Teague moved in closer, barely six inches from my face.

"Delilah, don't worry. Let them get the information they need, so they can find this boy's real killer. You can do this. It'll be alright."

I took a deep breath and nodded weakly.

Detective Lewis' office was a gray cubicle in a field of others, though some were decorated with children's pictures, calendars, and posters. Detective Lewis' walls were all gray, except for post-it notes. A miniature cactus sat by his computer. I could almost hear it sighing from boredom.

He pointed to a chair next to his desk. I took a seat. My skin prickled from the cool air and icy situation. Lewis' mustache twitched. He started with general information. Full name. Address. Phone number. Birth date. Maybe Teague was right. I needed to give Lewis information, so he could move on to the next suspect.

"So, what's your last known address?"

I recited the address of my former apartment in Durham.

"Leave any dead bodies behind in Durham?"

My mouth fell open, and a feeling of half-disgust and half-surprise swept over me. I'm sure it showed on my face. "No."

"Tell me about the gun."

"It's not mine."

His mustache twitched. "Then, how do you suppose it ended up in your vehicle?" He tapped his pencil against the table.

I shrugged. "Anyone could've slipped it in there."

"You said you knew the victim." Lewis referred to his leather book. "How well did you know him?"

My eyes narrowed at his tone. "Not well at all. He worked for Damon on the apartment. I didn't *know* him, know him. I've only ever seen him like three or four times in my life."

"He got into the building somehow. Did you let him in before leaving for the fireworks?"

"No, I did not. When I left, no one was in the building that I know of. I turned out the lights, locked the door, and left—"

"In the Jeep?"

"Yes, in the Jeep, which I then parked down by the boardwalk—easy access for anyone to plant anything." I wanted him to write that down, but he didn't give me the satisfaction.

"Did you see anyone around your vehicle?" he asked.

"No."

"Was anyone with you the entire time at the boardwalk?"

"Just Willie, my dog."

"You said you had a few interactions with Chambers over the last week?"

I explained all of my previous encounters with Darryl Chambers. "The last thing he said to me was that he would get the light finished before the grand opening, but he didn't, not before I left."

"Did you question him about why he hadn't gotten the work done?" Lewis fiddled with his mustache.

"No. Around six, I stopped hearing work being done upstairs, so I assume that's when everyone left. I didn't go up to investigate. I didn't even give the light fixture a second thought. I had other things to get ready for the opening."

"Any valuables in the store?"

"A zippered money pouch in the bottom drawer of the filing cabinet in the office," I said. "Is it still there? Oh, my gosh, I hope I wasn't robbed, too."

"We'll check for it. Anything else of value?"

"Just books. I don't have much."

Lewis handed me a few forms to fill out and left me buried in paperwork. With a sigh, I rehashed again, on paper, the events of the last twenty-four hours. When Lewis didn't return right away, I asked an officer at the next cubicle for the ladies' room.

I blotted my face with cool water. Despite my good night of sleep, I looked, and felt exhausted. I had done nothing but felt drained. Still, Teague had been right. This wasn't as bad as I'd thought it'd be.

Then, I reached in my pocket.

A live sand dollar differs greatly from one you'd buy in a beach store. Live ones are never white. They're blue or gray or even purple. White sand dollars that wash up on shore and become treasures are merely beautiful skeletons.

One of those beautiful skeletons was still in my pocket. I'd stolen evidence from a crime scene!

Cringing, I pulled the sand dollar from my pocket, and eyed it like a ticket from my windshield. I'd made another huge mistake.

Aside from the blood that had stained one side of it, the sand dollar was beautiful. The painting was more detailed and delicate than I'd originally noticed. Orange and yellow hues birthed an incredible sunset scene over a bluish-gray seascape. A black silhouette stood staring at the sea. In the bottom corner, three black dots formed an upside-down triangle. Across the bottom, delicate brush strokes spelled out, *For God so loved the world... John 3:16.*

A knock on the door made me jump. The sand dollar slid into the sink.

"Ms. Duffy? You in there?" Lewis sounded impatient.

"Yes, I'll be out in a minute." I picked up the treasure, wiped off the excess water, and shoved it back in my pocket. I had to tell Detective Lewis. I took a deep breath before leaving the bathroom.

Lewis tapped his pencil against a file on the desk as I came around the cubicle. I took my seat and slid the completed forms over to him. He didn't seem to notice. Ready to confess about the sand dollar, Lewis stopped me.

"Your move to Tipee isn't without controversy, Ms. Duffy. Why did you come here, exactly?"

"I have family here, and my great-uncle Joe made me a great job offer," I said, robotically.

"You were a high school teacher?"

"Yes."

"How come you aren't teaching any longer?"

"Wanted a change."

"Ms. Duffy, isn't it strange to switch careers like that?" A smile edged up on his mouth.

"People switch careers all the time."

"Were you fired from your teaching position?"

"My contract wasn't renewed."

"On what grounds?"

I took a deep breath. "What does this have to do with anything?"

"Ms. Duffy, a murder has occurred at your residence. We found the murder weapon in your vehicle. I can ask whatever I want. Let me decide if one has anything to do with the other."

"I assure you, it doesn't," I said. "That should be good enough."

"How long did you work for that school?"

"Seven years."

"You must've done something terrible. Did it involve your students, Ms. Duffy?"

I scoffed. "I'm not answering these questions."

He grinned. "I thought you might feel that way." He reached for the file under his pencil and took out a picture.

Jonathan had taken it when we were together. I was on the bed wearing a skimpy black negligee. I was giving Jonathan a 'come hither' look—the only look I know after a few glasses of wine. A handful of my disgruntled students had mysteriously gotten a hold of that picture and posted it everywhere online. I thought I'd hunted all the pictures down and eradicated them from cyberspace existence. What I couldn't erase, I'd thought I'd outrun, moving to the island.

"This is you, isn't it?" Lewis asked.

My anger and humiliation boiled. "Yes."

"How did this picture end up on an eighteen-year-old's

Instagram?"

That was a question I'd asked myself a million times. I didn't know. "Not the way you're inferring." I folded my arms across my chest.

"The young man wrote, '*Ms. Duffy will knock your socks off.*' What does that mean?"

"Not what you're thinking. I never had inappropriate relationships with students." I folded my arms over my chest, trying to control my anger.

"Then, how did he get this picture?" I remained silent. "I bet you got yourself fired because of this. Then, you came here to Tipee to escape your sordid past. So, when did Chambers get involved?"

I stared at Detective Lewis through squinting eyes and furrowed brow. "I told you. I have nothing to do with Darryl Chambers." I pushed the sand dollar deeper into my pocket. "You're wasting your time. My past has nothing to do with this. You should find out all you can about Darryl Chambers and look into my strange vandalism cases and the message written on my wall. This community is full of people out to destroy my business. What about them?"

"Ms. Duffy, I'll investigate all leads. I know what I'm doing."

"Really? Have you had a lot of murder cases in Tipee?"

His mustache twitched. "An investigation is an investigation."

"Right, I thought not." I remembered what Teague'd said to me. "Well, you have no reason to hold me. I'm leaving."

Chapter Thirteen

HALF SLEEP

"I HATE WHEN this happens!" Clark paced the back deck. "Damn paper comes out twice a week and the story of the decade happens on Saturday. I have to wait four days to report it. Shawsburg will scoop me on a murder in my backyard."

"Calm down, son." Grandpa Charlie manned the grill.

"This is just God's way of endin' this family squabble." Clara sipped her Mojito, fanning herself with her hat.

"Well, God didn't kill 'em," Betty said.

Clark took a deep breath. "At least, I have an inside man on this. I can get the real story with all the glorious trimmings—right, Delilah?"

"What?" I glanced up. I was sitting in the chaise lounge on the back deck with Willie snuggled at my feet, even though it was steamy hot outside. My glass of water sweated into my lap until my shorts were wet, but I hardly noticed.

I'd been thinking about dolphins, whales, and porpoises. When these celebrities of the sea sleep, they become aquatic zombies.

They shut down half their brains, enabling them to rest while still being conscious enough to surface for air. They function, but they're not all there. I felt like that—only half-aware and easily jolted.

Clark rolled his eyes and paced to my chair. "You'll give me some details, right? Tell me what you saw?"

Tears welled in my eyes, again. I'd walked home from the police station in time for the Duffy's weekly get-together, and my emotions had been yo-yoing. The more I thought about what I'd seen, the more upset I'd become.

"Leave her alone, Clark," Mamma Rose said. "She's weary to the bone."

"That Chambers boy was always at least knee-deep in trouble." Candy brushed out the wrinkles in her lap. "It really ain't no surprise, is it?"

"It's goin' to be bad for business, all the way around," Clara said.

"Are you kiddin'?" Clark asked. "Not for my business."

"It might sell papers, but it won't sell shoes. Too close for comfort." Clara sipped her drink.

"Or maybe they'll think it's cool," Rachel said. "I heard some boys at the beach talkin' about how they wanted to go peer in the windas. Heard it was all gross inside."

"Gross and perfect for a renovation. Tear it down and build it up again. Expanding Top to Bottom into that space will wipe the slate clean," Clara said.

I rolled my eyes and jolted from my seat. "A boy is dead! He isn't even in the ground yet, and all anyone can think about is business. Don't you even care that a life has been lost?"

Candy sighed. "Delilah, he was trouble. Came from a broken home and had nothin' but strikes 'gainst him his whole life—"

"So what? That makes it okay? He should've had his whole life to make up for whatever mistakes he'd made, but it was taken away from him, and no one here seems to care."

"Delilah's right. He's gone. I can't believe it. Ya'll are awful!" Raina stood up from her seat near the back of the deck, tears peppered her cheeks. I'd forgotten she was there. "Ya'll are being disrespectful, and—and—and un-Christian-like!"

She stormed off inside the house. Clara shrugged, turning back to me, one hand on her hip.

I took a deep breath. "The last thing Darryl Chambers did with his life was help me. I'm not bowing out now, and I don't think Darryl would want me to. As soon as the police give me the all clear, I'm opening Beach Read."

Raina had had the right idea—disappearing into the house. I moved toward the sliding glass door, determined to find some kind of peace in the sanctity of my temporary rooster bedroom. Clara had other ideas.

"We understand how you feel, Delilah," she said, almost in a singsong voice. "But, opening the store won't make up for it."

"Excuse me?"

"Surely, you realize that this unfortunate death—well, it's a great deal of guilt to carry. If you'd only listened to reason—"

"You're blaming me?"

"If you hadn't started this ridiculous venture in the first place, then maybe he'd still be alive. You said yourself that he was there doing work for you—"

"That's right!" Charlotte said, pointing in the air. "That poor boy. He could've been safe at home or at the movies or anywhere. Oh, bless his soul!"

Clara smiled. "As I say to my customers, Delilah, if the shoe fits, then charge it."

Part of my resolve crumbled. Guilt had found a place in the mixed-up brew of emotions stirred up by everything that'd happened. Still, it wasn't Clara's place to highlight it. I stormed over to where she stood and stared her down. The urge to strike her surged in me.

Instead, I slapped the drink from her hand. It shattered daintily on the deck. Everyone turned and stared like statues, mouths hanging open.

"You're the one who's incited everyone against me. If he died to send me a message, then his blood's on your hands as much as mine." I turned away from her, sick of her face. "Want to know a detail, Clark? The killer left me a message. *Go home*, written in blood on the wall."

"Holy shit!"

"Sounds like a message you'd send, Clara, if not in action, at least in spirit. You're a devil, and I hope to God you had nothing to do with this."

Chapter Fourteen

DEATH & BLASPHEMY

THE NEXT MORNING, Grandma Betty made the mistake of dragging me to church where I accidentally blurted out "shit" loud enough for the entire congregation to hear. In my defense, the shoes I borrowed from Candy's closet were a size too big. I tripped getting into the pew, banging my knee hard against the mahogany. My pain mattered little to the aghast congregation and my embarrassed family.

Grandma Betty was still mortified on the drive home. It was unbearably silent. Betty fidgeted. Charlie's hands tightly gripped and then loosened on the steering wheel. My curse in church had pushed my generous hosts over the edge.

I scanned my brain for something of interest, something to share, to lighten the heavy tension that had settled between us, but Betty beat me to the punch.

"Pastor Bill and Joanne went to visit Mavis yesterday afternoon."

"How is she?" Charlie asked.

"Fair to middlin'. She didn't want meals, or yard work, or visits or anything."

Charlie nodded. "She's never been one to take handouts."

"I know, but this is different from charity. We're a church family. We have to do something."

"When's the service?" Charlie asked. "We could send flowers."

Betty shook her head. "No service. Mavis didn't want one."

I sat up and leaned forward. "What do you mean, no service? No funeral? No memorial? No wake?"

Betty's eyes pinched together at my interruption. "She's having her son cremated. She told the pastor that she and Ronnie will do something special on their own."

"That's crazy. How can you not have a service?"

"Services aren't mandatory, Delilah. Arrangements are very expensive. The Chambers family—well, they've always been tight with funds."

"Plus, it's a lot of hubbub," Charlie said, "and they've never liked attention, either. Always been that way."

"Still! How are people going to pay their respects? How are his friends going to say goodbye to him? He's young. Surely, he has friends."

Grandma Betty shrugged. "He was very popular in high school when he played football. Even had colleges interested in him, but he made some bad life choices. I'd guess that Mavis is tryin' to stay away from the bad element his funeral may have attracted—"

"The funeral could've brought out his killer, and maybe he would've slipped up and given himself away—"

Grandma Betty laughed. "You sound like a mystery novel. Mavis knows what's best. I respect her courage, frankly."

The word *shit* echoed in my mind, but this time, I didn't say it. Whatever sadness I felt for Darryl Chambers quadrupled. His family choosing not to have a service felt like choosing not to remember him.

"Delilah," Grandma Betty said after a moment of silence. The way she said it showed trouble ahead. "Um, dear, I know you're goin' through a time right now, but I cannot abide foul language, especially in church. A young lady as privileged as yourself shouldn't talk like you're common. It's inappropriate for a lady. Oh, the phone calls I'm goin' to get!"

I wanted to argue. One tiny bad word uttered in pain shouldn't be such a big deal. Besides, I didn't consider myself *privileged*. Nor did I believe she'd get any phone calls. Still, as upset as I'd made her, I didn't want to further the insult by arguing.

Grandma Betty fixed chicken salad sandwiches, fruit salad, and iced tea for lunch. She prepared it all in plastic hula-girl dishes she'd got from the Dollar Store in Shawsburg and topped it off with paper umbrellas in our sweet iced teas. Sitting down to her creation, she grinned widely.

That's when the phone rang the first time.

Grandma Betty left the table and took the call in the kitchen. Grandpa Charlie started eating, so I followed his lead, hoping the call wasn't about me.

"A Wiccan?" Grandma Betty's voice carried to the table. "Of course, she isn't!"

Grandma Betty returned to the table with a forced smile on her face. She placed her hula-girl napkin on her lap and picked up her sandwich. I was about to apologize. The phone rang again.

"No, she had nothing to do with the murder," Grandma Betty told the caller, "except that she reported it like a law-abidin' citizen… No, to my knowledge, God doesn't send messages through dead bodies, for goodness sakes!"

This time, when Grandma Betty returned to the table, her plastered smile looked as if it pained her. She ate one bite of the sandwich before the phone rang again.

"Just say she was drunk," Grandpa Charlie said as she left the table again. I nodded enthusiastically.

Within minutes, she exclaimed, "No, she's not demon possessed!"

Returning to the table, Grandma Betty told us, "You know, I'm just goin' to leave the phone off the hook for a while."

"I'm sorry. I messed up. Again. If you want me to deal with the phone calls, I will. If you want me to go stay somewhere else, I will. No hard feelings. I should probably just get off my high horse and reconsider this whole thing, anyway. It's been one nightmare to the next. What've I been thinking?"

I dropped my head into my hands. Willie moaned at my feet. My grandparents sat in stunned silence. A million negative thoughts raced in my head, each vying for top position, but the most poignant one was that I had upset everyone's life, even those who were on my side.

Grandpa Charlie shifted in his seat, set his fork down, and wiped his mouth. "Well, there's only one thing to do then."

I glanced up hopefully.

"After lunch, Dee and I'll go fishin'."

My eyebrows pinched together. I hadn't been fishing since I was a teenager, given my love/hate relationship with the water. Still, the matter had been decided, without me, and again, I thought it best not to argue.

Death and blasphemy spread fast. After lunch, Grandma Betty replaced the receiver and checked the voicemail. All day, she fielded calls about my mental and spiritual state. I suppose that I don't blame them for being so skeptical about me. Stranger in town, same name as a Biblical evil temptress, involved in both death and blasphemy within almost twenty-four hours of each other. Business-wrecker of the year. They didn't even know about my expert mistake-making, yet. My shit-pit was deepening, and there was little I could do to stop it.

Chapter Fifteen

BATTLING

"GIVE ME SOME kind of estimate here," I said after ten minutes of getting nowhere with Detective Lewis. "I have a business to open. When will the police work be done on the store?"

"Hard to say."

"A day? Two days? A week? Just give me a window."

"Hard to say."

"What about the upstairs? Since it's separate from the crime scene, can that part be released so that Damon and his men can continue working on it?"

"That could happen sooner."

"When might you know?"

He shrugged.

"Can I get into the store for some of my belongings? To hold me over?"

He shrugged again. I wanted to punch his shoulders. "Possibly."

"And the Jeep? You must be done with it."

"Ms. Duffy, this isn't a TV show," he told me. "Things take

time. Exercise some patience. Should you be cleared in this matter, then all of your items will be returned to you, except of course that lovely picture. We'll have to keep that, for the file."

His mustache eased up in to a grin. My face flushed hot red.

Detective Lewis sat up in his chair. "Your former boss speaks highly of you."

I cringed. He'd spoken to Jonathan Dekker, my assistant principal, former boyfriend, and the guy who'd fired me. Jonathan was a little too keen on talking to strangers about me.

"He verified your story," Detective Lewis went on, "at least the part about not having inappropriate relationships with students. He said your students liked you until you screwed them over."

He laughed. Anger burned in me, but I had nothing to say.

"Dekker's sending me your personnel file," Lewis said. "He said it would clear up all my questions, though he wouldn't go into details on the phone."

My mouth dried up. I could feel my face go pale. Lewis' grin grew wider with my reaction.

"All will be known soon enough." After a short pause, he said, "Did I tell you how much my wife loves hats?"

"Delilah Duffy," Jonathan Dekker answered on the first ring.

"We need to talk." I moved off under the shade of an azalea tree outside the police station. Blades of grass tickled my ankles.

"I had a feeling you might call," he said. "Miss me?"

"I know you've been talking to some people. People have asked you questions."

"You're a hot topic. Nothing's changed."

"I understand that you have to answer their questions, but the murder has nothing to do with me except geography. Knowing about my past will make things harder for me than they already are, and worse, it'll keep the police on the wrong track. What I'm getting at is—"

"You want me to keep the Tyler Kettering incident a secret."

"Yes. It would lead them to false conclusions about me—"

"The Kettering incident is what it is, Delilah," he replied. "Gotta call a spade a spade."

I sighed silently. "Then why didn't you tell them already?"

"Wanted to see if you'd call."

I cringed. "If Lewis knows what happened with Tyler Kettering, then he'll definitely think I'm capable of something awful."

"You are, aren't you?"

My heart thundered. "Please. I'd never kill someone. If I could, wouldn't it have been you, Jonathan?"

He laughed. "That's true, I guess."

"I'm in a bad place here. I'm asking you, as someone who shared so much with me, to show a little mercy. I'm trying to start over—"

"What about that, Delilah? You weren't even going to let me know where you are?"

The question took me aback. "Why would I?"

"I get vacation time, too, you know," he said. "No reason I can't come see you, now that this whole mess at school is behind us."

I nearly dropped the phone. "Jonathan, I… we're done. You wanted nothing to do with me, remember?"

"Ah, Delilah, that's water under the bridge now. We should reconnect. Come for a weekend every once in a while. We had a lot of fun together, didn't we?"

"I'm sure you have others to play with, Jonathan."

"Not at the beach. I hear Tipee's gorgeous."

"No, that's not—"

"How important is it to you to keep this Tyler Kettering thing quiet?" I plopped down on the grass, silent for many seconds. "Delilah?"

I couldn't form words, digesting his insinuation, not that it surprised me.

He cleared his throat. "Come on, Delilah. Say yes and I'll lose that file. As long as he doesn't go over my head to Becker, you'll be safe. I'm thinking Labor Day weekend. That'd be perfect."

"Whatever." I clicked the phone shut.

Teague arrived at Betty and Charlie's house late Monday afternoon, before his evening shift. After my futile talk with Detective Lewis, I'd called Teague for advice. A few hours later, he'd arranged to take me back home to get some belongings—with a police escort.

"Thank you for doing this," I told him when he'd settled into the driver's seat.

"No problem."

"Lewis is such a tool," I said. "He's delaying the store on purpose. He mentioned how much his wife loves hats. How'd he ever become a detective?"

Teague smiled. "He's been there a long time."

"What about you? You'd make a much better detective than that guy."

"He shows up when everything's over. I love being a first responder, jumping right in to a situation and diffusing it. I honestly don't care to advance."

"I felt the same way about teaching." I sighed.

"He's messing with you," Teague said. "He's waiting for lab reports to come back. He wouldn't let us go in if there were more evidence to collect. Once the reports come back, there's no reason to keep the place sealed."

"How long do you think?"

"A day or two now," he said, pulling into the lot beside the store.

We got out of the truck and crossed the alley. The front door was plastered with yellow crime scene tape. My heart sank. Teague cut the tape with a straight edge from his utility belt, and then unlocked the door with my key—labeled with a tag, courtesy of the police department. The pennies and nickels smell had lingered and was the first thing I noticed when I followed Teague inside.

"You'll need to hire a special cleaning crew," Teague said, nodding to the large bloodstain on the wood floor and the words still sprawled on the wall. "I know a guy in Shawsburg who's reasonable. I'll give you his number."

I sighed. "Yes, I'd appreciate that." I avoided the stain and made my way to the back. I had my suitcase and other supplies stowed in the office and bathroom.

"The place looks awesome, aside from the obvious," Teague said from inside the store.

"Thanks." Nothing in the office appeared out of place or missing. I filled up my duffle bag with enough clothes for a few days and emptied my toiletries from the bathroom.

"You've really worked hard."

My eyebrow crept up at his compliment. It seemed out of place, given what we were doing.

Teague kept talking, his voice carrying to the office, though I couldn't see him. "A little free time might be fun, like the old days, you know."

I plopped down on the floor beside the filing cabinet, curious to hear where this might go, but even more curious to make sure that the zippered money pouch that held my register's start-up cash was still there.

"Any ideas on what you might do the next couple of days?"

I pulled the bottom drawer open and grabbed the red pouch.

"Um, no, not really." I counted the money, laying it out in my lap as I went.

"I was thinking about driving out to the Point," he said.

I stopped counting. My eyebrow peeked up on my forehead. The last time I'd been to Tipee Point was with him. It was the last time I went swimming, and the first time, not the last, that I'd been foolish with men. My shoulders sank. He paused. I could hear his footsteps pacing around the store.

"Is that so?" My eyes dropped. An object stuck out from underneath the filing cabinet, almost like an arrow pointing toward the office door. I pulled it out, revealing an odd metal tool.

"Yeah, I thought it'd be fun," he went on, "surfing, swimming, collecting shells."

I smiled, slightly. On our day together, we'd done all those things. I remembered how impressed he'd been when I'd known the difference between cockle, clam, and scallop shells.

The metal object looked similar to a nail file, slightly thicker. The handle extended into a thinner three-inch point and the tip curved into a snake pattern. I'd seen nothing like it.

"I could pack a cooler and some sandwiches for lunch."

Could it be Darryl's? Or the killer's? I dropped the tool into my lap like a hot potato.

"Sound like fun?" Teague asked.

My brain scrambled like eggs on the stovetop. If I made a big deal about the strange object, the police would start over with the store. They'd delay the opening, again. It could've been here for ages. Chances were that it had absolutely nothing to do with the crime.

My shoulders slumped. But, knowing me, I would've seen it. Wouldn't I? I'd been all over this place. I'd swept the floor and cleaned the floor, even slept on the floor.

"Doesn't that sound like fun, Delilah?" Teague popped his head round the doorway. I folded my arms over the stash of cash and the tool now piled messily in my lap.

"Um, yeah," I said.

"Everything okay?"

"Lost count." I grabbed a few of the ones, burying the tool underneath the rest.

"I thought maybe you'd like to go," he said, "with me."

"Oh, I don't know." My brains were both scrambled and

chopped at this point. The metal tool poked my leg, as if telling me to do the right thing, but Detective Lewis' stupid face kept flashing in my head. *Did I tell you how much my wife loves hats?*

Teague's eyes scrunched together, confused. "I messed up with the breakfast thing, but I promise I won't let anything mess us up this time." I cast him a stern look, mainly because I was contemplating several things at once. "I know you're a believer in second chances."

"Yes, I am, but, you know, I don't really swim."

"What?"

"I don't. I know I did, *that* day, but as a rule, I don't. I know how to, but I choose not to. I, um, have a thing about the water."

"You're kidding. You're like a fish in the wat—"

"I'm good at it. My father made me learn, but I can't."

"Why? Because of the nightmares?"

I gave him a shocked look. "You remember that?"

"Course," he said. "Do you still have them?"

I sighed. "Yes."

"We don't have to go to the Point. We could go to dinner, movies, anything."

"Can I think about it? And finish counting this money?" I asked with a smile. He nodded and disappeared back into the store. Feeling all around conflicted, I took the metal tool and slipped it back under the filing cabinet in exactly the same position as I'd found it. Perhaps I could pretend that I never saw it.

I couldn't put Teague back where I'd found him and pretend he wasn't there, though. I wouldn't want to. Still, I wondered what he could think, wanting to relive a day with me that ended with his rejection. Well, technically, the day ended with him dropping me off at Grandma Betty's house and a long, sweetly awkward goodbye. I'd thought he'd kiss me. He didn't. His words to Candy the next day ran through my mind. Returning to the Point with him would be like opening up an old wound and pouring lemon juice on it. Wouldn't it?

I finished counting the money. It was all there. I packaged it back in the money pouch and locked it in the cabinet.

Teague stared out the front window of the store. I moved beside him. I set my bag down and pulled my countdown sign off the window. Blood smeared its front from the splatter on the glass.

"I'll make a new one. Don't know what to put on it, anyway."

I set it against the wall. Teague turned to me, looking confused.

"You really don't swim?" His eyebrows pinched together, his blue eyes diving right into me.

I shook my head. "I almost drowned once." The words just spilled out, though it wasn't something I shared often.

"I had no idea."

"See? You don't know me as well as you think."

"How old were you?"

"Six. I fell into a friend's swimming pool, got tangled up in the tarp. Took her dad two minutes to get me breathing again, and no, I didn't have any supernatural experience. That's usually what people ask, when I talk about it."

"Tell me more. What time of year was it?" Teague asked.

I gave him an odd look. "Um, it was fall. The sky was a captivating blue color, leaves were turning, but it was warm. Lisa and I were outside, trying out the fairy wings she'd gotten for her Halloween costume, taking turns racing around the yard. We had this crazy notion that if we went fast enough with those wings on, we could fly."

I smiled at the memory.

"Bet you looked beautiful in those wings."

I chuckled. "Oh, yeah. I was fairy-tastic."

"Our day together must've been hard for you."

I shrugged. "I thought it would be. I predicted an embarrassing succession of panic attacks, followed by you inevitably ending the date early and kicking me to the curb at Candy's house with a cranky, wincing look on your face, like you'd just tasted dog food or something."

Teague laughed. "That'd never happen."

I cut him a confused look because that's almost how it had felt. I shrugged again. "Anyway, it turned out okay, even though I haven't been in the water since."

"Why did you do it?" he asked. "Why, if you were so afraid of the water?"

"Why do you think?" I huffed, figuring it best to be vague rather than admit I was crazy enough in love with him to jump into the thing I feared most. Candy'd convinced me that a surfing lesson was the best plan for arranging time together. Though I'd argued, she was right. Surfing was what Sam Teague was known for back then. Candy'd told me he often went surfing at dawn to get hours in before school started. He'd go to class with his hair still wet. Shy of walking right up to him, introducing myself, and asking him out, it was the only plausible scheme.

A grin eased up on his mouth. I tried not to look at him. Suddenly, the tips of his fingers dangled with mine, mingling like old friends. Tingles scurried up my arm. My heart quickened.

A loud tap, tap, tap interrupted us. I jumped, snatching my hand away. Uncle Clark peered in through the glass door, grinning widely.

"We should go," I said too quickly. My cheeks flushed. Teague grabbed my bag and followed me out to the sidewalk.

"I've been hunting for you," Uncle Clark said, "but I guess I'm not the only one. Mom told me where you were."

"I guess we're done here," I said, glancing at Teague who locked the store.

"I have to get to work, anyway. You'll drive her back to Betty and Charlie's?"

Clark nodded. "Anything for a story. I'm starving. Let's get some dinner."

Clark pulled me down the sidewalk, but I hesitated.

"Could you put my bag in your car and give me a second?" Clark took my duffle and left Teague and me alone again.

Teague leaned against the brick by the doorway, staring at me like I was a puzzle he wanted to solve only he didn't have all the pieces.

I smirked at his perplexed expression and then shrugged. "I'm frustrating and strange—I know. I also know that since I've been back here, I've smiled a total of about four times. Each one was thanks to you. I don't take you lightly. But, no mistakes, remember?"

He was about to say something, but I stopped him by leaning in closer. Almost too close, I realized too late. His eyes captured me like tractor beams, drawing me in. I put my hand up to his chest, more to stop myself than to touch him, though that was a pleasant side effect.

"Please, understand. When I was sixteen, you were the absolute best and worst thing that happened to me. They're still battling it out." I punched his steel chest lightly and grinned. "I'll let you know which side wins."

His face pinched, looking even more confused. "Wait. I don't get it. How was I the worst?"

I leaned to the left to see Uncle Clark pointing to his watch down the sidewalk. I nodded. "I should go."

"Delilah, we need to talk about this," Teague said, "soon."

"Okay." I turned toward the street.

"Have a nice time with your uncle. And watch what you say."

Chapter Sixteen

SPONGES

SEA SPONGES ARE deceiving. What looks like a lovely underwater plant is really trouble in disguise given they're toxic to the touch. That's how I felt about most of the Duffys.

We beat the dinner rush at The Crab Shack and were seated street side, facing the pier and the ocean. Clark pulled out his leather notebook and pen from his back pocket. My shoulders drooped.

"I hear there's new information about to break at the station. Wanna give me the scoop? I'm sure I can spin it better than Lewis."

"Lewis isn't getting any new information," I said with more confidence than I really had.

"How do you know?"

"I just do."

"Lewis is circulating the picture. He expects it to be printed. He likes you for this, you know."

"He's misguided and a poor detective."

Mandy arrived and took our drink orders. Despite Clark's encouragement, I insisted on a Diet Coke rather than a mixed drink.

Clark said, "You're right about Lewis. This'll be his second big case this year—the robberies being the other—and he hasn't moved forward on either. The Granny Bandits have hit almost a dozen houses. They've gotten so comfortable with their crime spree that in the last few, they haven't bothered trying to hide the thefts. They used to get in, take specific items—mostly jewelry and collectibles, things people might not notice right away—and then lock up behind themselves, as if they hadn't been there at all. It's almost impossible to narrow down when those robberies actually happened. Now, they just break in and take whatever. No finessing. They've probably realized Lewis' ineptness, like everyone else. Saying you're his lead suspect won't really amount to much."

"Doesn't matter. Most people have already decided it's me— *stranger in town, trying to mess things up for the Duffy sisters, the one who cursed in church*—"

Clark laughed. "That was classic!"

"Well, now the town thinks I'm a devil-worshipper. Murderer isn't a stretch."

"I love it here. People are crazy, and they still read the paper. If you want to tell your side, then you have the perfect opportunity to do it."

"My side is that I didn't do it."

Our drinks arrived. Clark scribbled in his notebook. We ordered our meals.

"Tell me what happened that morning. What did you see?"

Clark listened, asking questions periodically, as I described finding Darryl's body. I left out a lot but gave Clark enough to satisfy him. Our dinner arrived, and we continued to talk as we ate.

"So, what's the deal with you and Teague? Seems like you were getting kind of cozy."

"I'm not sure I should talk about that with you."

Clark rolled his eyes. "Your love life isn't interesting enough to print, Delilah."

"You're right about that. Nothing's going on. He asked me out, but I kind of froze—"

"He was married before, you know."

I nearly choked on a piece of lettuce. "Married?"

"Yeah, married."

"No, I didn't know." I took a sip of my drink, but my mouth still felt dry.

"Back in Nags Head," Clark said. "Do you want me to do a background check, find out more for you?"

My blood flow must have stopped. I felt suddenly cold. I'm not sure why I reacted so strongly to news that a few days ago, I'd specifically said would be okay and none of my business. My emotions ping-ponged around my head.

"No, no spying," I said. "Like I said, nothing's going on. He's a friend—"

"There's nothing wrong with being divorced, you know. Everyone makes mistakes."

"Yes, I know."

Still, Teague was married. It didn't seem like a congruent sentence somehow.

"How's everything, folks?" Mike Ancellotti stood at the edge of our table. He shook hands with Clark and smiled warmly at me.

"Delicious," I answered.

"Delilah, I'm sorry about what happened. I can't believe it. The police called me to check on your whereabouts Friday night." Mike folded his arms over his chef's jacket.

"I'm sorry, Mike. You're kind of my alibi."

"She didn't do it," Clark said grinning, "in case you were wondering."

Mike's eyes widened. "Oh, no, I wasn't. I mean, I'm sure she'd never—"

"At least, she says she didn't do it. I'm not sure I believe her."

I rolled my eyes at Clark.

"He wishes I were the killer," I said, "so he'd have a scoop."

"I better believe you're innocent." Mike chuckled, turning to Clark. "Did she tell you about our plans for tomorrow night?"

Clark's eyes widened behind his glasses. "She didn't, Mike." My mouth fell open at Clark's sudden joy in knowing about our date.

"We're still on, aren't we?"

I smiled. Teague popped into my mind again, like a song running through my head. He'd been married. I still couldn't digest it. "Um, sure. Can you pick me up at my grandparents' house?"

"I'll be there at eight."

Mike excused himself to go back into the kitchen. Clark's raised eyebrow reminded me of my mother.

"Perhaps I spoke too soon," he said. "Your love life gets more interesting by the second. How... buttery."

I shrugged. "So, tell me, what should I expect with the story on Wednesday?"

"I'll report that you're a suspect, that they've questioned you, and that they found a weapon in your vehicle. These are all facts, and I wouldn't be much of a reporter if I didn't report them. That naughty picture has become compelling, too."

"Oh, come on. You know it has nothing to do—"

"I have to bring it up in the paper or it'll seem like we're avoiding it," Clark said. "Do you want to make an official statement about the picture?"

I shook my head. "No. I shouldn't have to defend it. It was a private moment with my then-serious boyfriend. No matter what I say about it, people will make their assumptions. I've been down this road before and it never ends well."

Chapter Seventeen

PUFFER FISH

MIKE ANCELLOTTI ARRIVED at my grandparents' house at 7:55, driving a blue Prius with the license plate CRBSHK. He drove us to the other side of the island to a hopping three-story joint called Lucy's View. The structure sat against the Cape Fear, piers lined with boats jutting out in three directions. Marshes surrounded the parking lot, which was loose gravel. I heard music playing when I got out of the car.

"I'll own this place one day," Mike said, looking up at it admirably. "Best kept island secret. Delicious food. Cool atmosphere. You'll love it."

The building was cinder block and siding, rustic and slightly dilapidated. We climbed a flight of concrete stairs to a door that led to a huge, open dining room. Unfinished floors. Graffiti-covered walls. A long bar sat to the left. A space for dancing on the right. Straight ahead was the water—no windows, no wall, just the open night.

Mike grabbed my hand and led me across the busy dining floor to an empty table in the back corner, against the wall-less view. I sat against the side wall and ran my hand across the scrawled messages of hundreds of visitors. *Jenny loves Jason. Tina and Carly BFF. Bobby was here '07.* I could have spent hours reading them all.

The bartender arrived with two beers, and Mike ordered for us.

Beautiful Day began playing over the speakers, almost drowning out the sound of crickets and frogs in the marshes below. I thought of my one day with Teague years ago. I always did when I heard this song. Fortunately, Mike didn't give me much time to think. He took a swig of his beer and then stood up.

"Dance with me."

I shook my head. "I don't dance."

"Tonight, you do." He grabbed my hands and led me to the dance floor. One couple practically made out, while another slow danced tightly. People leaned against the wall nearby, laughing and drinking beers.

Mike held my left hand outward, put his other on my waist, but didn't pull me too close. I put my right hand on his shoulder, and he guided me around the space, dipping me a few times for fun. My smiles slowly gave way to laughter.

The air was stuffy, but for once, I'd picked the perfect dress—a little blue sleeveless thing. A sea breeze drifted around the tables like a ghost, bringing sweet relief.

"See? You dance," Mike said.

"You're the one dancing. I'm just hanging on."

"Having fun?"

"Yes."

"Perfect."

"Do you do this often?" I asked, as he twirled me around.

"Dance? Yes, often."

"No, I mean bring girls who have their own drinks named after them to Lucy's View to go dancing."

He spun me around again, landing in a dip. "I come here often.

I mostly dance at home when no one's looking. But, no, usually not with a girl who has her own beverage namesake. What about you? I know you don't dance, but do you often date devilishly handsome chefs?"

"You're the first."

"I'm honored." He flashed me his knee-weakening smile.

The food arrived at the table before we did. A bucket of blue crabs, three dipping sauces, short ears of corn and two buttery corn muffins, two fresh beers, and a pile of napkins. Mike, our dinner, this place—nothing was what I'd expected from him, in a good way.

"So, what's it like to be in the restaurant business?"

Mike told a story about how he loved to cook, spent his college years studying abroad, and knew that he'd own a restaurant one day.

"My parents helped me raise some capital to start The Crab Shack, but since then, I've done so well that I've made them investors. They pull in part of the profits each month. Helps with their retirement. They're in Wrightsville."

"So, the next step is expanding, then? Buying a place like this?"

"I've always loved this place. I'd buy it in a heartbeat. I love The Crab Shack, of course, but I'd like to have both ends of the spectrum—the upscale, touristy gourmet Crab Shack and the low-end no-overhead life of Lucy's View."

I glanced around Lucy's View and didn't feel that it was low end at all. Sure, there was dirt on the floor and graffiti everywhere, but it was charming.

"I've been talking too much." Mike reached over to help me with a tough crab. "Tell me about you. What brought you here?"

I gave him the watered-down version of how I ended up in Tipee.

"Wow, that's so brave, to change careers like that," he said.

"Brave isn't the adjective I'd use. Foolish is better."

"Oh, I don't think so. The town needs a bookstore. They just don't know it yet. Once you get over this situation, it'll be amazing. Give it time."

"I hope you're right."

"Work on a niche," he said. "That's what islanders love. Your aunts have a good one. Don't just sell books. Make it some kind of experience."

I nodded. Silence fell between us as I worked on my dinner and thought about his advice.

"So, why aren't you married?"

The question caught me in the middle of a beer-chug. I let it pour down the wrong hole, choking a little. Mike laughed and handed me a napkin.

"Touchy subject?"

"No, it's just surprising how much you sound like my mother."

Mike grinned. "You seem relatively normal. You're intelligent and educated, self-sufficient, obviously beautiful—"

"That's debatable."

He shook his head and squinted his brown eyes. "Maybe you're crazy."

"Sometimes I think so."

"Ah, if you were crazy, you wouldn't realize it. So, why haven't you been snagged up yet with so much in your favor?"

"I could ask you the same question."

"I asked first."

"Honestly, I'm a bad judge of character, especially men, so that I'm enjoying our date doesn't really bode well for you."

He laughed. "Wow, had some real idiots, huh?"

"A few. Your turn."

He folded his arms over his chest and leaned in closer. "I want the whole package. I want someone who can make me crazy and keep me sane. I have a lot of *Seinfeld* moments, you know. She separates her peas and carrots, so suddenly she's not right for me,

113

or she has big hands, or she's a low talker. I know it sounds ridiculous, but—"

"No, I get it," I said, laughing. "*Seinfeld*'s ruined it for all us normal, imperfect girls."

"I haven't found a thing wrong with you," he said. "Can't imagine I will."

I rolled my eyes. It was just a matter of time.

Puffer fish aren't particularly intimidating. They're scale-less and look buck-toothed. But when threatened, puffer fish suck in water, growing several body sizes bigger and becoming about as edible as a soccer ball. Predators are easily turned off by the transformation.

If I'd that ability—to grow big and bold when intimidated—it would've happened twice on my date with Mike.

Ronnie Chambers sat alone at the bar, slouched over a half-empty pitcher of beer and a bowl of pretzels, eyeing a ballgame on the flat screen TV. When Mike left the table to check in with work, I seized the opportunity to say something to him. I'm not usually so bold, but I felt pulled in Ronnie's direction.

"Ronnie, I wanted to tell you how sorry I am about your brother."

He turned to me, beady eyes flashing. Taking a swig of beer, he sloshed it around in his mouth and gulped it down. Then he belched.

"Who the hell are you?"

"Um, I'm Delilah," I said weakly. This was a mistake. "I, um, found him."

"You wanna prize or something?"

"No, of course not—I just thought—"

"You wanna give me a sympathy lay?" Then, he chuckled. "That'll make me feel better. Otherwise, back off!"

Ronnie went back to his beer. I raced back to the table.

"What's wrong?" Mike asked when he returned. I nodded in

Ronnie Chambers' direction.

"Do you know him?"

With lowered eyes, Mike said, "Yeah, he worked for me once. Little bastard stole two cases of lobster."

"Seriously? You caught him?"

"Delilah, the kid was literally putting the boxes in his truck."

"Did you call the police?"

Mike shook his head. "I should've but didn't. He was seventeen at the time and had only been working for me for about two weeks—him and his brother, Darryl."

"They both worked for you?"

"Those boys've worked everywhere. They were kind of a package deal. Darryl was the one who talked me out of pressing charges."

"Darryl had nothing to do with the theft?"

"Well, he wasn't there that night, so he had nothing to do with *that* theft. I'm sure Ronnie got away with other stuff before I caught him."

"How'd Darryl convince you not to press charges against Ronnie?"

"Hard life story, no father figure, all that jazz. He said that if Ronnie went to jail, it'd crush his mother's heart. So, I fired them both, banned them from the store, but didn't press charges."

"That's a shame."

"What's worse is that Darryl had potential," Mike went on. "He was great with his hands. One time, the ice machine went out in the middle of dinner rush on a Saturday night. The distributor couldn't send anyone out to service it. I didn't know what to do. Darryl pulled it away from the wall to look at the machinery, and a second later, told me he could fix it. I didn't believe him. But I had nothing to lose."

Mike took a long swig of beer.

"He fixed it, didn't he?"

"Within twenty minutes." Mike smiled. "I was freaking amazed. He was a keeper, but I couldn't trust him after the lobster thing."

After dinner, we took a few more turns on the dance floor before leaving. Mike suggested a walk along the pier. Conversation dwindled as I thought about Ronnie and Darryl's relationship, and their fight at my dumpster. Now, I knew what Darryl'd meant when he'd said he'd always tried to do his best for him. Perhaps getting him out of trouble, like he'd done with Mike over the lobsters, was a habit for Darryl.

"You okay?" Mike asked. We'd stopped walking. I stared out at a black mass speckled with reflected moonlight.

"Sorry. Got distracted."

"You were a million miles away."

"Not that far. Lost in thoughts, I guess."

"Ah, I know exactly what you're thinking. You're thinking how perfect this date has been, and how sexy and charming and smart and funny I am, and how you don't want it to end. How you feel conflicted—"

"Conflicted?" I asked with a raised eyebrow.

"Conflicted because—look at this place." He motioned to the moon and the water. He stepped closer to me. "It's the perfect spot for a first kiss, but making the first move isn't your style… or is it? You're wondering, hoping even, that I will, but you can't count on me because I'm a man, after all. Should you take matters into your own hands, or lips, as it were? What to do? It's a difficult dilemma."

I couldn't help but laugh, even though my puffer fish instincts were kicking in. He was charming, and pleasant, but the idea of a kiss petrified—

That's when he went for it. Softly. Easily. He leaned down, hesitating just before our lips met, and then, there it was. My woman parts cheered. My little gray cells, however, stood at attention like soldiers and beckoned me to stop. All I could think was *shit, shit, shit*.

I pulled away. "Wait. I don't—um—maybe this isn't a good idea. I'm sorry, Mike."

We didn't talk on the way back to the car. Five minutes into the drive, I guessed that I'd reached the *Seinfeld* side of Mike's brain.

Finally, he sighed. "I'm sorry if I upset you. Sometimes I come on too strong, like a Ferrari when I should be like a tricycle. If I make you feel uncomfortable next time, please feel free to hit me. A slap to the cheek will set me straight."

I chuckled. "Next time?"

He glanced at me like I was crazy. Maybe I was. It was the best date I'd had in years. Still, something was off.

He asked me for a second date on Thursday night, and strangely, I agreed.

Chapter Eighteen

INTIMACY

I SLEPT IN, caught up in tidal wave dreams. They crashed into me, tossing me against buildings and cars and streets like a rag doll. My perfectly enjoyable date with Mike had left me feeling rather hung-over, and not because of the drinking. Dates and bad dreams combined to make me uneasy.

Honking outside pulled me from my room after lunch. My Jeep sat in the driveway. Teague emerged from the driver's seat. I raced out of the house, nearly tripping down the porch steps, Willie in tow.

"Oh, my gosh! I've never been so happy to see that Jeep."

Teague smiled. He wasn't in uniform. A pale-yellow polo shirt accentuated his blond hair and blue eyes. He handed me the keys and then bent down to give Willie his due affection.

"The lab's finished. Just took a little convincing."

"Well, thank you. You've been a lifesaver. Want to come in for coffee?"

Teague nodded. As we walked toward the house, he shoved his

hands in his pockets. "I think he'll release the upstairs later today. The downstairs will take longer, but it's better than nothing."

"You're right. If I can get Damon back upstairs, I can at least move forward on the apartment. My grandparents have been great, but I don't want to overstay my welcome."

"Are they home?" Teague perched himself on a barstool at the kitchen counter. I reached for the coffee.

"Grandma's shopping, and Grandpa's fishing."

"So, how'd it go last night?"

I stopped my coffee preparations and cocked my head at him.

He shrugged. "I know you went out with Ancellotti. Just wondering how it went."

"You stalking me? How d'you know?"

Teague grinned. "Mandy, honeypot. She called and told me. Guess Mike's been talking you up around work. How'd it go?"

"It was nice."

"He's a nice guy," Teague said, "a little cocky sometimes, but generally nice."

"Don't do that."

"Do what?"

"Plant little negative suggestions in my head. Now, I'll think about that word 'cocky' and look for it in him. Not that he is."

The evening swirled back to life in my head. Perhaps he had been cocky with the whole kiss thing. My shoulders sagged.

"Seriously, though, he was a gentleman?" Teague asked.

I laughed. "What, are you going to beat him up if I say no?"

"Maybe," he replied. "How did the night end exactly?"

My mouth dropped open. "How can you ask me that?"

"Why can't I ask? I told you about Mandy. All's fair, right?"

"Did you know that idiom—*all's fair in love and war*—actually comes from the line *the rules of fair play do not apply in love and war*. It's changed since John Lyly wrote it during the Renaissance. Everyone thinks it's Shakespeare, but it's not. Although

Shakespeare read Lyly and liked his work—"

"Are you dodging the question?"

"Maybe it's fun seeing you get upset. Though, I don't understand why you'd care. The night ended with me curled up in Grandma Betty's rooster bedroom with a good book. Alone. I'm offended you'd think otherwise, especially on a first date."

Teague's face relaxed. "Well, you were so taken with his stupid drink-naming thing. Who knows what you might fall for?"

I chuckled. "Want to know a very sad fact about me, Teague?"

"Tell me." He leaned forward across the counter.

"I'm twenty-nine years old, and I've been with two men. I suppose your number is higher. Everyone's number is higher. Mine should be, I guess. Makes me feel like a loser. But sometimes I don't feel bad because I regret them both. I filled my bed with a warm body one night only to replace it with cold regret the next."

"My number's higher," he said, "but one, the right one, would've been enough."

I glanced over at him. He didn't say it, but I felt like he meant me. I brushed off the thought, deciding that I was being the cocky one.

Thankful for a distraction, I poured the coffee and offered Teague cream and sugar. He accepted both.

"When I think about it," I began awkwardly, "I don't like to count my number that way—by sex. Intimacy is more important."

"What do you mean?"

"Intimacy's what we all want—to feel uniquely connected to each other. Sex is just one very narrow way that can happen, and sometimes, intimacy isn't achieved that way at all." My eyes fell when I considered Jonathan Dekker. "It's more important to count how many times you've felt an amazing soul connection. That's true intimacy. Much harder to come by."

I stared into my coffee cup, realizing that I'd just bumbled into a conversation I didn't want to have. I hoped he'd change the subject.

"Two." Teague said it without hesitation. "That's my number, then."

I smiled softly. "My number's four."

"What counts as intimacy for you, then?"

I shook my head.

"Hey, you opened the door." Teague smiled. "Can't close it now."

I huffed out in one breath, "When I was fourteen, I made out with Charlie Baker behind the lockers at school. First boyfriend, first kiss, and once he actually showed me his... well, you know."

Teague's mouth dropped. "No, I don't know. What did he show you? His baseball card collection? A picture of his mom?"

"Cut it out!" We both laughed. "You know."

"What d'you do?"

"I laughed and ran away."

"You sure know how to hurt a guy."

"Yes, Charlie's in therapy now because of me. I didn't know what else to do. He broke up with me." I shrugged. "Anyway, I consider Charlie my first intimate experience because he shared something personal."

"No kidding," Teague replied, still laughing.

"And, poor Charlie taught me not to jump into things without taking it seriously because you never know when someone might— well, be ready for something you're not."

Teague nodded. "What about the others?"

"Well, um, the losers I mentioned before. My college boyfriend and my last boyfriend. I was very intimate with them. They weren't so much with me. One-sided intimacy still counts."

"You said four," Teague reminded me, though he didn't have to. "Please don't say Ancellotti."

I smirked. "No, dummy. The second one was you. Guess that's why I can't seem to keep my mouth shut when you're—"

My words stopped when Teague left his barstool and met me on my side of the counter. He stopped a foot in front of me, penetrating me with his gorgeous eyes and sweet smile.

"I was hoping you'd say that. You were my first."

I crinkled my eyebrows together and considered laughing and running away, like I'd done with Charlie Baker. This moment was becoming uncomfortably intimate, all thanks to me and my super big mouth.

Teague didn't come any closer, perhaps seeing my distress. "Delilah, I thought about what you said—the whole best and worst thing. I'm not sure I—"

"Teague, it was a long time ago. It's probably dumb to even—"

"It's still important to me. The best, I get. I can't tell you how many times I've replayed that day in my head over the years. It's been a light in some dark places in my life. But, the worst, too? How?"

"Seriously?" I edged by him, dumping my mug in the sink. Grandma Betty's car pulled the carport below us. Willie perked up. "We've got company."

"The worst thing about it was that we didn't do it again," Teague said. I raised an eyebrow and shook my head. "Is that what you mean?"

"I have to help Grandma. She'll have—"

Teague grabbed my elbow, bringing me and my mouth to a stop.

"Delilah, I really don't know. You have to tell me."

I raised my eyebrow at him. "I don't take rejection well. Coming from you, I could hardly take it at all." Grandma Betty honked her horn to hurry me along. "Let's talk about it some other time."

I pulled away and rushed down the hall.

"Delilah Duffy, you're in a world of trouble!" Grandma Betty slid out of the front seat of her car, holding up a copy of the newspaper. My seductive picture graced the front page, making my heart palpitate. Now, all of Tipee had seen my best bedroom eyes and come-and-get-me-nightie.

Next to my lovely portrait was Clark's headline: *Murderer?*

"You want to explain why you're half-naked on the cover of our *Gazette*? A dozen people came up to me in the grocery store. I about had a heart attack when I saw it. Your grandfather—well, thank goodness he's out fishing, because if he—when he sees this—well, I don't know what he'll do."

"I can explain."

"I can't wait to hear this. Oh, I didn't realize we had company."

Teague moved out from behind the car, so she could see him. "Can I bring in some groceries for you, Mrs. Duffy?"

"That'd be helpful, Sam, but I'm not sugarcoating because you're around. I'm pretty peeved, and I don't mind showing it."

I raced over to help Teague with the bags. Grandma mumbled as we followed her into the house. She slapped the paper on the counter and waited, hand on hip, for me to address her questions. Teague busied himself by putting the groceries away. In a small way, I was glad he'd stayed.

"Grandma, what do you want me to say? I trusted the wrong man. I loved him. I thought he'd ask me to marry him. He took this picture of me one evening after I'd had a little too much wine. A few of my students got ahold of it and plastered it all over social media. It's part of the reason I left Durham."

"You should've told me," Grandma Betty said.

"I didn't want to tell anyone. It's embarrassing. And private."

Grandma lectured me about using common sense, not jumping into bed with every 'Joe' that happened along, and if I should stoop to having sex before marriage, not allowing cameras in the bedroom. The speech lasted a solid ten minutes, during which she cited *Oprah*, *Dateline*, and the Bible several times, in that order. I kept my mouth shut.

123

"Cursing in church and now naughty pictures. What's next? You're not the young lady I remember or that my son raised you to be."

Her words hit me like stones.

The phone rang, stopping her. I ducked out of the kitchen to the back deck, tears slipping down my cheeks. Teague opened the sliding glass door, letting Willie out to dig in the sand. I wiped my eyes quickly.

"She's angry," Teague said. "She'll get over it."

"She's right. I was stupid, completely stupid." My new deal with Jonathan made my stomach queasy. I leaned over, placing my hands on my knees.

"You okay?"

"No."

"Delilah, it's just an article, read today, forgotten tomorrow."

"It's not your picture plastered all over town."

"I know it seems bad right—"

"Bad? It's like I've landed on one of the circles of hell." I sank to the sand.

As I pouted, Teague retrieved the paper from inside the house.

"Delilah, this isn't so bad." Teague sat next to me on the sand, scanning the article. "He basically says they have nothing on you. Lewis is under pressure to move the case forward."

"It doesn't matter what it says. All people will see is my slutty picture with 'murderer' beside it."

"Don't give up."

"That's what everyone wants. Maybe—"

"You're not a quitter."

"What do you—"

"Remember surfing?" he asked with a smile. "At the beginning of the day, you were the most ungraceful, uncoordinated person I'd ever seen. You were so stiff, it was like trying to teach a tree trunk to surf. The board was more pliable."

He laughed, and I couldn't help but chuckle in spite of myself. He was right. That day, I'd felt completely out of my element, at least at the beginning.

"I never thought you'd be able to pop up, let alone surf, but you did it."

I wiped another tear away, but smiled. "I had a good teacher."

"I can't take credit. It scared you to death, but you did it anyway. You have an unbreakable spirit."

"Feels fairly broken right now." I let my head fall against his shoulder, and his arm slipped around my back. Amid all the newspaper drama, something peaceful settled over me.

"No, not broken. Scarred maybe, but never broken." Teague tossed the paper to the sand like a Frisbee. Grains scattered over its surface. "This will pass."

Willie barked at passing seagulls. A breeze whipped up. And hope filled me up again.

"It'll be okay," Teague whispered.

"When you say it, it sounds believable."

Teague pulled me closer and rested his head against mine. "Delilah, does this count?" His lips brushed my forehead.

"Count?" I leaned closer to him.

I felt him smile. "Intimacy?"

"Seems like every time I'm with—"

Grandma Betty yanked the sliding glass door open and ordered me back inside. "I'm not done talkin' to you, missy!"

My moment of comfort ruined; I grew irritated. I was too old for lectures and too angry to listen, anyway. I jumped out of Teague's arms and strode over to the door. Teague followed, collecting Willie.

"I'm not talking about this anymore," I told Grandma Betty as sternly as I dared. "Am I still welcome here or do I need to make other arrangements?"

This time, I put my hand on my hip and stared her down. It

took her by surprise.

"Delilah, you're my granddaughter," she said. "Of course, you're welcome here."

"Thank you," I said. "I'm leaving. I'll be back later."

With no further explanation, I grabbed my purse and keys and headed for the door.

Chapter Nineteen

LOCKS

IF THE EMBARRASSING picture wasn't enough to make my head spin with regrets, the word *murderer* replayed like a bad song. I had to do *something*. Getting out of town, at least for a few hours, seemed like a good idea.

Willie and I headed toward the Tipee Island Ferry on the north side of the island, which crossed the Cape Fear to Shawsburg. A metropolis compared to Tipee Island, Shawsburg had the closest hospital, mall, Walmart, and schools.

Shawsburg High School—Home of the Pirates—was a massive three-story building with four decorative towers perched on the rooftop like widow's peaks—very beachy. Though out for summer, the lot was filled with cars. I tied Willie's leash to the Jeep's roll bar, gave him a treat from my glove compartment and went inside.

The office staff directed me to the English department, three stories up, where I'd find the department head, Mrs. Trojak, in room 323. The barren halls still held the typical school smell I'd grown so accustomed to but hadn't realized I missed. A strange mix of cleaner, school supplies, old books, and teenagers. It wafted through the air like ghosts.

I knocked on Mrs. Trojak's door. A woman in her mid-fifties looked up from a stack of papers on her desk. I smiled.

"Sorry to bother you. Are you Mrs. Trojak?"

She nodded and waved for me to enter, pulling off her reading glasses and standing up from her desk. I extended my hand, and she shook it warmly.

"I'm Delilah Duffy. I hope it's okay that I've popped in on you like this."

"Any relation to the Duffy-Saintlys? Rachel and Raina?"

"They're my cousins."

"Wonderful girls. What can I do for you?"

"I'm about to reopen a bookstore on the island. I was hoping to get a copy of your summer reading lists, so I could make sure I stock the titles."

"Great idea." Mrs. Trojak rummaged through her desk. "I'll give you our summer reading lists and our list for the year. Most students order their books online or through the school. But some still buy them the ol' fashioned way."

"Thanks."

"I read in the paper that you used to teach English." She smiled, and I nodded. "What grades?"

"AP seniors."

"Ah, me too. They cannot graduate without getting through me first."

"Oh, did you have Darryl Chambers?"

Her face soured. "I taught both the Chambers boys. Ronald was only in my classroom a few times before he dropped out. Darryl lasted most of his senior year, thanks entirely to football, but dropped out after the season ended."

"Difficult students, I take it?"

"I'm saddened about what happened to Darryl. I didn't know

Ronald long enough to classify him as anything, except to say that he slouched in class. I don't approve of slouching. On the other hand, Darryl was no slouch." Mrs. Trojak found the summer reading list and scribbled some other titles on it as she spoke. "He was best known for football. He produced little for me. I only recall one instance where he turned in anything of merit. He was a teacher's nightmare—able but unwilling."

"I heard he had some colleges interested in him."

"You should ask Coach Tucker. He's here, downstairs in the gym. He probably knew Darryl best." She handed me the list of books and I thanked her for her time.

I turned back to her at the door. "Oh, Mrs. Trojak, do you remember what the one thing was? The thing he turned in that had merit?"

She pulled the reading glasses off her nose again. "Oh, yes. It was the first and only time in my twenty-five years of teaching I'd ever seen this topic—the history of locks."

"Locks?"

"Yes, pin locks, warded locks, lock puzzles, and pin tumbler locks. It was fascinating material, difficult to forget."

"Sounds like an in-depth research paper for a slacker."

"No, it wasn't a research paper. It was an in-class free write. That's how I know he did it himself. I asked the class to write a descriptive essay on any topic of their choice. Darryl chose the history of locks."

The gymnasium smelled less like cleaner and more like teenager, but was open and empty. Light filtered in beams through high windows. Championship banners hung from the rafters. A narrow hallway led to Coach Tucker's office.

"Coach Tucker?" I asked gingerly. "I hope I'm not disturbing you." He was staring at what looked like financial records on a computer, which he quickly minimized. "Could I have a minute of your time?"

His wincing expression went unchanged. "Will it cost me any money?"

"No, not at all."

"Then, sure. Come on in." He pointed to the chair in front of his desk, and I sat down. "What can I do for you?"

"Mrs. Trojak said you knew Darryl Chambers?" I felt awkward asking, but Coach Tucker didn't mind. He scratched his chin and leaned back in his chair.

"Yeah, we were close, once upon a time. Chambers was a good kid. An excellent football player. Three colleges fought for him his senior year, each offering a full ride. For a kid like him, that was a sweet deal. He never had a daddy, you know. And his mom, well, she's a character."

"So, what happened?"

"The season ended, and Chambers let it all go. Grades fell. Stopped coming to school. They rescinded the offers. I spoke to him. He said he couldn't cut it. I didn't believe it for a second. I think he was having family issues. Either way, he never explained and dropped out of school not long after the incident with Mr. Ellis."

"What incident?"

Coach Tucker chuckled. "Well, that's sort of Pirate lore 'round here, but I reckon some of it's got to be true. When Chambers was a senior, our assistant principal was Logan Ellis. Chambers and Ellis hated each other. Nothing made Ellis happier than nailing Chambers on violations. Early in the season, Ellis benched him for a game because he'd acquired too many tardies or some other nonsense."

"He could do that?"

"Oh, yeah. He could do anything—or at least, he thought he could. Chambers sat out the game, and we lost. Everyone was angry at Ellis after that, even the higher ups. Anyway, Ellis came into his office on Monday morning to find someone had stolen his prized stuffed marlin. It devastated Ellis. He said that he'd caught that fish himself on a charter cruise with his father. Ellis was certain that Chambers'd done it."

"Did he call the police?"

"He did, but they had nothing to go on." Tucker leaned back further, making his chair squeak. "Probably didn't try too hard, anyway. The whole town was angry at Ellis for costing the game, so no one really cared if he got his dang fish back. Besides, Chambers couldn't have done it."

"Why not?"

"Are you kiddin'? This place was locked up tighter than Fort Knox. He would've had to get in the front doors, the office door, the inner office door, and then Ellis' door—all locked with different keys. The outer door had one of those electronic locks on it, too." Tucker folded his arms over his chest. "I've got keys and sometimes have a hard time getting in here. Geeze. I'm not sure what happened to Ellis' stupid fish. Maybe he stole it himself to blame Chambers. Who knows! But there's no way a kid could've stolen it."

I wasn't so sure.

Mike called while Willie and I were on the ferry and left a message since service wasn't great out in the middle of the Cape. Once on land again, I listened to his voicemail. He cancelled our date because one of his chefs was out with a stomach bug—so he said. I half-wondered if my embarrassing front-page spread had finally given Mike his *Seinfeld* moment.

I grunted. Instead of returning to Grandma Betty's where I'd inevitably face more fallout from my photo, we drove to Beach Realty, arriving minutes before closing. I found Candy packing up a briefcase-sized Coach bag on her desk.

She grinned slyly when I entered. "Nice picture in the paper."

I huffed, still not keen on talking about it. "I'm sorry about getting you in trouble with Uncle Joe."

She waved me off. "Ain't no trouble. It's my fault for not paying much attention to the building, that's for sure. Got bigger fish to fry—or at least, I *had* bigger fish to fry. Now everything's about Beach Read. Any idea when you'll be able to open?"

"No, but I'm hoping for next week."

"Ain't givin' up, huh?"

I shrugged, remembering Teague's words. "I'm not a quitter. At least, I don't want to be."

"I hear Momma bit your head off today," Candy went on, with a twinge of a smile. "I thought she saved all those lectures for me."

"Word travels fast."

"She called and asked if you'd come by. I think she's fixin' to apologize. Mamma heats up like lighter fluid on hot coals, big and fast. Then, she comes to her senses. She'll probably have something baked for you when you come home."

I sighed with relief and grinned. "Baked goods'll definitely be better than lectures on my love life."

"I'm sorry that things have been so shitty for you here."

"Really?"

Candy shrugged. "I felt squeezed in the middle, but yeah."

"It's okay."

She huffed, making her earrings jingle. "I get all caught up in tryin' to hold my own around here. It's so competitive. I've been here a dozen years and I ain't never been top seller, not once. Anyway, I'm sure things'll get better for you. They have to, right?"

"I can only hope." I rolled my eyes, making light of what I wanted to ask her. "Candy, you remember that summer when I was so ridiculously in love with Sam Teague?"

"What makes you bring that up?"

I laughed lightly. "Thinking about old times. I never thanked you for what you did that summer. It must've been a hassle dealing with me."

"That's what aunties do, I suppose."

"Do you remember when Sam came by your house and spoke to you after our date?"

She nodded, piling files into a stack on her desk. I could see the irritation creeping over her face, shadowing her usual peppiness. Her penciled eyebrows perked up, awaiting my question.

"What did he say, exactly?"

"Not this again." She huffed. "He said he wasn't interested in you."

"But why?"

"He wouldn't say why, only he wasn't. It was a good day, but that's all. That's what he said."

I nodded but couldn't shake my confusion over it still.

Candy sighed. "Sometimes people just aren't interested, plain and simple. It could've been a thousand different things, and you know what else? Men have very selective memories when it comes to that sort of thing. Damon's like that. It's amazin' what he's conveniently forgotten 'bout our datin' back then. I bet Sam Teague had himself 'nother honey. Come to think of it, I remember seein' him with some girl after that. Can't remember who it was."

I shrugged like it didn't matter but wondered if *that* girl ended up being his wife.

"Tell me you're not interested in him again."

I shook my head. "We're friends."

"Well, he's with Mandy Davis."

"He told me he wasn't."

Candy groaned, flicking her hair back behind her shoulders. "I've seen them out and about, not too long ago. Considering your history with men, you shouldn't trust your own feelings. You're like blinded or somethin'."

Candy grabbed her bag and headed out of the office. I followed. She switched off her office light and turned down the hallway where we ran into one of her coworkers.

"Megan, this is my niece, Delilah. She's tryin' to open Beach Read."

"Oh," Megan said with trepidation. "Pleasure to meet you, Delilah."

"You, too. I've seen you before. Weren't you talking with Darryl Chambers on my move-in day?"

Megan rolled her eyes under her poofy bangs. "Oh, I remember that. Yes, that poor boy. It's such a shame, what happened to him."

"Delilah found the body," Candy said.

Megan's face fell into shock. "Bless your heart! How disturbin'."

"It was. Did you know him well?"

"Oh, no," she said with a wave of her hand. "He'd come to me a few weeks earlier because he was interested in buying a house in the Tradewinds."

"Darryl Chambers?" Candy's eyes widened in shock.

"Yes, we looked at a great three-bedroom, two bath cottage at a terrific deal. Perfect for a young couple. Chambers said he had a substantial down payment, but the bank denied his loan application. Too high risk with his fluctuatin' job history and zero credit."

"How disappointing!" I said as we exited the building toward the parking lot.

"Tell me about it. I thought he'd blow a fuse. Instead, he said that he'd make a better offer, and that he'd secure a job that would make the bank change their minds. Well, in the meantime, someone else bought the house."

I shook my head. Candy beeped her BMW unlocked and opened the door to air out the heat.

Megan went on, "He came to me with a letter saying he was enlisting in the army. He also told me he'd raised $25,000 as a down payment. But it was too late. What could I do?"

"Where would a kid like him get that kind of money?" I asked.

"I don't know," Megan said. "He'd been working a couple of

jobs. I assumed he'd saved it up."

I didn't think so. Whatever he was in to could've gotten him killed.

Chapter Twenty

HOME

FRIDAY AFTERNOON. LEWIS released the building. The lab reports had cleared me, for now. Damon and his crew were back to work upstairs in the apartment. Downstairs, John Mack from Custom Cleaning Service was decontaminating the wood floors, walls, and windows.

Finally, there was progress. Not that it mattered.

Public opinion had mounted against me. My newspaper portrait had become window dressing for many local businesses. Anyone supportive of Aunt Clara's cause clipped the article and plastered it in their doorways, on their windows, or bulletin boards. People ogled me like a bearded lady.

Being back in the store felt strange, too. Death still hung there, a dark shadow looming, heavy on my shoulders.

So, I came to the sea, but found no relief.

Willie and I crossed the boardwalk and waited for traffic to clear on Atlantic Avenue. Ronnie Chambers passed by in a dark green truck, turning onto Coral Avenue. Though I'd rather take the alley than the business route home given that my picture was posted next to blood drive fliers, lost dog signs, and event announcements, we followed Ronnie.

Chambers parked at the post office at the end of the strip. He reached in the back of his truck, pulled out several packages, and awkwardly carried them inside.

"Come on, Willie." I picked up the pace. Peeking in the post office window, I saw Ronnie at the computerized self-postage counter, weighing each package and affixing the printed labels.

I tied Willie's leash to the nearest lamppost and went inside, eyeing the packages as I made my way to the man at the counter. One was heading to Nevada, another to Ohio. The return address was a post office box rather than a home address and didn't say Ronnie's name anywhere.

"A book of stamps, please," I said to the postman, taking my attention away from Ronnie. Turning to leave, Ronnie stood behind me, staring. I jumped at the sight of him—that he was so close to me and the weird, creepy smile on his face. Saying nothing, he gyrated his hips in my direction. I pushed by him and hurried out the door. Willie and I couldn't make it home fast enough.

Back at the store, John Mack told me the work was complete. Where the bloodstain had been was now an unfinished section of hardwood, perfectly round. John Mack had cleaned, sanded, and swept Darryl Chambers away, leaving what looked like an island.

Damon Carver came in the store as John Mack left. He examined the spot on the floor, rubbing his chin.

"I could take care of this for you," he said.

"Um, let's leave it for now," I said. "How're things upstairs?"

Damon smiled widely. "Done. Finished."

"Really?"

"Yep, come see." He waved me toward the door. Willie and I followed him.

"I can't believe it," I said as we rounded the corner. "It seems like it's been years since we started."

"We would've been done last Saturday, if not for—" He stopped himself. "Well, you know. I'd no idea Chambers planned to come back to put up the chandelier."

"He seemed like the kind of guy who did things his own way."

"He was. You know, I always heard all this crap about him—how he went from job to job because he stole or didn't show up or did something else stupid—but he was perfect for me. Always on time. Always a good worker."

I nodded. "I heard he was handy."

Damon's eyes lit up as we climbed the back stairs. "Hell yes. That boy could fix anything. You know, he insisted on doing all your cabinetry himself, custom. I was content just to buy you some mass-produced stuff, but he said, '*Oh no, Mr. Carver, isn't she family? Let's do something nice*'."

We stood at the top of the third floor in front of the glass and purple door.

Damon smiled. "Let's do it." He opened the door.

The sun was setting over the ocean and the orange lights streamed in through the windows, making the whole room warm and soft. The ocean side brick wall looked clean and bright with its fresh layer of white paint. The exposed beams and columns had been repaired and repainted white. The remaining walls, Damon'd painted sky blue, giving the entire apartment a true cottage feel.

I gasped, tears in my eyes.

"You like the color?" he asked. "I thought it'd be a nice surprise instead of borin' ol' white."

"It's perfect."

The kitchen had been gutted and replaced. Birch cabinets lined the walls, floor to ceiling. Darryl had created a beautiful, intricate latticework over the cabinet fronts. New countertops, sink, and faucet. The window above the sink had been completely replaced. There was a gap where the stove used to be and a small space for a refrigerator.

"You'll need to get yourself a stove and fridge," Damon said. "There's a Lowe's in Shawsburg."

Damon had already moved my Cotton Exchange finds in—the lamps, Charlie Brown mugs, and Mr. Coffee I'd bought from Lenny, an old kitchen table with mismatched chairs, and a long mirror with a thick black frame. New pendant lamps hung down the length of the apartment, shining against a floor that had been buffed down and refinished to its original dark wood glory.

"The bed's a gift from Rose," Damon told me. "She had my boys come by and pick it up for you. She wanted it to be a surprise."

Damon had moved Mamma Rose's spare bed into place against the far wall. It was a dark wood four-poster canopy bed—the most elaborate piece of furniture I'd ever had. I couldn't wait to thank her.

"Check out the bathroom." Damon opened the door, revealing a clean sky-blue bathroom with a pedestal sink, ivory tub, and freshly tiled floors. An oval mirror was flanked by two silver sconces. He'd even installed two towel racks because he said one was never enough.

I was home. *Really* home.

Damon handed me a tissue from his pocket. "What do you think?"

I wiped my eyes again. "I love it. I can't believe it's the same place. I feel like I'm on one of those dumb TV shows and the cameras will come out or something."

"Nah, no cameras. I'm glad you like it. I'll give you some time to get acquainted, unless there's something else you need right now?"

"No. Thanks, Damon. It's everything I wanted."

He smiled. "Welcome. Enjoy the new digs."

I pushed open the seaside windows and basked in the warm

glow of sunlight and ocean breezes. I couldn't believe it. For the first time since returning to Tipee, it didn't feel like another mistake.

I raced to get my things from Grandma Betty's and must've gone up and down the stairs a dozen times, carrying boxes from the office and storage room. I set up the kitchen, loaded the bathroom with my toiletries, made the beautiful bed, and hung up my clothes. Progress was grand.

By the time the fireworks blasted over the pier at 9:30, my activities had worn me down. I leashed Willie for a last stroll around the alley and then prepared for relaxation.

At ten, I climbed into the glorious bed and escaped into an Agatha Christie. Again, *Wuthering Heights* called to me, so I picked it up and alternated between the two. My eyes drifted into dozing sometime around midnight.

A low growl woke me up. Willie was on high alert, staring at my front door. The boom, boom of Via's rattled in the background. In the distance, a car alarm sounded momentarily. Still, I heard nothing that should've upset Willie.

I'd left the stair light on, so the gleam shone through the front door's slated window and dingy sheer curtain, producing a crisscross pattern on the floor. I looked over.

Nothing.

"What is it?"

Willie jumped off the bed, barking. The distinct sound of footsteps, thud, thud, thud, told me someone was coming up the stairs.

"Oh, shit." *Don't freak out, just think*, I told myself. I jumped from bed and searched for weapons. Dashing over to the kitchen, I grabbed the longest knife from the butcher block and retreated behind Willie.

Willie growled again. I grabbed my phone from the table. It was dead, and I'd left the charger downstairs. A large shadow moved by

SEA-DEVIL

the door's glass. It looked like Frankenstein's monster, broad in the shoulders and neckless.

The monster tried the door handle, turning and shaking it. When that didn't work, he rattled it back and forth, forcing Willie into a barking fit.

"Holy shit!" The phone slipped from my shaking hand, clanging against the floor. Any second, he'd break the glass or break the door down—I just knew it. The handle moved again. He banged on the glass, making me jump.

"Go away!" My voice didn't sound as forceful as I wanted it to, but he stopped. His shadow moved. His silhouette appeared at the kitchen window above the sink. I ducked, worried he might see how non-threatening I was and break in anyway. My heart rammed against my rib cage.

Tires squealed. A commotion erupted. Footsteps pounded down the steps. I scurried to the door, peeked, and seeing nothing, rushed out to the porch.

A hooded figure dashed into the bushes behind Via's and through their parking lot with Officer Williams right behind him. The Dodge Charger sat at my doorstep. Teague rushed over to the bottom of the steps.

"Delilah, you okay?" he asked.

"Yes. Go help Williams!" Teague jumped back into the Charger and raced to aid his partner. Willie and I waited atop the balcony. Though it was only a few minutes, it seemed like forever before the Charger reappeared down the alley.

"What happened?" I demanded when Teague and Williams stepped out of the car.

"Got away," Williams said, breathlessly. "Bastard was fast. Lost me in the park."

Teague made his way up the stairs. The knife tapped against the railings as my hand shook.

"You sure you're okay?" he asked.

"Yes."

"He didn't get into the apartment, did he?" Teague slid the knife out of my hand.

"No, he just scared the hell out of Willie, that's all."

"Should we go inside?" Teague pointed to my front door. I raised an eyebrow at him. Being alone with him worried me.

"Why? I can give you my statement right here. It's messy, boxes and dirty clothes everywhere. I wasn't expecting company, and there's no need for the two of us to be in there, anyway."

Teague didn't answer. Instead, he grinned and pointed down at my mid-section.

I was wearing a tank top, braless, and panties—my Tuesday panties even though it was Friday because I'd stopped caring about getting the days right long ago.

"Shit." I opened the door and slunk inside.

Chapter Twenty-One

GOOD GRIEF

TEAGUE SAT AT the tiny kitchen table with his back toward the bedroom as I made myself decent. Willie sauntered up to Teague, pushed his hand for attention, and received plenty. I pulled on some shorts and a baggy t-shirt, still shivering with fright.

I babbled as I dressed. "I was just reading, you know, a little Agatha Christie and a little *Wuthering Heights* because I can't resist. I drifted off to sleep. Next thing I know, Willie's growling. Then, footsteps came up the stairs, and it's like I'm in the middle of a cheesy horror movie. A big shadow's at the door, turning the knob, and when it doesn't open, he bangs on it. Bang, bang, bang. He moved to the window, but then you guys showed up and he took off."

"Did you see his face?"

"No."

"Anything familiar about him?"

"Based on this guy's serious creep-factor, he felt like Ronnie

Chambers. That weasel's freaked me out twice recently—"

Teague squinted at me. "What did he do?"

In a blur of words, I spilled out the two encounters I'd had with Ronnie Chambers, the latter one being only a few hours old.

"You should've called me."

I shrugged. "Didn't seem worth mentioning. Besides, this wasn't him."

"How can you be sure if you didn't see his face?"

"Wrong body type. This guy looked like Frankenstein's monster. Big, neckless, dark."

I started the Mr. Coffee, realizing that there'd be no sleep tonight.

"You want me to put out an APB for Frankenstein?"

"Frankenstein was the name of the very normal looking doctor who made a creature out of used body parts. I said he looked like Frankenstein's monster. There's a huge difference, literally. And obviously, it'd be silly to do that. I'm only giving you a frame of reference."

"You read too much. And you're doing the nervous talking thing again."

"Can you blame me?" I went to grab the coffeepot, but my hands still trembled. Teague got up and took the coffeepot from me. He placed his other hand on my arm and let his fingers roam back and forth.

"Everything's okay now. Let me get this." He took two Charlie Brown mugs from the cabinet and filled them both with coffee, adding the sugar and creamer without asking, which is exactly how I take it. He handed me the mug that said *Good Grief* along the side under an upside-down picture of Charlie Brown. *Fitting*, I thought.

We sat down at the table.

"Did he say anything?"

"No."

Teague grabbed his walkie-talkie off his belt and asked for dispatch to send a crime scene technician to 111 Starfish Drive. I rolled my eyes. "We'll take fingerprints. We need to know who it was."

I huffed. "I'm sure it was nothing. Probably some drunk guy."

"Drunk guys don't run that fast."

I held my finger up. "Could've been the squatter."

"Could've been the guy who sent you that note."

"No, it wasn't. I'm sure." I clamped my lips shut.

"So, it wasn't a bill, after all?" My shoulders slumped. He said, "Who sent the note and what did it say?"

"I did get a note in the mail, but it wasn't threatening, just annoying, and nothing to do with this or Darryl—"

"Why not tell me?"

I groaned. "If I do, can we move on and not discuss it anymore?" Teague nodded. "My former boyfriend thought it'd be cool to send me a sticky note that said *Miss me?* I suppose he wanted me to know that he knows where I am—"

"You don't think that's threatening?"

I sighed. "Teague, he's a jerk. A control freak. That's all."

My new deal with Jonathan came to mind like needles jammed in my eyes. He'd have no reason to come here in such an underhanded way, given that we already had an arrangement. Course, I couldn't tell Teague that.

"Look, I know him, and he wouldn't scare me. He's more of a controller than an intimidator. When we dated, he insisted that I straighten my hair." Teague looked confused. "You know, my hair's kind of unruly. Jonathan insisted that I straighten it out."

Teague raised an eyebrow.

"I know it sounds ridiculous, but I did it. Took hours every time. Maybe it looked better. Anyway, I eventually realized that it wasn't about hair, really, if that makes sense."

I stopped to shake my head and run my hands through my very

messy hair. "Jonathan likes to do things like write stupid notes or tell me how to look or hold things over my head. But he's never been violent or scary. Jonathan would've knocked and tried charming his way in. This wasn't his style."

I shoved my face in my coffee cup to shut myself up. Teague was silent for a moment and then cleared his throat.

"This must be your first night in the apartment. Who knew you'd be here?"

I took a heavy breath. "Family. Damon's crew. Or anyone who saw me moving in."

Teague jotted down notes. "I want to check downstairs. You have your keys?"

I handed him the keys from the counter. "Should I go with you? To check on the money and, um… you know, I'd be the one to know if things are as they should be, anyway, since they're my things."

Teague gave me his best calming look. "I'll call Williams up here. I won't leave you alone. Once I do a sweep, you can check the money and make sure everything's in order."

Teague left to search the store. Officer Williams joined me in the apartment and accepted a cup of coffee.

"Still don't believe in curses?" he asked, chuckling lightly.

I grunted and rolled my eyes.

"Well, you ain't gotta believe in curses for them to believe in you," Williams said.

The technician arrived to dust the doorframe and windowsill. Moments later, Teague returned. Though he said things were fine, I wanted to see for myself. Teague guided me around the darkened building with his flashlight.

"Are you okay?" he asked. "I mean, really okay?"

"My heart's still beating a little fast, but I'm fine."

He gave me a coy grin. "You sure that's because of the attempted break-in?"

I laughed. We rounded the corner and stepped onto the sidewalk. Streetlights brightened up our path. Teague switched off his flashlight.

"You're perfect for this job, you know." I gave his arm a gentle squeeze before letting it go. "You have a calming way about you, and I'm difficult to deal with. I talk too much and think I know everything." He laughed. "I'm serious. You melt tensions, and not just when you're rubbing my temples to get rid of my headache."

We stopped in front of the store windows. Teague smiled, glanced down at his feet, and blushed like he didn't know what to say.

"You should know," I said, nerves rising again, "that you make things better."

"So, do you, Delilah." Teague looked back up and let a lock of my hair curl around his fingertip. "And you should know not to change anything, especially your hair. I love your hair."

I chuckled. "Wow, you've trumped my compliment."

"Since you were giving them out, thought I'd hand one over. You could use one."

"I won't turn it away."

Teague unlocked the front door and flipped on the lights, bringing the store to life. Nothing was out of place. My would-be intruder hadn't bothered with the store, thankfully. Still, I checked everything. Teague followed me to the back office. I gathered the money bag from the bottom of the filing cabinet. The cash was still there. I was about to tell Teague that all was well, but his attention was diverted.

"What's this?" He leaned down by the base of the filing cabinet, eyeing the metal stick jutting out from underneath the left corner. With a handkerchief, he eased it out from its hiding place. My heart rammed into my throat.

"Um, that's mine. I must've dropped it."

Teague looked at me with a raised eyebrow. "Yours, huh?"

"Yep."

"What is it?"

"It's a nail thingy, for my nails." I wiggled my fingers, though I hadn't done my nails in ages. Teague stood upright, holding the tool delicately in his handkerchief, and cocked his head at me.

"You want to stick with that story?" His left eyebrow perched high on his forehead.

Nervous acids boiled in my stomach. My shoulders fell. "No."

"Why lie about it?"

"Because if it doesn't belong to me, then it might belong to Darryl," I said. "Or the killer. And if your nimrod coworkers overlooked it, then that means they'll come back in here again, and that'll mean another delay."

"You knew it was here?"

"I saw it when I came in to get my clothes."

"And you said nothing?"

I shrugged. "I didn't think it was important. It's probably been there for years. Probably belonged to Uncle Joe or something. I didn't want to further complicate matters by wasting more time on something that was nothing."

"Delilah, this is a lock-picking tool. It's called a snake rake. It's part of a set of tools. Just possessing them, unless you're a certified locksmith, is illegal."

The word 'mistake' reverberated through my skull like it was sounding off a gong. I bit my bottom lip and cocked my head.

I shrugged weakly. "Then you should probably know that my fingerprints are on it."

Teague called Detective Harlan Lewis to report the snake rake. Lewis asked to see me again in the morning. The technician upstairs dusting my door for prints came down to collect the new evidence.

"Ms. Duffy found it," Teague told the gentleman, "and picked it up."

The technician admired the tool. "Haven't seen a snake rake in ages. Did you see any others lying around?" Teague and I shook our heads. "We'll do a more thorough search. I'll call in a few other officers. Hope we won't have to pry up any of the floorboards."

My mouth dropped. "What?"

"Well, it's a lot of work and it gets messy. Hopefully, we can avoid it." The man smiled. I fumed.

"I'll take Ms. Duffy back upstairs and finish taking her statement." Teague escorted me away from the scene.

"I'm sorry. I shouldn't have lied to you," I said once we'd turned into the alley. My mind flashed to the painted sand dollar I'd stolen from the crime scene, and my heart leapt once again. Presently, it was safely tucked away in my make-up bag in the apartment.

"Tell Lewis that you found it tonight and picked it up," Teague said with irritation.

I shrugged. "Okay."

Back in the apartment, Teague worked on the rest of his paperwork, seething under his collar. I sat down next to him, bringing one knee up to my chin. I hated that he was so angry.

"I didn't know what it was," I told him, "honestly."

"I know."

"I didn't think it was important."

He stopped writing and tossed the pen down. "Obviously not."

"I'm sorry," I said. "Don't be angry at me."

"I'm not angry. I don't like lying."

"You don't have to protect me."

"Is there anything else, Delilah?" he asked. "Any other thing you're keeping from me, even something you think isn't important?"

Possible answers to that question swarmed in my head. I was selective.

"I may know why there was a snake rake near Darryl

Chambers," I said, weakly.

"What do you know?"

"Well, the other day I went to Shawsburg High School, and asked a few questions—"

"About Darryl Chambers?"

"Well, yeah. I mean, he's been on my mind, and since I was there for summer reading lists anyway, might as well bring him up to people who knew him."

Teague stood up and leaned against the kitchen counter, arms folded. "What were you thinking?"

"They were harmless questions—"

"Really, Delilah? Let's consider what happened tonight and then rethink the word *harmless*."

"Just listen, okay? I think I can help."

"Fine, I'm listening."

"I spoke to Darryl's English teacher, Mrs. Trojak," I said, "and he wrote a paper on the history of locks. It was a free-write, which means he wrote it off the top of his head, Teague. She said it was very specific."

"So?"

"So, did you know that during his senior year, Darryl allegedly stole the assistant principal's prized marlin right off his office wall? Coach Tucker told me that if it had been Darryl, he would've had to break in to four different locks, including an electronic one."

I stood up and went over to Teague. "I think Darryl Chambers knew all about locks. That tool, the snake rake, was his. He used it to get into the store after I left, so he could put the chandelier up for me." Refilling my coffee cup, I took a hurried sip of coffee. "He had high spatial intelligence. He could solve puzzles and work with his hands. Mrs. Trojak said that Darryl Chambers was no slouch. I believe her. I also think whoever killed him knew about his lock-picking skills—"

"Because they tried taking the tools with them when they left through the back door," Teague said, "but one slid out—"

"And landed under the filing cabinet."

Teague said nothing for several seconds, eyeing me in contemplation. I sipped my coffee, feeling both wired and exhausted simultaneously.

"I need you to do two things for me," he said. "First, share this information with Lewis—"

"Oh, come on. He's so unreasonable."

"Give him a chance," Teague said. "He wants to see you tomorrow. Tell him what you found out. It'll help him get on the right track with the case."

"Fine," I said. "What's the second thing?"

"No more asking questions about Chambers. You're in danger." I was about to protest when he said, "Delilah, please."

My time was evaporating. Lewis would grow impatient with Jonathan's failure to send my personnel file. If he went to a higher up for it, I'd be done. The only way to prevent that from happening would be to push the police to the right suspect. If Lewis had no reason to get my file, then my secrets might be safe.

Still, Teague's pleading face wore on my heart, and felt abrasive, like sandpaper, against my resolve.

"I'll talk to Lewis," I said, "and I'll be as safe as possible—"

"By not asking questions."

"By being smart," I said. "I don't want to lie to you again. Making that promise would be lying. Don't make me. I'm trying to protect myself here."

"From what?"

"From being called a murderer, for one. Isn't that enough?"

He shook his head. "It's more than that."

"Teague, I don't want to talk about it."

He stood up and gathered his things, shaking his head. "Maybe you should open up to the people who want to help you, if only to save you from the ones who don't."

Teague left. I stared into my coffee cup in exhausted contemplation. I'd learned more about Darryl Chambers than I'd told Teague, and the sand dollar still nagged at my guilt. I don't know why I didn't tell him about the conversation with Megan Masters. If the police were doing anything right, they'd already know about Darryl's attempt to buy a house. After all, I told them that he'd had an argument with Megan Masters myself. Had they checked into it?

Putting the pieces of Darryl's lock-picking abilities together, I decided that Darryl must've dared to disturb his universe. Whatever bad business he'd gotten himself into, he was trying to break from it. But the army seemed like a stretch, especially for someone who'd had full rides to college a few years ago. Why not then? Why now?

I thought of T. S. Eliot's *The Love Song of J. Alfred Prufrock.*

"*And indeed there will be time,*" I said tiredly. "*There will be time to prepare a face to meet the faces that you meet... And time for all the works and days of hands... Time for you and time for me... And indeed there will be time to wonder, 'Do I dare?' and 'Do I dare?'.*"

I sighed, lamenting that Darryl's time ended, perhaps because he'd dared.

Chapter Twenty-Two

ANGELS & DEVILS

"IT'S THRILLING TO see you again, Ms. Duffy," Detective Harlan Lewis said as I approached his gray cubicle. He shook my hand but didn't smile. "I appreciate you meeting me like this."

"Did I have a choice?" I sat down in my familiar seat.

"Thanks for alerting Officer Teague to the snake rake," he said. "We're a small department. Our crime scene techs are laypeople. That's the way it is with small towns. You use what you can. Our crime scene photographer works for the local paper. Our coroner is also our town doctor. Our evidence collection guys are only part-time. They're all trained, mind you. But they aren't policemen, like the rest of us."

"Why are you telling me this?"

"Evidence can sometimes get overlooked, especially by laypeople."

"I'm a layperson."

"At any rate, I'm sure your uncle doesn't have to hear about our oversight." Lewis shuffled in his rolling chair and grabbed his pencil. I smirked, thankful that having a journalist for an uncle had finally worked to my advantage.

Looking uneasy, Lewis went on, "Thank you for being so observant. If witnesses could be more observant, like you—well, it'd make my job a whole helluva lot easier. Take the damn granny bandits, for example. The reason they've been so hard to catch is because the victims didn't even realize someone had robbed them—"

"How could they not know someone had robbed them?"

Lewis shrugged and leaned forward. "No forced entry. Nothing outta place. Always specific items taken. Unless those things were in plain sight, owners didn't notice right away. Not everyone checks on their pearls and old coin collections every time they walk in the door. They're ghosts, but I'm hot on their trail. They've gotten sloppy, expanded their take. Won't be long now."

My eyebrows felt like mountain peaks on my forehead at his casual, conversational mood, such a change from his usual antagonism. "Well, anyway, I hope this means you've eliminated me as a suspect. You've already wasted—"

"Let's not get ahead of ourselves, Ms. Duffy. I'm still waiting to get that information from Mr. Dekker. I've put in a call to your former principal as well."

"Knock yourself out." My stomach twisted into tight knots.

Lewis asked more questions about the would-be intruder, the snake rake, and events surrounding the discovery. I answered diligently, even revealing what I'd learned about Darryl Chambers from his coach and English teacher. He jotted down notes but said little.

Seeing that I hadn't impressed him much, I said, "Darryl tried to buy a house, according to Megan Masters. He claimed to have a sizable cash down payment. You should investigate his money."

"Don't involve yourself in this case, Ms. Duffy," Lewis said after he'd written what he wanted. "Folks watch a lot of TV these days, have illusions of grandeur about their abilities, and wind up wasting their time and, worse, wasting mine."

"Teague's already had this talk with me. For the record, I didn't involve myself. The case involved me."

Lewis pulled his arms back behind his head, as if he were under arrest. Sweat circles stained the underarms of his shirt.

"Officer Teague suggested a protective detail for you."

I shook my head. "I don't want anyone following me around."

"Fine. Some extra security at your apartment might not be a bad idea. It's not a safe location anyway, behind the strip club." A short grin eased up on the corner of his mouth. "You know, I hear Via's hiring. You should think about it. After that picture in the paper, I'm sure you'd make a pretty penny there."

Disgusted, I got up, ready to leave. If I stayed any longer, I might feel sick.

Lewis said, "They've already got their eyes on you."

I stopped. "What do you mean?"

"Lenny Jackson at Via's called in your intruder last night," Lewis said, glancing at the file on his desk. He smiled slyly. "Looks like you already have friends in low places, Ms. Duffy."

Outside the entrance of Via's Sports Bar and Gentleman's Club, I took a deep breath and tried to shake off my nerves along with my preconceived notions. It was late Saturday afternoon. It had taken me several hours of extreme self-convincing to get here. I carried a store bakery tray of assorted cookies and a growing feeling of stupidity.

The street side of Via's isn't like most stores. You can't see in. The windows are blocked out by black silhouettes of naked ladies against hot pink backgrounds. A tubby bouncer stood guard at the door, arms folded and expression grim. He reminded me of one of Tolkien's trolls.

"Hot ladies get in free," the troll said gruffly as I walked up. I entered the dark cavern.

I expected the place to smell like beer, puke, and semen, but it was strangely normal. The stage could've been home to comedians or singers, if not for the poles. A stripper in a red devil outfit danced to an extremely loud *Devil Inside* by INXS. I averted my eyes.

Round tables and chairs dominated most of the red-carpeted room. A bar took up the far wall. Private rooms lined the right side. A disco ball hung from the ceiling, pretzels littered the tables, and it smelled like French fries. Only a few 'gentlemen' were in attendance, quietly drinking and observing the show. It was all rather, well, boring.

A suited man at the bar, uninterested in the show, struck me as the man in charge. His dark hair was slicked back, gangsta style, and about two days' worth of stubble peppered his face. He was thin, not unattractive, approaching forty, and not as greasy as I would've expected, or maybe hoped.

"Excuse me," I said. His head bobbed up with a sigh of annoyance. He set his eyes on me and smiled. I shivered.

"I'm Delilah Duffy," I said, nervousness gripping my stomach as his eyes went up and down. "I'm the manager of Beach Read, the store behind you."

He brought his attention back to my face. His smile dropped. "Oh, what's the problem?"

"Nothing. I wanted to stop by and introduce myself. And thank you."

"That's a first. For what?"

"I live in the upstairs apartment. Last night someone tried to break in. Your bouncer, Lenny Jackson, saw the guy and called the police. He really saved my ass. I wanted to come by and say thanks. I brought cookies."

He extended his hand. "I'm David Via."

"Delilah Duffy."

"Drink?" He snapped his fingers for the bartender.

"Diet Coke?"

"The alley poses a problem from time to time," David Via said as the bartender placed my frosty Diet Coke on a red coaster. "People trying to gain access to the club by the back-exit door. Others trying to slip out without paying their tabs. Drugs being sold. Hard to run an honest business with so much devilry going on."

I almost choked. "I can imagine."

"My security team checks the perimeter every hour on the hour during our night shifts as a crime deterrent."

"That's a very smart policy," I said. "It saved me from, well—who knows what?"

"I'll pass along your gratitude and the cookies. Lenny's shift doesn't start until nine."

"I know Lenny," I said. "He sold me some lamps. Looks like Mr. Clean, right?"

Via chuckled. "Yeah, that's the guy. Selling junk's his side job."

"After last night, and of course the murder, it's comforting to know that you guys are protecting the area."

"More than we can say for the damn cops." David Via nodded, looking me over a second time. "That's right. You're in the building where Chambers was killed. Oh, I know you. I saw that gorgeous shot of you in the paper. My, oh, my. You're like a celebrity around here."

Inside, I cringed, but I kept a smile on my face.

"Thanks. Chambers worked here, didn't he? I'm sorry for your loss."

"That rat fuck son of a bitch? He wasn't an employee of mine anymore. He quit three hours before a Friday shift. Left me hanging out to dry, bastard."

"He quit?"

"Days before he got off-ed. His brother still works here, though, but not for long. He's useless."

"Why's that?"

"He doesn't have the physique for the job. I only hired Ronnie because Darryl begged me, said they worked better as a team. I'm such a softhearted guy. But, nobody's intimidated by a hundred-pound weasel."

The bartender laughed in support.

"Well, you seem to know a lot about people," I said. "Any theories on who killed him?"

David Via grinned. "I thought you did it, sweetheart."

"No, it wasn't me."

"Police jacking you up? They do that shit to me all the time. I don't know who killed the bastard. Talk to his old girlfriend. Miss Angel. She's backstage. I'll show you."

Teague had asked me to leave it alone, but I couldn't refuse Via's offer. My tummy did somersaults as we neared a narrow hallway. Lighting was scarce. The walls were littered with pictures of stripping stars.

"You know, you've got just the right physique for Via's. You ever dance before?"

"No."

"If you need to make a little extra money, let me know. Delicious Delilah… Dangerous Delilah… Delilah the Dancer." He licked his lips, and I felt queasy. Alliteration was ruined forever.

"No, thanks. I'm trying for Delilah the Decent."

I didn't live up to that name, either.

"Wake up, ladies." David Via barged in through a closed door at the end of the hall. "You have a visitor." He turned back to me. "I'll be at the bar if you need me. Have fun." He winked and left.

"Who the hell are you?"

Two scantily clad women occupied chairs in front of large, well-lit vanities in a cluttered, cramped room.

"I'm Delilah."

"Great, a new one," the gruff one said. She wore a turquoise sequined baby doll dress, heavy make-up, a dragon tattoo on her left arm, and about one hundred more pounds than an average stripper (I'd guess). "What the hell are you staring at?"

"I'm looking for Angel."

"You got a problem with my weight?" She slammed her powder puff down on the counter. A plume of dust billowed up from it. "Guys love fat girls."

"I know they do," I said. "You're a Renaissance woman."

"What's that supposed to mean?"

"In the Renaissance, they preferred larger women. That's why all their art shows women with more to hold on to. You would've been a supermodel then. Larger women represented wealth and status. Higher class. Nobility."

A wide red smile blanketed her chubby face. "Nobility?"

I nodded. "It's no surprise to me you're a dancer here. Beauty comes in many forms and sizes. It's an honor to meet both of you. I've never met dancers before."

I extended my hand to the heavyset lady. She shook it daintily.

"I'm Sadie. What d'you say your name was again?"

"Delilah, and I'm not here for a job."

"Then why are you here?" the other stripper asked meekly. She wore a white negligee, platform thigh-high boots, Christmas tinsel in her hair, and silver gems around her eyes. She had delicate features, a petite frame, and heavy red lipstick.

"Your boss said I could talk to Angel," I said. "You must be her."

"I'm Angel." She checked her face in the mirror. "About to go on, so you better make it snappy. I gotta make rent tonight."

"I'm opening the store across the alley, Beach Read."

Angel sat back in her chair. "That's where Darryl died."

I nodded. "Yes. I heard you used to date."

"For a while, about a year ago. He was sweet. I like the big, burly type. Used to buy me nice presents."

"What presents, if you don't mind me asking?"

"Got me a foot soak. He knew my feet hurt when I came home. Got me a pretty white mink coat once. That was the nicest thing he gave me, but the thing I loved the most was a gorgeous angel pin. It had diamonds for eyes and a gold halo. So cute. He never asked for none of it back either when we broke up."

"Why did you break up?"

"Most guys can't handle what we do, get jealous and act stupid. He wanted me to quit, but I like working here. I make great money." She shrugged. "What am I going to do? Be a doctor? Sweep floors?"

"Was the break-up friendly?"

"Yeah, it was kind of mutual. I mean, he was sad about it for a while, but he got over it. I'm pretty sure he was seeing someone."

"Who?"

"I don't know. No one here at the club. But, someone. He started acting different."

"Yeah, he was actin' like an idiot lately," Sadie said. "Hummin' and smilin' all the time. You'd think he'd won the lottery or something—kind of annoying, actually." Sadie's eyes widened. "Maybe he was seein' a married woman. A jealous husband could've killed him."

Angel adjusted her hair. "Nah, I doubt Darryl'd do that. If I had to guess who killed him, I'd say his brother. He's a creep." Angel got out of her chair and checked her backside in the mirror. "I gotta go."

"Thanks for the help, you guys." I turned to leave.

Sadie held up a long, turquoise fingernail. "You're that chick from the paper, aren't ya?"

My shoulders slumped, but I nodded.

"Oh, my gosh, you've got stripper written all over you, girl," Sadie said. "You want to learn how to dance, you come see me. I'll teach you everything."

The sticky humidity felt like a baptism when I finally exited Via's. I looked up toward Coral Lane in time to see Aunt Clara driving by, staring right at me with her coy smile. I could almost hear her dialing her phone. I wondered which relative she'd call first. Probably my mother.

Chapter Twenty-Three

WHALES

WALKING DOWN THE alley from Via's, my phone rang. A glance at the tiny screen on my flip phone showed it was Mike. I huffed, opting not to take it for the sake of getting over to Grandma Betty's *nearly* on time for family dinner. In his message, he apologized again for cancelling our date and asked me to stop by The Crab Shack later. I didn't know if I wanted to given how uneasy I'd felt about our date. With family to face, I pushed Mike out of my head.

Willie and I arrived to a full driveway, forcing me to park on the sand near the street. All the regular cars took up the spaces under the stilted house, plus one. Teague was there, standing on the back porch holding a bottle of beer and wearing casual clothes. He smiled from the railing. Willie bounded up the steps to greet him properly.

"You look good," he said. "Did you sleep?"

"A little. What're you doing here?"

"Betty invited me the day she drove me home, when I dropped

off your Jeep and you took off." I bit my lower lip. *Oops.* "Hope you don't mind."

I shook my head. "I don't mind, but it feels a little like you're stalking me, Teague."

"Might be." Teague followed me down the hallway toward the family room. "How was Lewis?"

I shrugged. "He was himself."

"That bad?"

"It's over," I said, "but I did everything you asked." He smiled as we moved into the grand living room.

"Rachel'll be fine. She dates like you try on shoes. You keep going till you find the right fit. Raina, well, she'll be the death of me. But I swear if my daughters aren't married by the time they're twenty-nine, I'll shoot myself," Aunt Clara said to Aunt Charlotte and Aunt Candy as we walked in. My shoulders dropped.

Willie bounded from one person to the next, extracting as much attention as he could. Candy's girls, Neisha and Nikita, asked to take him outside to play. Willie and I both agreed.

Aunt Clara smiled warmly. "Delilah, we didn't hear you come in. Officer Teague, always a pleasure to see you." The usual round of greetings and hand shaking swept across the room. No one mentioned the strip club. Maybe Clara hadn't seen me.

"I don't think they know," Teague whispered, as if reading my mind. I glanced at him quickly. "About your break-in last night. You didn't tell them?"

"No, I've been busy," I said. "They'll just make a fuss. Do we have to tell them?"

Teague shrugged and shook his head.

Dinner was served. We sat at Grandma Betty's enormous table, decorated in red, white and blue hydrangeas, white candles, red place mats, and rooster dinnerware. Stuffed salmon was the main course, but she had a myriad of side dishes to satisfy even the picky eaters at the table. Teague sat between me and Mamma Rose.

"So, Delilah, when's the new grand opening going to be?" Clark asked midway through dinner.

"Tomorrow."

"You're goin' to have your grand openin' on a Sunday?" Aunt Charlotte said.

"Yes."

The aunts exchanged glances.

"Terrific," Clark said. "It's about time."

"No, that's not terrific. That's completely unacceptable," Aunt Clara said. "Openin' on Sunday is just wrong."

"What's wrong about it?" Clark asked for me. "Sunday sail, never fail!"

"She'll open for business while the good folk of Tipee are at church?" Clara asked. "After all that's happened, you should restore your reputation, Delilah. Not make it worse. People think you're a building-stealing, filthy-mouthed murdering floozy. This won't help."

"People are sayin' you're like the devil," Aunt Charlotte said.

Not to be left out, Candy said, "I heard someone say she's the bride of Satan."

"Girls!" Grandma Betty huffed.

"I'll open after church," I said, "so as not to offend all you upstanding Christian people."

"That's a considerate compromise, Delilah," Grandma Betty said with an approving smile. "Now, can we eat our meal?"

Teague leaned over, whispering in my ear. "Wow, the Duffys in their natural habitat. Kind of scary. Let me know if you want me to get my gun."

Laughter spurted out of me along with the water I'd been sipping. I smiled at Teague, thankful for the comic relief, and we got caught up, grinning at each other. Course, the pleasant distraction was short-lived.

"So, how'd the job interview go today, Delilah?" Aunt Clara

asked, her voice louder than necessary.

My giggles stopped. "What?"

"You had a job interview, right? I mean, why else would you be at Via's strip club?"

Grandma Betty's fork dropped with a clang to her plate. Clark gasped. The twins' mouths dropped, and eyes widened. Mamma Rose shook her head. Damon Carver laughed. Candy's hand went to her mouth, while Charlotte went pale. Grandpa Charlie looked confused, and Clara's husband Peter kept eating.

"What?" Grandma Betty cocked her head at me.

"I saw her with my own two eyes, Mamma," Clara said.

I rolled my eyes. "Obviously, I wasn't there for a job."

"So, you were there?" Grandpa Charlie asked.

"Yes, but I have a perfectly reasonable explanation."

"This better be good," Betty said, sitting back from her food as if she'd lost her appetite. Clara smirked. I seethed. I'd have to tell them about the break-in in order to explain the strip club which meant opening a whole new can of worms I'd hoped to avoid.

"We're waitin'." Clara smiled slyly.

My stomach rumbled and churned. The whole table heard it. I breathed heavily, in and out, and started to speak. Teague stopped me with his hand on the back of my shoulder.

"Delilah wasn't there for a job. She has a job, reopening Beach Read," he said to the waiting audience. "Jumping to ridiculous conclusions like that isn't fair to her, and we all know Delilah isn't the stripper type, anyway. She comes from a better family than that."

Around the table, heads nodded in agreement.

Clara huffed. "There're black sheep in every family."

"Troublemakers, too." Clara winced at Teague's words, but he didn't give her a chance to argue. "Granted, Delilah's been in strange and difficult circumstances lately, but she's handled it gracefully. You should be proud of her. She's even helped the police. It may seem odd that you saw her at a strip club, but they share an alley and a dumpster. It's reasonable for the two businesses to communicate with each other, however distasteful that'd obviously be for Delilah."

Unbelievably, Teague turned the tide back in my favor, much to Clara's dismay.

Teague glanced over at me, smiling, and said, "It's none of our business why she was there. We all know her. She'd never be there for the wrong reasons. So, let's all just ease up on her."

"Samuel is absolutely right," Mamma Rose said. "I'm sick of this shit. Delilah's a good girl."

Gasps circled the table, and all eyes fell on Mamma Rose.

"I'm old. I can cuss whenever I want to," she said. "Shit. There, I said it again. And, I've wanted to say it in church a thousand times, but I've never had the balls."

The Blue Whale is the largest mammal ever, beating out all creatures, including the dinosaurs. Blue whales live in all our oceans; the seas belong to them. They are beautiful, musical, gentle creatures, and most of them live solitary lives. Their hearts alone weigh over a thousand pounds more than jet skis. With hearts so big, it's no wonder why they stay alone.

Teague either had a big heart or a serious save-the-damsel-in-distress complex. Again, he'd saved me, and I wasn't sure how I felt about it.

After dinner, Teague suggested a long beach walk. Eager to get away from the Duffys, I agreed. Teague held Willie's leash as we headed to the shore.

I nudged Teague's elbow with mine. "Thanks for coming to the rescue back there. You've made it a habit—taking care of my headaches for me."

He smiled. "It's my pleasure. You need someone on your side, especially at that table. So, why don't you tell me why you really went to Via's?"

Though I knew he'd be upset with me for continuing to press my luck with the case, I told Teague everything—why I ended up at Via's and what I learned there—hoping that more information about Darryl might offset his disappointment. It didn't.

Teague huffed. "You can't keep doing this. You're dealing with questionable people and one of them's a killer."

"I can't sit back, twiddling my thumbs while Lewis ruins whatever chance I have left of making a life here." The surf circled my feet, running up my legs. I darted around Teague to get away from it. "Wouldn't you do the same thing?"

"Maybe." Willie barked at a passing poodle while Teague held the leash tightly. We hurried on to relieve his temptations. The sun produced a soft orange glow on the sea, making everything softer, taking the pinch off the heat.

"I guess it's unfair, asking you to back off, but I'm worried, Delilah," Teague said after a few minutes. "I don't know what I'd do if anything happened to you."

I stopped walking. His words felt heavy on my heart. I stared at him, confusion etched on my face, and said exactly what I was thinking. "I don't get you."

"What do you mean?"

"Tell me something. What's hanging from the visor mirror in your police car?"

He looked curiously amused, as if surprised I might snoop there.

"Is that what I think it is?" My irritated tone caused him to crinkle his eyebrows together and take a small step back. "So, Williams has pictures of his family on his visor, but you have my ankle bracelet."

"You gave it to me."

"What does it mean?"

"I told you, that day's been a bright spot in some dark places in my life. The bracelet's a reminder, my good luck charm."

He pulled his hand out of his pocket to show me the tattered bracelet tangled between his fingers. He smiled. "It's been all over the world. When I was in the army, I took it to battle, kept it in my shirt pocket, right here." He pointed to his chest. "Whenever life was shit, I took it out and thought about our day together. It gives me peace, Delilah, remembering how good life can be and how much I want that again."

"How could you possibly feel that way about that bracelet?"

"It's not the bracelet, Delilah. It's that day. It's you."

This time, I crinkled my eyebrows together and took a step back.

Teague smiled uneasily, as if about to tell me a secret he wasn't sure I wanted to hear. "Everything's been crazy since the news hit that you were coming back, especially for me. The thought of seeing you again—it thrilled me." He stopped to chuckle. "But, made me nervous, too. Maybe I'd taken our day, and you and built you into a dream. I feared I'd idealized you, that I'd see you and you'd be different. I'd feel differently."

I stood there, cemented in place and unable to say anything.

Teague shook his head. "That didn't happen. Everything I remembered became real again. You're the same girl I came to know on a beach thirteen years ago, but better. You're everything I thought I'd imagined, only more beautiful, more brilliant than—"

"Please, stop." I tried walking away, but he grabbed my hand, holding me there.

"I can't. You say you don't get me? I don't see why. We're the same, me and you."

His words brought tears to my eyes. Had Great Aunt Laura been there, she would've pushed me to him with all her scrawny might, especially since I'd said the same thing to her about him. But I couldn't move, couldn't let go of all the mistakes I'd made. However beautiful it was that our day had meant something to him after all, I couldn't feel anything but ashamed.

I shook my head, tears spilling. I pulled my hand away from his. "We're not the same, at all. You've been so kind and sweet, but I don't deserve your devotion. You've put me on this cloud, Sam, but you know nothing about me. If you knew the things I've done—"

"I don't care about your past, Delilah. I care about you."

I scoffed. "It's easy to say my past doesn't matter when you don't know what's in it."

"Then, tell me. Tell me anything, everything. Thirteen years apart didn't change the way I feel about you. Nothing you say'll change it either."

Water closed in on my feet again, but I stayed still, locked in place by the disarming look on his face. He took my hand back in his, running his thumb along my fingers. He nodded encouragingly. "You trusted me enough once to walk into the ocean with me. You can trust me with this. What've you got to lose?"

Over his shoulder, the sea curled against the shoreline, reaching for whatever it could pull into its dark and mysterious depths. The memory of being trapped, choking for air, and sinking helplessly into nothingness stirred my anxieties.

Still, this scared me more.

I took a deep breath. "I accused a handful of my seniors of cheating. I believed that one of them was writing papers for all of them. My proof was solid, I thought, but wasn't enough for their affluent parents, the administration, or the school board. After a closed hearing, I was told to apologize, fix their grades, and drop it, which I did. My students, though, weren't satisfied. They started a shame campaign against me, which included that stupid picture somehow. My reputation was ruined. I had zero control of my classes or anything else. So, when Tyler Kettering—the eighteen-year-old football player and ringleader of the group—confronted me after school one day to rub it all in, my temper took over. He got in my face, so I punched him in his."

"Sounds like he deserved it."

"No, he didn't. I let things get out of hand. And I paid for it. Jonathan brokered a deal with the Ketterings that spared me official assault charges but cost me a nice apology fee for Tyler and, well, my job. And that's not even the worst part."

I swiped away the pesky tears that wouldn't stop flowing from my eyes and hesitated. It was an odd relief—unloading my terrible mistakes. It was also scary knowing that he'd never look at me the same way again.

"What's the worst part?" When I didn't answer right away, he said, "You've come this far. Might as well tell me everything."

I pulled my hand out of his and folded my arms over my chest. "Jonathan didn't help me out of the goodness of his heart. That cost me, too. We'd been broken up for months. He'd dumped me as soon as I started making waves about our future. My awful mistake scared me back into his bed. What does that make me, huh?"

Teague's eyes pinched together. "Human."

More tears escaped. "He's got me again, keeping my secrets for me. Labor Day weekend he's coming to collect, if I'm not in jail by then, of course. What's worse? Letting Jonathan have me or letting the world know my secrets? My life'll be ruined here before it's even started."

"That won't happen."

"It's already happening." I scoffed. "See, Teague? I'm not that girl anymore. I haven't been that girl since that day. And the funny thing is, it's all your fault."

"My fault?" He stepped closer, slipping his hand around my waist. "Wait, what'd I do?"

The breeze kicked up, sending my hair dancing in the wind. His gentle smell tickled my nose. His fingers pressed against my back, making my knees tremble. Another tear slipped out. He wiped it away with his finger.

I took a deep breath, staring up at him. "What do you think one perfect day does to the rest of them? You ruined me."

Teague's free hand brushed my cheek. He lifted my chin, and when our lips met, I swear I heard the sweet sounds of whales singing.

Chapter Twenty-Four
SERENADE

THOUGH WHALES SOUND ghostly and strange, they are singing songs. They repeat the same rhythmic patterns, which change during mating rituals. However romantic, the songs sound sad to me, and in their enormous ocean home, they don't stay together, continuing their slow serenades.

Teague's kiss was as I'd always imagined it would be. Soft and strong. Delicate and passionate. Locked in his arms, my past and everything else was locked out, lost to the beauty of his touch. My legs tingled. My heart pounded. I found his chest, then the back of his neck, and then his chest again. His fingers traced my face, slid down my neck, scooping up my hair, dragging down my back. I was intoxicated.

I broke away. "We have to stop." Then, I kissed him again, melting into him, suddenly starved for something I didn't know I'd been without.

"Why would you ever want to stop?" he said, when I pulled back a second time. He rested his forehead against mine. "I've wanted to do that for thirteen years."

"For thirteen years, I've wanted to know why you didn't." A little breathless, my lips found his again. His hands tightened around my back, pulling me closer.

When we separated, he smiled sheepishly. "I wanted to. You made me nervous. The perfect day with the perfect girl—I was afraid I'd mess it up."

My brow furrowed, but I pushed out a curious smile. "Then why d'you reject me?"

He pulled back. "Reject you?"

"I'm a big girl. I can take it. Was it the nervous talking? Or the distance? Was it someone else? Whatever it was, I'm sure—"

"What makes you think I rejected you? I don't get it."

I gave him a bothered look. "You came by the house the next day. Candy gave me your message."

Teague cocked his head at me. "What message exactly?"

"That you weren't interested in me. You said that it was a nice day, but that's all it was."

His mouth dropped, and his eyes widened. "I gave Candy a message, but that wasn't it. Damn, is that really what you've thought all these years?"

"She told me repeatedly. It devastated me."

Teague grabbed my hands in his. "I couldn't wait to see you again. I came by the next morning hoping for another perfect day, determined to get that kiss. When Candy told me you'd gone back to Wilmington, I was crushed. I couldn't believe that after the day we'd had, you'd left without so much as a goodbye—"

"I didn't go home. I was at the bookstore with Great Aunt Laura."

"Candy said your folks picked you up that morning, that your summer vacation was over. I had a present for you. Did she ever give it to you?"

I squinted. "No."

"Damn, Delilah, I'm sorry. I don't understand this. I told Candy it was the best day of my life, that I had to talk to you. Candy insisted that I'd get you in trouble with your mom if I called, and after what you'd told me about your parents, I believed her. So, I trusted Candy to tell you I'd come by, to give you my present, to be the link between us—"

"That can't be true." I folded my arms across my chest and shook my head.

"I pestered her every day. She promised me she'd talked to you, told you everything, but that you didn't care. After a few weeks, she told me you'd moved on with someone else."

"No, she never would've said that—"

"I didn't believe it, either—didn't want to, at least. So, at Christmas, I hid outside the Duffy house because I thought you'd be there. You never showed."

"We went to my mom's family that year."

"I called your house anyway, to hell with getting you in trouble. Your mom always told me you were busy. I finally decided that this was your way of getting rid of me."

"She never told me you called." My Mom 'forgetting' to give me messages from boys wasn't unusual, but I still found all of this hard to believe. I pulled my hands away from his.

"Well, I did. In the spring, Candy happily told me you and your very serious boyfriend were going to the prom. You went to the prom. I enlisted."

"So, what you're saying is Candy's a liar? That she lied to us?"

"Yes!"

"That doesn't make sense. Why would she do that?"

"Let's ask her. We can clear this up right now." He pointed up the beach and started walking toward the house. I stopped him by grabbing his arm.

"I asked her about it the other day. She's never changed her story. Why would she lie?"

Teague's eyes narrowed. "Either she's a liar or you think I am. Why would I lie?"

"Candy set our date up in the first place. Without her, we never would've had our day together. She encouraged me to go through with it, and she was there for me through the crushing rejection."

"I didn't reject you. I've never given you a reason to doubt me. You have to believe me."

"Right, because my judgment is just spectacular."

"Delilah, you remember that day. How could you think I wouldn't want to see you again? I told you I wanted to, remember? In the sand?"

"I can't think!" My mind muddled with memories and words, and I couldn't sift through it all. "Candy wouldn't do that to me. I know Candy—"

Teague shook his head. "You know me."

"Really? Do I? Then how come you haven't told me about being married?"

His eyes fell. "Hasn't come up."

I laughed. "Was I supposed to ask?"

"That has nothing to do with this. Being married before doesn't make me a liar."

"It's evidence of broken promises. That's as good as lying—"

"You don't know anything about that. If that jerk Jonathan'd asked, you would've run down the aisle, so don't be so quick to judge me. You're changing the subject."

"So, we're victims of an elaborate lie—one that arguably ruined our lives—perpetrated by my aunt for no discernible reason? That's what you expect me to believe?"

"Maybe she had a reason. I don't know. But, yes. I expect you to believe the truth."

"You weren't there, Teague. I was inconsolable. Candy never would've let me go through that if it wasn't true. She's right about me. It's like I have blinders on when it comes to men. That day—

that kiss—nothing's ever that perfect. Getting involved with you again was a mistake."

"I'm the mistake?" He took a step toward me, anger brimming in his pinched lips and icy blue eyes. "How can you say that? Your aunts have treated you horribly since you got here. How can you possibly believe her over me?"

I grabbed Willie's leash from Teague's pocket. "I'm going home." I headed up the beach. He followed, steaming.

I huffed. "Please, stop following me."

"I'm not. I'm going inside to talk to Candy."

"No!"

"Yes!" He headed up the back-deck stairs, taking two at once.

I scrambled to catch up with him. "Don't you dare cause a scene!"

"Who cares if I do? Your family's used to 'em."

"I care. Please. Everything about my life's been turned into a dramatic, dirty exhibition lately. Don't give them something else to shake their heads at."

He stopped.

I moved in front of him, putting my hand up. "I'll bring her to the front porch. Then you can ask her whatever you want. Okay?"

"Fine." He took Willie's leash and circled around the wraparound porch.

I slipped through the sliding glass door. Candy stood in the kitchen, tasting whipped cream on her finger. I pulled her to the front porch where Teague waited with Willie on the steps.

Candy's penciled eyebrow perked up on her forehead. "You look hotter than a jalapeno, Officer Teague. What's this all about?"

"Why d'you tell Delilah that I wasn't interested in her after our day at the beach?"

She gave him a baffled look. "Um, because that's what you said. Don't shoot the messenger."

Teague's hands went to his hips. "You know I didn't say that. I could never say that."

Candy shrugged, fumbling with her seahorse necklace. "I've told her everything you said verbatim. Over and over again, as a matter of fact. You showed up, told me to pass along the message, so that's what I did."

"No, you didn't. I told you it was the best day of my life. Where's the present I asked you to give her?"

Candy shook her head, and to me said, "He didn't give me anything."

Teague took two steps up the stoop. Candy backed up, her grin falling. Teague gripped the railing so hard that I thought he'd break it off. "Look, I don't care what happened back then. It's all forgiven, okay? Just tell her the truth now. Our first chance didn't work out, but don't ruin our second. Please. She thinks I'm a liar."

Candy flicked her fingernails in the air and huffed. "How many times do I have to say the same thing?" She turned to me, shaking her head. "I told you everything. Well, I guess there's one little thing I left out, but that was only to spare your feelings."

My heart sunk. "What?"

"I had to bribe him to give you that surfin' lesson in the first place." Candy rolled her eyes. Teague looked down at his feet. "That's why he stopped by. Cost me a whole day's work, but you know, you were so happy about it."

"Seriously?" My face flushed red-hot.

Teague's anger softened. "I didn't accept the money."

I stormed down the steps, snatched Willie's leash, and rushed to the car.

Chapter Twenty-Five

SAND

WHITE SAND IS actually ancient bones and shells, thrashed and beaten into tiny grains. Though it's little more than a graveyard, the sand felt warm and soothing filtering through my toes.

Willie jumped in and out of the foamy surf. Night had long since claimed the sun, the tourists, the heat. But the peaceful scenery didn't quell my frustration. I felt thrashed and beaten, like the island itself was trying to break me into pieces and bury me in the sand. Worse, I didn't know how to stop it.

My emotions bubbled inside me. I'd handed Sam Teague my secrets, like an idiot, letting myself fall into his trap, again. What was I thinking, falling for the same guy who'd wrecked me once already? Our 'perfect' day'd been a lie. Why couldn't I feel his deception in his kiss or see it in his eyes? Why did that stupid kiss keep replaying in my mind like a naughty treat?

I gave up on the ocean; it wasn't helping. I huffed, rounded up Willie, and headed back to Starfish Drive through the alley. I longed to crawl into bed with a good book and forget all about Teague.

Course, that wouldn't happen. Teague waited for me, sitting on the steps.

In a heavy sigh, I said, "I don't want to see you."

Teague stood up as I approached. The kiss flashed through my mind and my knees felt weak again. I closed my eyes to blank out the image.

"I know. I'm sorry," Teague said softly. "I have news—"

"What?"

"They picked up your intruder loitering at the state park. His name is Henry Bellows, a local homeless guy. He's relatively harmless. Detective Lewis believes that he may be your squatter."

Teague followed me up the stairs.

"Did he come up with that all on his own?"

"When we ran the prints off the door and window, his name came back quickly. He's been arrested a few times for various misdemeanors."

"So, what'll happen now?"

"He'll be charged, given a court date, and released until he's required to report to court," Teague said. "Since he's had charges before, he'll probably get a little time for this one."

"In jail?" I filled a glass with water and gulped it down.

Teague nodded. He stood near the door, unsure. "At least you can sleep better tonight."

"Doubt it." I took a seat at the kitchen table and rubbed my eyes.

Teague stepped closer to the table. "Delilah, I—"

"Please, don't. I can't handle any more about us." I swiped away tears that suddenly flooded my tired eyes. "Only I have to ask for your discretion. I'm on borrowed time here as it is because Lewis'll never solve Darryl's murder, which leaves me at Jonathan's mercy… and now at yours. Please, don't tell my secrets."

"Delilah, I'd never betray your trust. Your past makes no difference to me or how I feel about you."

I took a breath, relieved, at least, by the sincerity on his face. Maybe he wouldn't tell. I gave a weak nod.

Teague hesitated. "I knew you'd want the news about Bellows right away." Teague smirked. "One less thing to bother you, you know." He moved toward the door. "I'll, um, go."

I shook my head. "But he is bothering me," I said before he could leave.

"What do you mean?"

"If I hadn't been so freaked out by Ronnie Chambers and Darryl's murder, then I wouldn't have gotten so scared about Bellows. He wasn't going to hurt me. He just wanted a place to crash and didn't know I'd moved in. Is that mistake jail-worthy?"

"It's unfortunate, but he broke the law," Teague said.

My shoulders slumped. "Can I see him?"

"You want to see him?"

"Can I?"

Teague sighed. "I'll drive."

The police station was much quieter at night. A uniformed officer worked the front desk in the lobby. The cubicle room was gray and empty except for a two-person cleaning crew. Downstairs, another officer guarded four jail cells. The lights were low and the mood quiet.

"You bring all your dates to lock-up, Teague?" the officer said, smiling as he eyed me.

Teague huffed. "Ms. Duffy's a witness. Keep your eyes on your own paper, officer."

He led me to the third cell where a large lump lay on a cot near the wall.

"He's sleeping," I whispered.

"Right, it's late." Teague banged his keys against the bars. The loud clang made me jump. The lump moved. "Bellows, rise and shine. You have company." The dim lights made it hard to see anything but a dark shadow rising from under the wool blanket. I moved behind Teague.

"What do I say to him?" I asked in a whisper.

"Beats me. I'm sure something'll come to you."

The burly man grunted. He lifted his heavy body from the small bed. His Frankenstein's monster-like stature made my mouth go dry. What was I thinking?

"*I grow old.*" He cleared his raspy throat. "*I grow old.*" He stood up. "*I shall wear the bottoms of my trousers rolled. Shall I part my hair behind? Do I dare eat a peach?*"

I pulled myself from behind Teague's protective shoulder and closed in on the bars. Bellows stepped toward me. He had the beard and body of an aged biker gang member. He wore a dark overcoat, boots, and knit hat that held his straggly hair in place.

"*I shall wear white flannel trousers, and walk upon the beach.*" His voice was deep and strong. "*I have heard the mermaids singing, each to each.*"

Teague rolled his eyes. "He's always spouting—"

I shushed Teague. "*I do not think that they will sing to me,*" I said.

Henry Bellows smiled. He took a step closer. "*I have seen them riding seaward on the waves combing the white hair of the waves blown back when the wind blows the water white and black.*"

I grinned warmly. Closer, his face was less menacing—gentle blue eyes, a friendly grin. He was in his fifties, I guessed, though he looked weather beaten.

Together we said, "*We have lingered in the chambers of the sea by sea-girls wreathed with seaweed red and brown till human voices wake us, and we drown.*"

I giggled and clapped. Teague looked at us like we were idiots.

"Teague, he knows T. S. Eliot." I chuckled, turning to Henry. "You recited Prufrock beautifully." He nodded and bowed his head. "I want him out of here, Teague. Now."

Teague grabbed my arm and pulled me to a nearby corner. "What the hell?"

"Teague, he's harmless," I said. "I don't want to press any charges or whatever."

"You know nothing about him, Delilah."

"That poem has significance to me. Call it a nudge." I tapped Teague's shoulder softly and went back over to Henry's cell. He reached for a lock of my long hair and played with the end.

"You look like a mermaid," Henry said. "I've seen them, you know, in the ocean."

"Harmless, but crazy." Teague gently removed my hair from Henry's grasp.

"Crazy I can handle," I said, grinning.

"This is a bad idea," Teague told me for the millionth time. I sat in the middle, squeezed between Teague and Henry Bellows in Teague's Toyota pickup truck. Henry hummed, eerily content to be riding off with strangers. The skies were still dark, the moon gone, and morning threatened. In his lap, Henry Bellows held all his earthly possessions in a *Dora the Explorer* book bag.

"I'm just letting him come in for a while," I said, again. "Let him eat and get a shower, maybe some sleep. Right, Henry?"

"I know better than to get involved in these domestic disputes," he said, grinning.

At the apartment, Willie checked out our guest thoroughly before we leashed him for a walk. I hoped to pick up breakfast at Britt's Donut Shop on the corner, if it wasn't too early. I set Henry up with towels and told him to make himself at home. He thanked me with one of Shakespeare's sonnets.

"If poetry's the way to your heart, I must start reading up." Teague smiled lightly as we walked down the alley.

"You don't have to babysit. You should go."

"And leave you alone with—"

"I'll be fine."

Teague let out an exasperated sigh. "Delilah, let me explain. Please."

He stopped me in the middle of the alley. I folded my arms and tried not to look at him, though I was curious how he could defend himself. "Yes, Candy offered me fifty bucks to teach her niece to surf. She said you had this silly crush on me. I pictured an annoying, thirteen-year-old townie with pimples and braces. Why else would she have to pay me?"

I raised an irritated eyebrow.

"I said no," he went on, "but she begged me to do her this favor. Said it'd finally give her one day of peace. To help her out, I agreed."

"That's a terrific story, Teague." I huffed, walking away. He stopped me again.

"Listen, please."

His pleading eyes kept me in place. Listening seemed easier than arguing, anyway. Willie drifted to the dumpster by The Crab Shack, content with the delay.

"When I first saw you—the very first time—it wasn't at your grandparents' house when I came to pick you up. It was on the fishing pier." A light smile crossed his face. "You were lying on the bench at the end, one knee up, one leg hanging over the side, hair falling down through the slats of wood. You were holding a book up to the sky, reading."

My eyebrows crinkled.

"I stopped and watched you. Watched your face change as you read over the words, hints of a smile. Then sadness, I think. It was the most beautiful thing I'd ever seen—you reading that book. I had to talk to you but couldn't for the life of me think of something clever. I've never been so intimidated." He stopped to laugh. "I mean, girl with book. What's a guy to say?"

He shoved his hands in his pockets, looked down at his feet, and then back at me. "I almost came up with something really good, too, but you shut the book, sat up suddenly, and then speed-walked down the pier. Blew right by without even seeing me."

"I would've noticed—"

He shook his head. "No, you didn't. I followed you down the pier. You crossed the street and turned down Starfish. By the time I rounded the corner, you were gone."

I nodded weakly. "I remember that. I was in the middle of *Wuthering Heights*, and Catherine had died, and suddenly there was a baby. So, I rushed off to ask Aunt Laura about it."

Beyond the alley, across Atlantic Avenue and over the sand and sea, the sun rose, casting a warm glow on everything and melting the slight chill of the darkness. Sweet scents from the bakery wafted in the air. Teague caught me in his gaze and held me there.

"I hoped I'd see you again. Looked for you everywhere I went." He smiled. "When you came down those stairs, everything fell into place. The perfect day started with the perfect girl. You have to believe me, Delilah."

I felt a little breathless. "I-I do. I mean, I want to. Only everything's been so upside down since I got here. I don't trust myself, let alone anyone else."

"I get it, and I'm sorry to give you more to deal with, but you're important to me." His voice was soft and warm, like the sunlight slipping over us. "However long it takes, things'll work out for us. I know it will. Until then, I'm here for you." He shrugged lightly. "And maybe you can try not to hate me?"

I breathed out heavily, smirking. "I don't—"

A crash cut through the peacefulness of the early morning. Breaking glass smashed and chinked into what sounded like a million pieces, echoing down the alley. A second explosion of glass followed the first.

Teague handed me Willie's leash and took off running. Tires squealed in the distance. Already on his phone, Teague rounded the corner of Beach Read. Willie and I followed, reaching the apartment stairs as Henry Bellows raced out, wearing nothing but one of my towels.

"We're under attack!" Henry raised his fist in the air.

We dashed to the front of the store. Henry was right.

Chapter Twenty-Six

LIGHTNING

"**M**ARAUDERS!" HENRY FUMED as we circled to the front. Glass glimmered in the new sun, covering the sidewalk and spraying the street. Beach Read's windows were shattered. Glass sections dangled from the tops and corners, but the bulk had fallen, leaving pieces everywhere.

"Henry, get back upstairs. Your feet. And please, take Willie with you." I handed him the leash.

He accepted the responsibility and left the disaster.

When cloud to ground lightning hits sand, the heat scores the earth, melting the grains together in a split second. Glass tubes called fulgurites form, branching out into beautiful sculptures. Instantaneous art. Beauty formed by violence.

Again, my Beach Read hopes'd been shattered. But, like instantaneous art, something beautiful appeared.

The glass crunched under my sandals as I moved in closer. In the first window, a stone lay among fallen books and bits of glass. I reached for it, leaning in.

SEA-DEVIL

"Delilah!" Teague yanked me back. A two-foot-long section of glass tumbled off the top pane and crashed down where my head'd been. Teague shielded me as more glass shattered.

The noise stopped. I held onto Teague's arm, grasped around my shoulders. Blood wet my fingers.

"You're bleeding," I said. A six-inch cut graced the top of his forearm. Blood oozed and dripped to the ground.

"It's okay," he said. "Are you alright?"

I nodded, eyeing the window. A bloody shard, still hanging on to the pane, showed where he'd been injured reaching in to grab me.

My eyes scrunched together. "I wasn't thinking. I'm sorry."

Teague shook some glass out of my hair. "I don't even feel it." I held his injured arm in both of my hands, the blood passing through my fingers. He lifted his phone back to his ear.

"Ask for an ambulance."

He shook his head, but then obeyed, grudgingly. "Sorry about the store."

With Teague's blood dripping onto the pavement, Beach Read was the last thing on my mind. "Your handkerchief?" He handed me the embroidered handkerchief from his pocket. I wrapped it around the wound, but it wasn't enough. Blood soaked through quickly.

I eyed him, worried. "Feeling dizzy, yet?"

A coy grin stretched over his face. "Only because you're touching me."

I allowed a brief smile. Pulling him to the curb, I kicked away glass and urged him to sit down. I sat next to him, holding his injured arm and applying gentle pressure.

Two police cars arrived, followed by the ambulance. I relinquished my hold on Teague. Billy Mott showed up with his camera. The regular craziness ensued. Only this time, Teague was hurt—a fact that strangely pained me more than him.

187

"Chuck, I'm not going to the hospital." Teague sat against the tailgate of the ambulance.

The paramedic huffed. "You need sutures, lots of them."

"Don't be a dick, Teague," the other medic said, coming around the side of the truck. He wore a baseball hat to hold back his mass of dirty blond hair. His name tag read Jake Nelson. "Won't take long."

"Yeah, right. Just wrap it up. I'll take care of it later."

I stood in front of Teague with my hands on my hips. "What do you mean? You need stitches. Why are you being stubborn?"

"Delilah, it's a cut. I've had worse. Besides, Aunt Bev's a nurse. She can sew it up."

Jake and Chuck shared my irritated reaction. Chuck cleaned the wound and wrapped it over and over with gauze for a temporary fix.

"Ms. Duffy, we've collected the rocks," an officer said.

"Anything special about them?"

"No, ma'am. Know of anyone who might take such an action against you or your property, ma'am?"

I glanced at Teague with an exasperated laugh. It was too much to explain, and at the moment, I didn't care, anyway. "I have no idea, officer." Teague chuckled and shook his head, like he could read my mind.

"The photographer's done. We'll get the glass on the street and sidewalk cleaned up. You must board up those windows as soon as possible."

"Okay." I nodded over at Teague, "but first, I'm taking him home."

The drive to Teague's house was quick and quiet. Aunt Beverly was still in her nightgown, fixing coffee when we arrived. At the sight of all the blood on our clothes, she gasped. Then, seeing Teague smile, she shook her head and pointed to the kitchen. Within seconds, she lay an impressive first aid kit out on the table.

She washed her hands. "You know, Sammy, there will be a time when you won't want this old lady sewing up your cuts. My hands aren't what they used to be."

Teague waved her off with his good hand. "Ah, they're fine."

She cut off the soaked gauze. "Oh, my word. You shoulda gone to the hospital for this one." She asked him how he did it.

I explained that it was my fault. "I encouraged him to go to the hospital, but he's stubborn."

"He hates hospitals." She sat beside him, arranging her tools.

Teague leaned back against the wall and closed his eyes. "Aunt Bev, come on. Let's not get into that."

"Took him to the emergency room when he was eight years old. He'd jumped from the bow of the boat to the driveway. Sprained his ankle."

"Please, don't—"

"He threw an absolute hissy fit in the parking lot. All I wanted was to get an X-ray, make sure it wasn't fractured. Couldn't even get him in the door."

"Sam Teague, afraid of something?" I said with a soft smile. "I can't imagine."

"I'm not afraid, just don't like them. And I'm bleeding to death here, so could you get to it, Bev?"

I held Teague's free hand. With every push of the needle into his skin, his fingers tightened, and face clenched. Still, he smiled when he looked at me. Simultaneously, it was the best and worst feeling. Teague being hurt and going through this pain because of me made my heart sink. And yet, my anger washed away. I knew that this injury, or worse, he would've gladly accepted on my behalf if given the choice. Not only that, but anything I wanted or needed. It was a strange, beautiful, achingly difficult feeling—this trust creeping into me.

"When we're done, I'll help you with the store," Teague told me.

"No, no. You need sleep."

"What are you going to do?" he asked.

I shrugged. "Call Damon to get my windows boarded up." I looked down at my clothes. "Take a long, hot shower. I look like I just walked out of a Stephen King novel. Then I'm going to bed. I'm dead on my feet."

My phone chimed. I tugged my hand away from his, but he wouldn't let it go. I fumbled to answer it with my free hand.

"Thinking about me, darling?" Jonathan said, his voice smiling.

"Nope." Sitting with Teague while he got his arm sewed up, blood oozing, wasn't nearly as nauseating as Jonathan's voice. "What's up?"

"Lewis called Becker. I misplaced your file here, but Becker will probably reach out to HR for a copy. Nothing I can do then."

"Okay."

"I'd guess you have a couple more days before—"

"I get it. Thanks."

Jonathan chuckled. "Good thing I had the foresight to file your incident with Kettering as an altercation, not an assault. To get the full story, he'd have to talk to Tyler or get it from me. Course, I won't talk, not with Labor Day weekend to look forward to."

I sighed. "I have to go." I clicked the phone shut before Jonathan could protest.

I left Teague once the pain medications kicked in. I walked to the Jeep, the heat of the sun burrowing into my shoulders. The events leading up until now circulated in my head like a whirlpool. The snakes. The petition. The clippings. Darryl's death. My newspaper debut, and the endless accusations. The stings of my past. Broken windows, and Teague's bloody arm.

I was sick of being the sand and ready to be the lightning.

Chapter Twenty-Seven
ORDER & METHOD

A PLAN FORMED during my shower and phone calls. I headed to Shawsburg. Everything came down to this—to salvage my life here, business or otherwise, I needed to clear my name, and time was running out.

On the ferry, I parked behind a green pickup truck filled with junk. I got out of the Jeep to take in the scenery, once Willie's leash was securely tied to the roll bar. Strolling by the junk-loaded truck, someone called out.

"Hey there, missy!"

Lenny Jackson emerged from the driver's seat with a wide smile and gleaming head. I said hello. He followed me to the front of the boat where the ferry winds whipped through us, keeping us cool.

"Headed to town for some shoppin'?" he asked.

"I have a few errands. You?"

"Gotta truck load of goodies to sell to some other flea markets there. Sometimes I got so much junk, I don't know what to do with it all."

"Where does it come from?"

He leaned closer. "Well, I don't tell a lotta people this, but my mamma, God rest her soul, was a mental case. She had whole rooms filled floor to ceiling with junk. So, when she died, I figured I'd sell it all off piece by piece, the same way she got ahold of it in the first place."

"Oh, sorry to hear about your mom."

He shrugged. "That's life, you know."

"Thanks so much for calling the police for me about the intruder."

He waved his thick hand in the air. "No problem."

"They caught him—a homeless man looking for shelter. Can't be too careful these days, especially since the murder."

"Well, you're more than welcome, honey. That's part of my job."

"Were you friends with Darryl?" Asking questions about Darryl Chambers had almost become too natural, but I couldn't help myself.

"Worked with the boys at the club."

I tilted my head, trying to gauge how Lenny felt about his coworkers without luck. "Any theories about the murder?"

Lenny shrugged, looking thoughtful. "Well, everybody at work liked Darryl, except for the ruffians he dealt with, course."

"What about his brother?"

"Oh, you mean Pipsqueak?" Lenny chuckled. "That's what I call him."

"That word is roughly a century old," I told him, "and it's supposed to mimic the sound of a weak animal."

"Then it fits. Pipsqueak's alright, except being kinda lazy. 'Course, Via fired him, so I don't know what he's doing anymore."

"I'm not surprised. Via hated both of them."

"Well, Via's got all kinds of hate for everybody. I heard talk that he was interested in buying your building."

I perked up. "My building?"

Lenny scratched his head. "Yep. I overheard Via talkin' with his lawyer about it at the bar."

"What'd they say?"

"Well, Via was asking the lawyer about offers and counteroffers or whatever, and the lawyer was spitting out all these numbers at him. Via mentioned something about Clara Duffy-Saintly. The suit said that she'd have the obvious advantage, being family, but that Via had the more lucrative offer, somethin' like half a mill. The lawyer said something about disguising the offer. I'm not sure what he meant."

"Uncle Joe said there was another party interested. Why would Via want Beach Read?"

Lenny shrugged. "Dunno. A larger parking lot, maybe."

Could Darryl've been killed for a larger parking lot? I considered Lenny's information the rest of the way to Shawsburg. Learning about Via's offer on the building was compelling—he had as much reason to sabotage Beach Read as Clara and Charlotte. I was also hung up on Pipsqueak. Ronnie Chambers didn't seem like a weak animal to me. He'd intimidated me twice. Perhaps he was tougher than everyone thought.

Freddy Weaver's snake farm was a huge plot of land against a swamp. A double-wide trailer and three feeble sheds comprised the base of operations. Two broken down trucks decorated the landscape, and a third, closest to the house, seemed to be the only working vehicle as it wasn't surrounded with weeds.

Mr. Weaver, a tall, spindly man wearing a dirty t-shirt, jeans, rubber boots, and a wide smile, greeted me as I exited the Jeep. I held my wallet in my hand, expecting that information from him would cost me. Willie barked his disapproval that I made him wait in the car.

"What can I do you fer?"

I smiled. "Are you Freddy Weaver?"

"Yes, ma'am."

"Okay, then I'm where I should be. Where are the snakes?"

"You interested in a snake?" he said, eyes lighting up under his ball cap. "Got some dandies!"

"No. I mean—they're like caged, right?" I glanced around at the unruly grass.

"Oh, yes, ma'am. Don't you worry your pretty little head."

A heavy breath escaped me. "I've dealt with enough snakes lately to last a lifetime. Someone vandalized my store with about twenty dead ones—black, copperhead, water moccasin. You're the only snake guy within fifty miles—"

"Anybody can get snakes—"

"With all due respect, Mr. Weaver, it's highly unlikely that someone would've tracked down and collected so many varieties of snakes without being a professional."

He folded his arms across his bony chest and cocked his head.

"What someone *would* do, however, is think of something creepy to do and then hire a snake guy to do it."

"You're talking a bunch of foolish nonsense!"

"No, Mr. Weaver, I'm not. You came in to Tipee that day and left a few hours later in that truck." I pointed to the truck behind him. "The ferry captain confirms it."

"I ain't gotta tell you nothin'. You think I'm goin' tell you any different from that blasted cop that kept callin' me?"

"It could be your lucky day, Mr. Weaver, because I'm not a cop. Whatever fee you collected from your employer, I can match it. All you have to do is give me a name."

"I ain't fallin' for that trick. Now, get off my property." He turned to head back to his house.

"Wait, Mr. Weaver. Please. I'm desperate."

"I don't care if you're—"

"Daddy?" Over his shoulder, a lovely little girl, dressed to the nines, bounded down the stairs. She giggled, twirled, and skipped over to us, a beautiful smile on her face.

"Hi, gorgeous." I knelt down to her level. She beamed at me. "What's your name?"

"Olivia. I like your hair." She reached for my long, dark tresses and fiddled with them in her fingers.

"I love your hat. Can I see it?"

"Olivia, get back in the danged house," her father said weakly, but my attention won out. She handed me the hat. It was hot pink with a floppy brim decorated with a fancy boa, purple beads, and white daisies.

"I asked the lady to make me a *Fancy Nancy* hat," Olivia said.

"It's beautiful. I love it." I handed it back, glancing up at her father with a determined smile on my face. He shoved his hands in his pockets. I opened up my wallet and showed Olivia a picture of the Duffy family. We'd taken it last Christmas on Grandma Betty's deck.

Olivia looked. "There's you!" she said.

"Yep, and where's the lady who gave you the hat?"

With a giggle, as if we were playing a fun game, she pointed to Aunt Charlotte.

At a coffee shop in downtown Shawsburg, I sat against the window. I pulled out a small notebook and pen from my purse. I guzzled down my *Big Gulp*-sized coffee, mind already racing.

Hercule Poirot is my favorite Agatha Christie detective. He solved his cases using order and method, exactly what I needed now, even with no sleep and minimal skills.

For order, I wrote everything I knew about each event at the store. About the snake prank, I filled up the page. At the end, I wrote in bold letters, *Aunt Charlotte.*

Clara and Charlotte, along with all the Duffys, were well-aware of my snake distaste. It was a safe bet that snakes would send me packing, and maybe the old, less desperate me would've given up then. I didn't go in Grandpa Charlie's garage for two years after spotting a black snake stretched out under his boat. My screams had upset the neighbors and ruptured the foundation. Sometimes, the Duffys still bring it up, even though I was only eight at the time.

If Charlotte and Clara were responsible for the snakes, the articles taped to my storefront and the broken windows were probably their doing, too.

But, murder?

Darryl Chambers flooded my mind. I wrote everything I'd learned about him since I arrived in Tipee. My phone rang, and I answered without looking.

"Where are you?" Teague asked, irritated.

"I'm out."

I glanced out the window and spied a short strip mall. Tucked between a Subway and a Fashion Bug, there was an Army Recruitment Center.

"I can see that," he said. "What are you doing?"

"I'm right in the middle of something. Are you feeling better?"

He sighed. "I'm fine, though bothered that you aren't here like you said you'd be."

"Look, I'm not far. I'll be back. I have to go." I clicked the phone shut, leaving him no chance to argue.

The Army Recruitment Center reminded me of the dealership where I'd bought the Jeep—standard cubicles with desks, chairs sitting in front, computers, phones—nothing to write home about, except that the salespeople wore military uniforms.

A man in beige army dress clothes approached, hand pushed out. He was tall, my age, with a slightly receding hairline and bulgy eyes.

"I'm Jeremy Marcus. Thanks so much for stopping by today." He gripped my hand like he didn't want to let go.

"I'm looking for some information about—"

"Well, I'm sure I can answer questions you have. Why don't

you come over here and have a seat?"

I obeyed, hesitantly. He pulled up something on his computer and then glanced over at me.

"So, tell me your name."

"Wait," I said. "I'm not here to join anything. I'm here to inquire about a friend of mine who may've come in recently."

"Are you a college graduate?"

"Yes."

"You could enter as an officer. Respectable pay. Great benefits. Have you ever longed for adventure in your life?"

I chuckled. "I get plenty of adventure, believe me. Have you ever met a man named Darryl Chambers? Twenty-one years old from Tipee Island?"

Jeremy Marcus rolled his eyes and huffed. "Yes, didn't even have to give him my usual spiel. All he asked for was a letter outlining his intentions, and then he pulled a no show. Do you know him?"

"He's dead."

Marcus sat up in his chair. "Oh, well, that explains it then."

"Did you offer him a signing bonus to join?"

"No," Marcus said, shaking his head. "He'd get a small bonus once he made it through basic, but nothing upfront. He hadn't even been to college."

"Did he explain why he wanted to join?"

"Said he wanted to settle down and get his life in order. That's a shame. He would've made an excellent soldier, had great skills. Not everyone can handle it, you know." Marcus chuckled a bit, leaning back in his chair. "I bet you could, though. You have this rawness about you—this beautiful strength, like a steel magnolia."

I left, deciding I didn't want to hear any more of Marcus' spiel.

Chapter Twenty-Eight

CONSTRUCTIVE WAVES

I ARRIVED HOME a little after eight and took Willie for a walk. He'd been a patient passenger all day, and we both needed to stretch our legs. At the end of the block, the dishwasher from The Crab Shack smoked a cigarette outside. His thick arm boasted a brilliantly colored dragon.

"I've seen that tattoo before," I told him when I got closer.

His Cheshire cat smile widened. "Me and my lady has matchin' ones."

"I've met her," I said, stepping over to him. "Miss Sadie."

"That's her." He flicked the cigarette into a puddle. "I'm Benny."

I introduced myself, but he said, "I know you. Boss man can't stop talkin' about you. Neither can my Sadie. You told her she was like royalty?"

"Guilty. Sometimes I talk too much."

"She's been going on and on 'bout it ever since. You wouldn't think a beautiful queen like her would get down 'bout herself, but she does. It was nice, what you said."

"Good. I'm glad."

"You've been asking 'round about Darryl Chambers, huh?" He lit a second cigarette and tilted the pack to me. I shook my head.

"Yes. Did you know him?"

"We played football together. Used to keep his ass safe from gettin' tackled." He grinned at the memory. "You should know that Angel ain't no angel. She swapped out Darryl with Ronnie 'cuz he gave her many presents. Girl a gold digger. Still messin' with Ronnie some, but she's gettin' bored with 'em."

"Where might Darryl get $25,000?"

Benny shrugged. "He hated drugs, but he was no joke at stealin'."

"Yeah, I heard about Ellis' marlin."

"You shoulda seen his face runnin' up and down the halls lookin' for that damn thing, like it was goin' to be hidden in a six-inch locker or someone's book bag." Benny laughed. "I've seen Darryl steal other stuff, too, but that was back in the day. Money out of teachers' purses."

I cringed.

"Phones and shit from people," he went on. "You'd have to jack a bunch of phones for $25,000."

I nodded.

"You should come in," he said with a sly smile. "Make Mike's day."

I shook my head. "Can't." I pointed to Willie as my excuse but knew I wouldn't go in anyway.

"Then, come up to the house sometime," he said. "We like doin' cookouts on the weekends, get e'rybody over, make it like a block party. Beer and burgers."

I smiled widely and nodded. "Two of my favorite things. I'd love it."

"Good luck, book girl." He held out his fist to pound mine. I pounded it back.

"Thanks, Benny."

Constructive waves bring sand and sediment to the beach, building it up in tiny increments. They are the promised deliverers of what the beach needs to keep it sustained, to make it grow.

I was still riding the constructive wave of my information gathering when I woke up Monday morning. I'd slept through the night, felt refreshed, and made a long list of to-dos over my first cup of coffee. The items on the list fell into two main subcategories: 1. Get store open, and 2. Solve murder.

Beach Glass could come Wednesday to install my new windows. I checked the first thing under category one off. On to category two.

Uncle Clark answered his phone on the fourth ring, and I asked him to help me with some research.

"I'm exercising some curiosity here, but I could use some help."

"Exercising curiosity is what I do best. What do you want to know?"

"I want to learn all I can about the home robberies in Tipee. Is it possible to round up all the articles?"

"That's easy. Wrote most of those myself. Anything else?"

"Yes, actually. Should you hear from Lewis today, anything concerning me, could you give me a courtesy call?"

"Uh, oh. Sure."

"Do you know how long Darryl Chambers worked for Via? I heard he jumped around jobs a lot."

"Four to six months," Clark said. "Before that, he worked at the Piggly Wiggly. Why?"

"Not sure." I jotted down more items on my to-do list. "Thanks, Clark."

"Sure, no problem. But, Delilah, one thing."

"Yes, Clark?"

"If exercising your curiosity actually turns into something, can you please tell me about it first?"

I grinned. "Absolutely."

Uncle Clark asked me to come by the newspaper's offices by lunchtime, so he could give me the file.

I checked item one under category two off. Back to category one, which meant sweeping up the glass inside the store. Skipping that one, I went back to the murder category and called Great Uncle Joe. I only had one question for him, but he wanted an update on the store. I didn't have the heart or energy to give him all the heinous details.

"There've been a few kinks, but everything'll be fine. Uncle Joe, you mentioned that there was another party interested in the bookstore. Who?"

"The lawyers handled it, but it was Avid Corporation. Made a huge offer."

"Did the lawyers say what Avid wanted to do with it?"

"Nope."

I wrote the name of the company and got off the phone as soon as I could. Avid means keen or enthusiastic. It's also an anagram for D. Via.

I glanced at my phone to see the time. It was way too early to head to Via's club and ask him about the offer. So instead, I called Raina, who answered hesitantly after four rings.

"I'm not sure I should talk to you," she said. "Mamma's declared war."

"I know, but it's not about her. I really need to talk to you. It's important. Can you come to the bookstore?"

"No," she blurted. "I can't come there."

"Then, can I meet you? How about the pier?"

Reluctantly, she agreed.

The pier sways at the end ever so slightly under the pressure of the waves hitting against it below. I shut my eyes as it rocked, my vision filled with his kiss and my heart ached. *When I first saw you—the very first time… was on the fishing pier.* His voice echoed in my head. A soft smile snuck across my face.

"Delilah?" I looked up to see Raina standing over me. I grinned and patted the seat beside me.

"Daydreaming," I told her. "Sorry."

"It's okay. What's this all about?" Raina and Rachel are perfect beach babes—blond, tan, beautiful. But Raina didn't look herself. Her hair looked oily. She wore no make-up. Soft shadows hung under her eyes.

"Darryl Chambers."

She gave me a distant, vacant stare. "What about him?"

"You worked with him at the Piggly Wiggly. Right?"

She nodded.

"Did you know him well?" Asking Raina about Darryl was a long shot, but after the family'd been horrible after Darryl's death, Raina'd stood up for him. Of course, Raina had filled her young life with food drives and mission trips. Standing up for others was what she did best, next to her art.

"Um, a bit. He was a bagger for a while, but he got fired." Her voice cracked like a boy in puberty.

"What'd he do?"

"Stole money out of my till."

"Wow, did you catch him?"

"No, he admitted it. It was when I was on break. Anyway, that was it."

I rubbed Raina's back gently. "You look a little pale. You feel alright?"

"Been under the weather."

"I hear a stomach thing's going around."

"Maybe that's it," she said. "Is there anything else?"

"Well, what else can you tell me about him?"

She shrugged and fiddled with the unusual pendant around her neck. Her hair flapped in the wind, and her eyes looked empty.

"He was, um, a good person, I think. No matter what anyone says. I hope they find who killed him because it's the right thing."

After Raina left, I leaned against the pier railings, contemplating Darryl's sticky fingers. Benny described a skilled criminal, but at the Piggly Wiggly, Darryl had been bold enough to go for cash out of a register and got caught? I went back to the bookstore and added to my notebook in between cleaning up shards of glass.

Chapter Twenty-Nine

DECONSTRUCTING

THE TIPEE ISLAND Gazette sat in a short strip mall near the ferry, sandwiched between an insurance agency and doctor's office. I parked next to Uncle Clark's black Range Rover. A bubbly blond receptionist named Jeanette greeted me and led me to Uncle Clark's office. She presented his door Vanna White style. I smiled warmly and walked in.

Uncle Clark's office was plastered with framed pictures of Tipee. Sea oats against the baby blue sky. A frothy wave cresting. The pilings underneath the fishing pier. A starfish attached to the side of a boat. Sunset.

"These are incredible," I said. "You took these?"

"It's a hobby of mine, though I sometimes use them for the paper when we're desperate."

"Breathtaking. When I start making some money, can I buy some? For the store and my apartment?"

He chuckled. "Delilah, we're family. I'll make you some. Now, sit down. Let me give you what I have."

I took a seat as he flipped through a few folders. He pulled one out, opened it up, and leafed through it.

"I printed the articles we've done on the robberies, per your request." He handed over the folder.

I rummaged through it, eyeing the headlines. "This is exactly what I needed. Thanks."

"No problem. What exactly are you looking for off the record?"

I smirked. "I never thought I'd be in a conversation with someone in which saying 'off the record' was actually appropriate. I don't know what I'm looking for, honestly."

"I hear the police are talking to Via. Whenever anything goes awry in Tipee, they talk to Via. He's the catchall. But he doesn't have an alibi."

I perked up. "Darryl must've been killed at 9:30, when the fireworks were going off. That's how I would've done it. Use the fireworks to hide the gunshot. The bouncers check the perimeter every hour on the hour, so if the killer went through the back door, he would've had to have been careful not to be seen, unless he knew the schedule. Via would know when the alley would be empty. He had the best access. Where does Via say he was?"

"In his office at the club. No one laid eyes on him for at least two hours. He could've easily slipped out, killed Chambers, and come back in."

"He's sleazy, but I don't think he did it."

Clark raised an eyebrow. "How come?"

"Because if you kill someone, you won't tell a perfect stranger, like me, how much you hated the guy. If he'd killed him, you'd think he would've shut up about how much he disliked him."

"Good point," Clark said. "People are hardly ever what they seem, anyway. Via's probably like a sheep in wolf's clothing, you know. He probably goes home at night to an empty apartment, has several cats with names like Mrs. Whoopsy, bakes bread and cupcakes, and likes to read poetry."

I laughed at the image. "I don't know about that, but it's a nice thought."

Back to focusing on getting the store open, Tuesday morning, I visited the used computer store at The Cotton Exchange, where I bought a laptop for the business.

Rounding a corner in the labyrinth of hallways inside The Cotton Exchange, I spied Ronnie Chambers. I stopped short and ducked away before he saw me. Ronnie lugged an enormous blue and white marlin.

"What's he doing?" I whispered to myself.

Ronnie took the marlin into a shop on the left. Two minutes later, he exited the shop, still holding it. He crossed the aisle to the next shop.

"He's selling the fish!" I couldn't believe it.

Ronnie exited the second store, still holding the awkward prize. I bolted from my corner.

"Hey," I called out to him. "Are you selling that fish?"

Ronnie plastered on a mean face at the sight of me. "What of it?"

"How much?"

"You wanna buy it?" Ronnie asked. "Why?"

I shrugged. "I like fish. I'll give you $20 for it." I handed him a bill. Ronnie squinted his beady eyes.

"Fifty."

"$25 and I'll spare you the trouble of lugging that monster all around The Cotton Exchange. There's precisely four miles of shops, you know, if you stretch it all out."

Ronnie agreed, though irritated, and snatched my money away.

I shook my head at him, accepting my awkward prize. "I can't believe you'd sell Darryl's marlin after all he went through to get it."

Ronnie smiled. His teeth were yellow with tobacco stains. "You don't know anything, bitch, but I hope it'll keep you warm on your lonely nights. If the fish don't work out, call me. We like to keep it in the family."

He disappeared around the corner before I could ask him what he meant.

Destructive waves smash the beach, moving and pushing the shore with crushing force. Whatever normal waves have given, these storm waves can take back, reshaping the entire shoreline.

Teague waited for me on the stairs leading to my apartment. He wore plain clothes and a grim expression. Seeing him was a relief and a stress. Of all the balls I had up in the air, Teague's felt like a boulder. Whatever wave I'd been riding crashed at his feet.

"We need to talk." He relieved me of the marlin and followed me up the stairs. "Why haven't you answered my calls?"

"Been busy."

"Too busy to let me know you were okay?"

I rolled my eyes and unlocked the door, brushing past Willie to set my bags on the table. I pointed to the marlin and the computer as proof of my activities.

"Bought a computer for the store, finally. And you'll never guess. This is Darryl's marlin."

Teague's eyes narrowed. "Darryl's marlin?"

"Yes, remember? The one he stole from his principal?"

"Where did you get it?"

I hesitated, like a child suddenly in trouble. I leaned back against the counter. "Um, bought it off Ronnie Chambers at The Cotton Exchange. He was trying to pawn it."

Teague sat down at the kitchen table, rubbing his head. "Ronnie Chambers, huh?"

I nodded weakly.

"What were you thinking?"

"I saw an opportunity—"

"An opportunity to taunt Ronnie Chambers?"

"Well, it doesn't sound good the way you say it," I said, "but it seemed right at the time. This fish is a piece of Darryl's history. I felt inclined to preserve it."

"At your own risk?"

"I was in a public place" I couldn't help the irritation in my voice. "I was safe."

"What about tonight when you're here alone? Or when you take Willie for a walk? What about—"

"Okay, okay!" I put my hand up to stop him. "I get it. Maybe not one of my better ideas, but I don't get why you're so mad."

"It's not just that." Teague cocked his head at me. "Who called when we were at my house?"

I gave him a confused look, though I knew exactly what he meant. It's not like I get a lot of calls, and Jonathan Dekker's stand out.

I shrugged. "Don't remember. Probably Clark."

Teague breathed out heavily. He didn't believe me. "Delilah, I want what you want. I want you to be successful, to be at peace with your past, and move on. But you won't help yourself—"

"What am I supposed to do?"

"Be honest. That's all." Teague stood up, facing me. "Honest with me, and with yourself—"

I scoffed. "You're lecturing me on honesty?"

Teague's eyes widened. "Tell him you never want to see him again."

"So he can spill all to Lewis, ruin my life here, and put me on the hook for murder?"

"It's better to deal with all that—if it happens—than for you to keep making decisions based on your screw-ups. You're letting your past dictate everything."

"Only so I can salvage my future. What else can I do?"

"Stop recycling the same old bullshit with these choices you're making. You push me away even though I'm trying to help you. You lie when you don't have to. You promise to give yourself to that user again. Delilah, why?"

Teague's eyes penetrated me. I desperately wanted to move away from him. I tried, but he blocked me with his hands on the counter. I folded my arms, fighting back the tears burning my eyes.

"Why?" he said again. "When all you have to do is say no? So what if the news comes out? Whatever fight you have to face, whether it be against murder charges or public opinion, it has to be better than compromising yourself. I can promise, you won't fight alone."

"I'm only doing what I have to do," I said weakly. Teague shook his head, disappointed. I pushed by him. "I'm desperate, and tired, and you're crushing me."

"Crushing you?" Teague followed me to the door. "I've done nothing but support you, and all I get is your distrust. I've been worried sick about your safety, and you ignore me. I'm falling in love with you, again, and you've promised to give yourself to someone you don't love for the sake of a stupid secret. I'm the one who's crushed, Delilah."

He said nothing else but left without even looking at me.

I collapsed on the bed, drained. Willie jumped up with me and rested against my shoulder as tears plummeted from my eyes.

Chapter Thirty

SAM

I ANSWERED MY phone in a half-greeting. "Becker's on the phone to Lewis right now. He's sending the file this afternoon," Jonathan said. "You sound terrible. Been drinking?"

I hung up on him and called Clark.

"Clark, when is the latest you can submit news for tomorrow's edition?"

"Everything's electronic," he told me. "I can make changes until about five."

"Should you make any changes concerning me today, would you call and let me know?"

"What changes might I be making?"

"Seriously, give me a heads up?"

After two more attempts to get the information out of me, he agreed. My altercation with Tyler Kettering would end up in either tomorrow's paper or Saturday's. My reputation ruined along with Beach Read's chances, I'd be booted back up to the top of the suspect pool again.

The funny thing was—I didn't care.

Of course, I cared about Great Aunt Laura's store, my future, and helping Darryl Chambers get justice, but at the moment all I could do was think of Teague. He'd always been on my mind, through every bad boyfriend and every lonely night. I'd always had a back-of-my-mind longing for him, a wish to go back to that one perfect day. Examining my priorities, it all came down to one. If only one thing could work out right, I'd want it to be Sam Teague.

I stared at the ceiling. The afternoon sun beat through the side windows, warming my face. I could almost feel the sand on my fingertips. I remembered that day as vividly as if I was still in it, soaking it up.

After practicing popping up on the board and listening to Teague give me general instructions about surfing, all while standing on the beach, I had to get into the water. Teague'd been extremely patient with me. I'd talked his ears off, thanks to my anxious energy, making him explain everything at least twice. What he didn't know was that I'd been stalling.

"*Ready?*" he'd asked. I'd looked over at him, and he smiled. The hang-ups and insecurities circling through my head had dissipated.

Sam Teague took my hand and led me into the ocean.

Later that day, we'd set the blanket out and laid next to each other.

"*So, what do you do when you get fed up with your mom and you need to escape?*" he'd asked.

"*I get lost in pages. I can't go anywhere, so I read. What do you do?*"

"*I'm lucky. I can go anywhere, but my favorite spot is the marina. Watch the boats go in and out. Relaxes me.*"

Some mental bargaining later, I gathered Clark's file in my bag and left the apartment with Willie in tow.

Low tide made the air a comforting mix of marshes and fish. I walked the length of the first pier, sandwiched by two great fishing boats painted with the names of ladies and adorned with ropes and gear. No Teague.

The second pier was the same, though Willie got excited over a crab clinging to the piling amid a smattering of barnacles. He barked until I pulled him out of sight.

The more piers we went down, the smaller the boats became, and the more my hope diminished.

"Willie, this was a dumb idea." I looked up at the sky, shrugged and turned to head back to the Jeep.

That's when I saw him.

Teague sat on a bench near the base of the dock, looking out over the whole marina. It took my breath away a little to see him there. I'd been wrong about so many things, to be right about this one—well, I didn't expect it.

"Okay, I have to fix this. Come on, Willie. Be extra cute and cuddly for me."

Willie and I made our way over to where Teague was sitting. Willie greeted him with a lick to the face. I decided to reward Willie later with an extra dog treat or two. Teague smiled wearily, and I sat next to him. I looked out over the expanse of boats, lightly bobbing in the water, and could see what he meant. It was relaxing.

"Sam, the first time I saw you, the very first time, wasn't at my grandparents' house when you came to pick me up."

A light smile slipped across Sam's face as he glanced over at me.

"It was in the fun house at Jubilee Park. Candy and I went one night after I arrived in town. It was fun, mostly, but Candy kept disappearing on me—bathroom or snack bar or whatever, saying nothing first. She'd disappear for a while, leaving me waiting and wondering. Well, it got pretty irritating, so I finally went to the fun house without her. I half-enjoyed the illusions, but it wasn't much fun since I was alone. I worried I might miss Candy on her way back from wherever. So, I bailed halfway in. I took what I thought was a shortcut and ended up in a room full of mirrors."

I smiled, staring down at my feet. "One-way mirrors. I could see out, but no one could see in. I even went back later to make sure."

"What happened?"

"You happened. You came into view on my left side, you and a couple friends. You were carrying a little brown teddy bear with a red bow tie."

He chuckled. "I won it in a ring toss game."

"You remember?"

He nodded, looking almost shyly down at his feet. "Must've been the bear that caught your eye, huh?"

I laughed. "It *was* very cute."

A boat's engine roared to life on the docks, and the driver eased it out of its space. A few piers down, a charter boat loaded up passengers and prepared to set off.

I grinned. "At the last mirror, you stopped. Your friends slipped out behind you, but you just stood there, where I was. We were inches apart, separated by floor to ceiling glass. I swear, you looked right at me. Your smile held me there, locked me in. I put my hand up on the mirror, and you did the same thing, right on top of mine like, like magic."

I raised my hand to the air, mimicking the memory.

"You couldn't have known I was there, but somehow, you did. You became a great mystery I wanted to solve."

Glancing sideways at him, I spotted his smile and the hint of blushing on his face.

"Your friends called you away, so I found my way out, and searched for you. I had no plan, no hope of talking to you. My mother's overprotection had instilled me with paralyzing insecurities, though she liked to call it shyness. Anyway, I caught up and watched you and your friends walking along, through the maze of game booths and food vendors. Then you did something that really clinched it—"

Teague smiled. "Wow, I can't believe you saw that."

"You remember the little girl?" He nodded. "Whatever set that girl off with her fat tears, I don't know, but you slipped her the bear, so slyly that no one saw—not her parents, not your friends— and she stopped crying. My heart leapt."

"Your friends'd called you Sam. When Candy found me again, I told her all about you. She thought I was nuts, but she said, '*You must be talkin' about that Sam Teague. I think God spun 'em outta gold*'."

I sighed, looking out over the boatyard with a full heart and nervous stomach. "Sam, I don't know what happened thirteen years ago to keep us apart, but I know what brought us together and maybe that's more important."

"You've trumped my story."

"Ah, yours was good, too." I breathed out heavily and played with the hem of my shirt. "You were right, Sam. I'm sorry—"

"No, don't apologize. I pushed too hard. I shouldn't have said those things."

I stood up and walked to the edge of the dock, folding my arms as I looked out on the murky water. "Why not? My decisions have been based on fear and desperation—definitely not who I am, or who I want to be. I've lied to you, lied to keep my secrets, sold myself out to Jonathan—again, even flirted with Mike, knowing full-well that I—"

I stopped talking, my confession bearing down on me like the sun's heat on my shoulders.

"Knowing what?"

I faced Sam, but stared at the uneven planks of wood at my feet. "Sam, for every single thought I have of him, I have thousands more of you. It's always been that way. No man's ever spent time with me without having to vie for my attention, even if he didn't know it. My thoughts always come back to you. I know how crazy that sounds, but it's true."

My forehead crinkled when I dared meet his eyes, but the smile easing up his cheeks made my worries vanish. He met me at the edge of the dock. "True for me, too. You've always been on my mind, Delilah." He took my hands in his, his thumbs drifting over my fingers. "It's been a long time between that day and this one. We've both made mistakes. None of that matters beyond the fact that it brought us here—to our second chance. I hope you can trust me enough to take it."

I didn't answer with words, but squeezed his hands, pulling him closer. He leaned into me, touching his forehead to mine and delving into my eyes. It would've been easy to get lost in kisses, but we didn't, not right away. Rather, we delighted in staring at each other, as if our perfect day on the beach had been paused until now. I ran my fingers along his cheek, laughing and tearing up at the same time. He kissed my forehead, then the wetness under my eyes, before meeting my lips.

"Come with me," Sam said when we parted. "Let's go for a ride."

He nodded toward the boats docked along the pier. I cast him a confused look.

"Huh? You mean a boat ride?"

"It'll be fun, and Willie'll love it. Let's go."

My mouth went dry. "You have a boat?"

"I have access to a boat."

"You remember what I said about my water fears, right? About not swimming and all that?"

He grinned. "You won't have to swim. You'll be in a boat. Delilah, you're safe with me. You never have to worry."

I took his hand.

Chapter Thirty-One

DRIVING

"**N**ERVOUS?" SAM ASKED, making himself comfortable in the blue and white eighteen-foot bow rider. I nodded. Willie jumped on excitedly and perched on the bow like he was Leonardo DiCaprio. I shook my head at my brave dog.

The motor rumbled, and Sam eased the boat out of the slip. Slowly, he maneuvered into the inlet. Maybe it wouldn't be so bad. Once out of the vicinity of the parked boats, Sam pushed the throttle forward. The boat sped up.

I gripped the vinyl seat, closing my eyes. But nothing helped my anxious mind stop spinning.

Finally, Sam stopped the boat and extended his hand to me. "Come here."

"No."

"Come here." He grabbed my arm, lifting me up. The floor of the boat vibrated beneath my feet. I crossed over, and Sam pulled me in front of him, facing the wheel.

"The problem is that you feel out of control."

He put my left hand on the wheel and my right hand on the throttle. "Boats are easy to drive. Slowly push the throttle forward."

He guided my hands, and suddenly, I was driving. The boat skirted across the glassy water. Trees and houses skimmed by along the shorelines. The wind whipped across my face. My shoulders relaxed.

"Steer the boat between the two buoys," he said over my shoulder, pointing out the red and green buoys on either side ahead. "Good. See? Easy. Feel any better?"

I nodded. The boat felt powerful, the way it pulsed through the water, much different from driving a car. The resistance of the boat against the water reverberated through the deck and up my legs. I sped up. Sam chuckled. He gathered my long hair in his hand and pulled it to the side, out of his face. His lips brushed my neck, and I rested against him.

I curved away from the Atlantic, and we entered the bloated belly of the Cape Fear. With no boats nearby, I turned gently, doing a donut. Willie barked, delighted at the spray that doused his fur.

Sam laughed. "You're getting the hang of it. Hold on for the wake."

"Oh, shit." Up and down we went, the boat suddenly feeling entirely too small. My stomach flip-flopped. The nervous feelings flooded back. I turned my back on the cresting swells, burying myself in Sam's shoulder.

"It's okay." He took the controls. Boating over smooth water was one thing. Swells made for a whole new experience.

Once the water was glassy again, I lifted my head. A soft smile alighted on Sam's face.

I smirked. "Sorry, still learning."

"I'm looking forward to more lessons, but how about I take you to dinner?"

I smiled widely, still wrapped in his arms. "You can take me anywhere you want, except in the water."

Sam laughed. "Deal."

A little later, Sam drove up to a small dock at a Cape-side restaurant called The Watermark. The building looked like a converted country house. The lawn was littered with picnic tables, covered in vinyl-checked tablecloths and lit with citronella candles. Sam gave me a quick tutorial on tying up the boat and helped me ashore.

We ordered cheeseburgers, fries, and beers, and sat at one of the picnic tables under an enormous oak tree with outstretched branches and a knotted trunk. Willie rested at our feet, waiting for scraps. Two kids played at the water's edge, dumping buckets full of water on each other.

We both laughed, watching the kids play.

Sam said, "I always wanted a brother or sister."

"Me, too. I always thought if I had a sibling, my mom might divide her attention, giving me a much happier existence. That's why I loved spending summers here."

"Aunt Bev couldn't have kids," Sam said, "though she and Uncle Ken wanted them. They ended up with me instead."

"How did that happen?"

Sam shifted in his seat and wiped his hands on his napkin. "Um, my real folks were addicts." He said it as matter-of-factly as he could, but his eyes dropped, and brows crinkled like a sharp pain had ripped through him. "We lived out of a hideous green minivan that barely ran. We were nomads. My mom told me we were like Scooby-Doo and the gang in the Mystery Machine. I thought that was cool until I realized that the only mystery we ever solved was where the next score would come from."

Sam shook his head and took a swig of beer. My mouth dropped, trying to imagine what that kind of life was like.

"We'd drop in on Aunt Bev and Uncle Ken. Ken was my father's brother. Bev and Ken tried to get them help, but it didn't do any good. My folks would stay a few days, hit them up for money, overstay their welcome, and then be off again. Finally, when I was eight, Uncle Ken offered them $15,000—all the money he could raise—to leave me with them. They took the deal."

I squeezed his hand. "Oh, Sam. That's awful. How could your parents do that?"

"They weren't my parents anymore. My parents died the second they became addicts. I was living with corpses."

"What happened to them?"

"Don't know. Never heard from them again."

"I'm sorry."

"I'm not," he said, with a gentle smile. "I ended up much better off. Aunt Bev and Uncle Ken were—are—the best parents a guy could want. It was the right thing."

"Is that why you became a cop?"

He shook his head. "No, that was a last-minute decision. I thought I'd be a career soldier. I liked the army, but it wasn't a lifestyle I could keep up. Went to Iraq, Afghanistan, spent most of four years overseas. Uncle Ken died when I was on my last tour— working in the garage one minute, gone the next. Heart attack. I needed to come back home. So, I spent my next two years at Fort Bragg, got out of the army, and then went to the police academy."

He stopped to feed Willie the last bite of his burger. "I worked in Nags Head for a while. You know what happened there. Then, I just came home."

We lingered by the sea long after our burger baskets were empty and our beers dry. We talked and laughed, and it was easy. Sam refreshed our beers, and when he came back, he straddled the picnic table beside me, instead of sitting across.

"My uphill battle has ended in a mudslide, Sam. I've done all I can to keep my past from catching up with me, but I can't outrun it, and maybe I shouldn't. I have some information about Darryl."

I pulled my notebook out of my bag.

"What's this?"

"Order and method," I said. "I had to decide which is more important—victim or location. The 'go home' message makes it seem like the place is the important thing, that they killed him because of me. But this is ridiculous, because if it were truly about me, the killer would've just killed me."

"Unless the killer couldn't kill you."

"Well, there have been plenty of opportunities, so that's not the issue."

"Maybe the issue is that you're family."

"For argument's sake, let's say it's one of my family members. Killing one of their own *would* put a damper on our weekly dinners. They have motive. But there are other facts to consider."

"I'm listening."

"Well, if Darryl was killed because of me and Beach Read, then it'd follow that all the incidents are connected to the killing. The 'go home' message on the articles and then at the murder seems to link them."

"Okay, I see what you're saying."

"Freddy Weaver definitely did the snake prank, and Charlotte organized it." I explained how I figured that out. "My aunts must've done all three acts. Only you and family knew that I'd be opening Sunday at noon. It's not a coincidence that they broke the windows early that morning."

Sam's eyes widened. "That's right! I was at the table when you told them."

"Right. The second thing—the articles—well, my aunts have the easiest access. Any number of Top to Bottom followers could have posted the generic articles, but the personal article told me it had to be family. My Aunt Clara has regular conversations with my mom. I bet it wasn't too hard for her to dig up some dirt on me, even if it was only a vague article about my hearing."

"So, you think nailing them for the three vandalism acts

exonerates them from the murder?"

"Yes. My aunts are a lot of things, but they aren't killers."

Sam shrugged. "Maybe not, but all you have to do is tell Lewis. He can flesh it out with them. You're off the hook. If you aren't a suspect, you aren't in the paper."

"That story'll still make the paper. Besides, I can't sic Lewis on my aunts. They didn't do it. I can't ruin their reputations like that."

"They wouldn't be so generous. Speaking of your wonderful aunts, I've been busy, too. The devilish duo is actually a trio. Guess how much money Candy's supposed to make off the sale of your building?"

"Something like $20,000?"

Sam was surprised. "Well, yes. She'd also make top seller at her agency. She's been coveting that title for years. There's something else. Prepare to be impressed because I'm sure you don't know this."

I leaned closer. "What?"

"About three years ago, for apparently no reason, Clara and Charlotte made Candy a partner."

"A partner?"

"Her Top to Bottom shares are small, but she owns them. I spoke to other agents at Beach Realty, and that's when she stopped showing the building."

My eyes narrowed. "What are you suggesting?"

"Clara and Charlotte's success took time. I think they've wanted that building for a while and made Candy a partner, so she'd hinder its sale. If she kept prospective buyers away, then they'd have time to raise the money to buy it themselves."

I cast him a skeptical look. "They could've given her the shares as a birthday present or just because she's their sister."

"Or because all three of them are diabolical."

I grinned. "They're not killers, but okay. Maybe they worked together to keep the building empty. That explains why Candy didn't take care of the place like she was supposed to." I sat upright, straddling the bench like Sam was. "Knowing all that, we can turn our attention back to Darryl, which is where it should've been all along."

"Okay, so tell me what you've learned about Darryl."

I told Sam about my conversation with Megan Masters, and then later with Jeremy Marcus, the recruiter. I revealed how I'd acquired the marlin, and about my chat with Benny, the dishwasher.

"I have a theory."

Sam smirked. "Well?"

"The Granny Bandits. I've gone back and read newspaper articles from the first robbery until now. I strongly believe that Darryl was a part of this group."

"Why?"

"In the earlier robberies, the police couldn't pinpoint the method of entry."

"That's true. Locked up tight by the owners when they left and locked when they came home."

"Darryl was the lock-picker," I said. "He got them inside. They took predetermined items and then locked up tight, hoping the owners wouldn't notice right away. Only, Darryl pulled out of the team. When the others were left to their own devices, the method changed. The last three burglaries have been forced entry—broken windows, busted doors—no more picked locks."

"Why do you think he quit?"

"Darryl was working two jobs, trying to buy a house, and enlisting in the army. He was getting his life in order." I smiled. "He was in love."

"With who?"

"I don't know."

Sam took a long swig of his beer. "I was going to tell you this earlier, before I got distracted. Lewis got a search warrant for Chambers' residence, based on the new evidence, the snake rake. Since Chambers lived in his mother's home, they could only search Darryl's private bedroom."

"What'd they find?"

"No lock-picking tools. No stolen goods. But there was a picture... of the entire Duffy family."

"*What?*"

"It was a couple years old. Christmas, judging from Betty's reindeer sweater. It was on the deck of your grandmother's house. You were in it, your parents. Clark had a goatee. The twins had braces."

"Grandma Betty's Rudolph sweater. It lit up when you pushed the button on the cuff. Yes, it was two years ago. Why'd he have it?"

"I was hoping you could tell me."

"No clue. Honestly."

Sam winced. "It bothers me."

"What does that mean for the case?" I sipped my beer.

"Means you and Via are suspect buddies, unless you point Lewis in another direction."

"Well, Via has a motive other than hating Darryl," I said. "Turns out he's trying to buy Beach Read, too. Made an offer using a dummy company."

"Holy shit. How d'you—"

"Lenny the prevention specialist," I said with a grin. "I've no idea what he wants it for, but Great Uncle Joe said there was an offer from a company called AVID, which I'm sure is D. Via."

"In that case, Darryl's murder could've been about him and you both. Via could've been killing two birds with one stone."

"He has the best motive so far, but I don't—"

"The killer won't jump out and confess, Delilah. You gotta practice some self-preservation here. You've got to hand Lewis someone. If not your aunts, might as well be Via."

I shrugged. "I don't suppose you guys have found Darryl's money?"

"Nope, if he ever had it."

"I can't imagine that he kept it anywhere normal. Knowing him, he probably had some kind of intricate lock box for his money."

I grinned, and then it fell again. Sam finished his beer and let his fingers wander over to my knees. I eyed the bandage on his right arm.

"Does it hurt?" I asked.

"Nope." He smiled warmly.

"You know, if my theory is right, then Darryl's brother is definitely one of the other robbers. Their fight makes perfect sense now. Ronnie was pissed that Darryl was bailing out and joining the army. I also heard that Ronnie was messing around with Darryl's ex-girlfriend, the stripper. I'm not sure if that's true, but if it is, that makes him gross and not a very good brother."

"Maybe being an only child isn't such a bad thing after all."

"Agreed." I guzzled my beer down. The sun had long since disappeared, and the night sky had blanketed the island. Boating at night would be another adventure. I let Sam drive.

Chapter Thirty-Two

LIGHT

UNDERWATER WHERE THE earth is its darkest, there's a cornucopia of lights. Creatures turn the black sea into a brilliant light show using bioluminescence. Even though I was still in the dark about everything, I felt hopeful that I could shed a little light, too.

Wednesday. Detective Lewis showed surprise, what little he could muster underneath his shaggy mustache, when I showed up, bright and early, at his boring little cubicle.

"Was about to come looking for you, Ms. Duffy," he said. "I have questions for you."

"Fine." I sat down beside his desk and readied myself.

I shed as much light as I could on Lewis' questions, even when he taunted me with the Tyler Kettering incident. I told him the story as calmly as I knew how, like I'd explained to Sam.

When I finished, he said, "I should arrest you."

"You'd be wrong."

"We've the gun in your possession—"

"But no prints or residue to link me to it."

"You've got a violent past—"

"No charges ever filed."

"A shabby alibi."

"So, does everyone else."

"Blood on your clothes and hands."

"Which I explained."

"And your picture in the victim's possession."

"No clue how it got there," I said. "And thanks to you, the whole town has my picture in their possession. You've got nothing. Most importantly, you have no motive. But I can help."

I laid out my information, but Lewis barely listened.

"Alright, Ms. Duffy, I'll look into it," he said finally, "but, if nothing else pans out within the next twenty-four hours, I'm setting my sights on you. Don't leave town."

Despite Lewis' typical bad attitude toward me, I felt better about everything and turned my attention back on Beach Read.

The glass guys arrived to work on the windows.

Henry Bellows visited, and I offered him a job. It was, of course, contingent upon me being able to afford him. But I had a special plan for his exceptional talents, and he, dramatically, agreed. He also asked if he could put a tent on my roof.

I made a new sign for the window. *One Day Until the Grand Opening of Beach Read.*

At six, I found myself in the parking lot of Seaside Baptist, eyeing all the cars and golf carts. It was bingo night. I paid my entry fee and found all the usual competitors parked at the back table. I sat across from Sam, next to Grandma Betty and Mamma Rose. Mavis Chambers sat on my other side. Sam was in uniform.

"Hoping you'd show," he said, smiling.

"Need to make some money somehow."

"Delilah, Samuel told us you went out for a boat cruise yesterday," Grandma Betty said. "As afraid as you are of the water and how much trouble you gave Grandpa over fishing, that just shocks me."

"Well, Sam's boat was bigger, and I didn't swim." I set up my boards.

"You don't swim?" Mavis said. It surprised me to see her, like I'd felt seeing Ronnie Chambers at the bar in Lucy's View.

"No, the water scares me to death. Ms. Chambers, I'm so sorry about your—"

"Pish, posh." She waved me off.

"We're glad you're here tonight," Grandma Betty told her for all of us.

Mavis shrugged. "Can't play bingo with my dolls. Well, I could, but it's not as much fun."

Bingo was a dismal failure for me again, but that was okay. Tomorrow, Beach Read would open. Even Lewis had granted me a solid twenty-four hours of peace. Sam left for his shift at intermission, so I walked him out. I promised to take Aunt Beverly home for him again, and he said he'd come by the store tomorrow.

I chuckled. "Funny, I don't picture you as being much of a reader."

"I could be talked into it." With a smile, he kissed my cheek. I grinned.

"Be safe tonight," I told him.

He raised an eyebrow. "I'm always safe. Hoping to rub off on you."

Back down the long hallway toward the fellowship hall, I spied Mavis Chambers on her phone again.

"I'm finally ready to trade the Rose," she told the caller. "You will love her. All original parts. And I have another doll I want to show you, too. This one's very special."

I smiled at her as I passed and made my way back to my seat. Aunt Beverly gave me Sam's boards, but I still didn't win at bingo. Ray Crackle said I had "the curse of the devil on me."

When bingo ended, Aunt Beverly and I headed to the Jeep. She handed me something out of her purse—a white handkerchief embroidered with my first name and a tiny monarch butterfly in the corner.

"I make 'em when I watch my soaps," she said. "And since Sammy was singing in the shower this morning, I thought I'd make one for you."

I laughed. "Sam was singing in the shower?"

"Like he was Elton John or something."

"I love it. Thank you. It's beautiful." I laid it in my lap as I pulled out of the parking space.

"I figured you could use a hanky." I guessed she'd say something about how often I'd been crying lately, not that she'd been a witness to it herself. Instead, she said, "A hanky's much more useful than what my Sammy gave you way back when, especially since you don't even like the water. Doesn't make much—"

"Pardon?"

"He sang in the shower then, too."

"What do you mean? What did he get me?"

"Oh, you know. When he was leaving the house that morning, he had his old life jacket. I asked him what he was doing with it. I mean, it didn't fit him anymore. He told me you needed it. Delilah Duffy. That's a name that stands out."

My eyebrows creased together. "A life jacket?"

"You know, honey, like you wear on a boat."

I dropped Beverly off and thanked her again for the handkerchief. Instead of heading home, I turned toward Grandma Betty's house. Grandpa Charlie answered the door. I could tell he'd been dozing in front of the TV because he had sleepy eyes.

"Delilah, you okay?"

"Grandpa, I need to look for something." I came inside.

"What is it? Did you leave something?"

"No, it's something old. I'm not even sure it's here at all."

My mind spun with where to start. The huge house, with its closets, bedrooms, and even an attic, overwhelmed me. I paced the hallway, not sure where to go.

"Tell me what it is."

"It's a life vest." Regardless of how crazy this sounded, Grandpa Charlie nodded and held up a pointed finger.

"Let me get my shoes," he said, trudging to the hall closet.

With a flashlight, Grandpa Charlie led me out to the back deck, down the stairs, and then to the first-floor garage. Inside, he had a small storage shed that he unlocked with a key.

"Keep all my boat stuff in here," he told me as he opened the door. He pulled the string of an overhead light and revealed a storehouse of islander supplies, wall to wall. Everything was tidy and organized, but overflowing. He went inside, rummaged around, and pulled out a dark blue life vest.

"I think this is what you're looking for. Showed up down here one day, so I put it in with the rest and thought nothing of it."

I set it on the concrete floor, dropping to my knees. Grandpa Charlie handed me the flashlight. The light fell on a name written in rough lettering on the back of the neck. *Sam T.*

"Oh, you don't think it belongs to Officer Teague, do you?" Grandpa asked, scratching his head. "That'd be weird. Wonder where Betty is. She's late."

I sat back on my legs, teary-eyed and a little breathless. I waved the flashlight over the vest once more and noticed a zippered pocket on the upper left side. I opened it, stuck my fingers in and felt around. A piece of paper said:

What to do the next time you have a bad dream:

1. Grab vest to feel safe and realize it's just a dream

2. Think of me and smile

3. Go back to sleep and have good dreams (hopefully with me in them)

Let me know if it works. Love, Sam

I stood up, vest and note in hand, and kissed Grandpa Charlie on the cheek.

"Thanks, Grandpa." I handed the flashlight back to him. "I have to go."

"Okay, Bean. Glad you found what you were lookin' for."

In the alley behind the store, I parked the Jeep. Parking from Via's had overflowed into my side because of a strange truck, but I hardly noticed it. I fixated my thoughts on Sam, and all the things I wanted to tell him.

I got out of the Jeep and reached in to get the vest. In doing so, I dropped my hanky. I bent down to get it, mentally kicking myself for being so careless. That's when someone whacked me over the head, hard. My vision blurred. My legs gave way. Darkness took over.

Chapter Thirty-Three

CURRENTS

THE BLOW KNOCKED me out, but the pain woke me up, like an electric drill burrowing into the back of my head behind my right ear. I tried to touch it, but my hands were bound. So were my feet. Enclosed in canvas material, dark and solid, I couldn't even see shadows.

The floor was hard. A squishy pool of blood puddled beneath my head. The distinct roar of a motor reverberated through me. Holy shit, I was on a boat.

Terror joined the pain, and they seized me together. The currents of my life had mounted against me.

Except for my heart pounding over the hum of the motor, it was quiet. Images from childhood spat through my head—how the plastic tarp had magnetized my skin, leaving me trapped, unable to breathe, unable to see.

I had to calm down. Breathe. Think.

My rope bindings were well tied, but loose fitting. With my teeth, I worked at untying them. The boat skirted over choppy waves, and my body thumped against the floor. Pain ripped through my head. I stifled a scream.

My covering wasn't Saran Wrap tight, but snug, with no apparent opening. In micro-movements, I tugged at the rope around my wrists, further loosening it.

The boat halted abruptly, jerking the vessel forward, banging my head against the side. Pain surged through me, but I stayed quiet and still. With the motor idling, my captor circled the deck, hard steps. My head vibrated with each one, sending stabbing sensations across my skull. My heart raced. The footsteps stopped right in front of me. Then I was airborne. I wasn't in a blanket; it was a duffle bag. Panic struck me as I hit the water.

The quiet night split open with my screams. Water saturated the bag, my clothes, my skin. I couldn't spread my limbs enough to kick or thrash. I was sinking. The boat revved up and sped off as I belted out one last shrieking curse.

A deep breath later, I sank. I was a six-year-old girl again, wrapped up and disappearing into nothingness, kicking and thrashing, choking. My heartbeats boomed as if knowing this was the last hurrah.

My peace I give to you… I have overcome the world.
Think.

I couldn't tell how fast I was dropping, but I felt heavy. I stretched as far as I could in the bag. Frantically, I searched for a zipper. Too much time was passing. My back landed on the seafloor. My fingers landed on a seam and followed it.

Be calm. Think.

A double-row zipper went down the length of the front. A pull-tab poked through on my side. I grabbed it securely—only one chance—and pulled.

The bag fell off me like a cumbersome dress. The ropes around my wrists dangled but held. My feet were sewn together. My lungs screamed for air. I set my tied feet against the seabed, bent my knees, and pushed as hard as I could.

Up I went. And up and up. Too slowly. Water filled my mouth. I choked. The salty water slid down my throat and burned my eyes. I chopped at the water with my tied hands.

A light, glorious and majestic, high above me, caught my eyes. It was the moon. I thrashed my arms, one last dash, swallowing more water.

Then I burst through.

I gulped up the air, coughing and gagging. Then I threw up, spitting out the wretched salt water along with dinner. The nausea lingered. Dizziness and pain scourged my head.

Still, between bouts of sickness, I untied my hands with my mouth and fingers. My shoes felt like bricks on my feet, so I kicked them off. With one hand treading, I used the other to work on the ropes on my ankles. Twisting my legs, I felt them chafe against the roughness. I cried out. My head wound throbbed.

Breathe. Think.

With one hand, I felt the ropes and pictured them in my head. After many painstaking minutes, the bindings fell to the ocean floor.

The relief was temporary. My head in agony and nausea plaguing me, I gazed out at my surroundings. The moon stared at me in its waxing gibbous form. In a day or two, it'd be in its full glory. I wished that could've been tonight. Still, its light brought comfort. Perched about seventy degrees in the sky, the moon still rose. I couldn't have been unconscious long.

To my left, far in the distance, the string of lights on the Tipee Island Fishing Pier dotted the night. To my right, red lights blinked on the bridge over the Intracoastal Waterway—miles away. In between the two, I bobbed, spying tiny specks of light here and there with no particular meaning, except that they all seemed incredibly far away.

The currents pulled me along, making the lights move like cars before my eyes. I was being dragged toward the black greatness, the Graveyard of the Atlantic, and so I started to swim.

Before I hated the water, I was a child of the beach. My father'd bring me to the shore whenever we visited his parents, and we'd stay all day. He'd fish. I'd play tag with the waves. I'd start out at his side wading in thigh deep water. Before I knew it, I'd be yards away from him, running through water to get back to him again. Waves would come in, little ones, then medium-sized, and then suddenly I'd get barreled over. My entire body would tumble. My face would smash against the sandy bottom. For one nanosecond, I'd be afraid. But Dad's hand would reach into the water and pull me out.

Bean, kick faster. Stroke.

The tiny lights on the island became fewer, extinguished by a cruel god. My body ached for rest, but I plowed onward. The moon sat high in the sky now, like the star atop a Christmas tree. Time crept by, taking pieces of hope with it as it vanished. It already felt like I'd been in the water for an eternity. My skin prickled in the salt and felt tight, stretching across my bones.

My childhood pool accident forced my mom into a state of hyper-vigilance. My father balanced her out with a stern determination to make sure nothing like that ever happened again. For swimming lessons, Dad took me off a pier that jetted into the Cape Fear, where the bottom was mushy and gross between my toes, when I could touch it. "*It's just water, Bean,*" he'd said when I refused to jump in. After many minutes of begging, Dad'd finally snapped. He surged from the water, grabbed my arm, and yanked. *Just water* echoed in my ears, along with the splash.

Pretend your feet are flippers. Legs straight like scissors. Kick, Bean.

I fixated on what I thought might be the nearest light, still a great distance away, and couldn't tell if I'd moved any closer to it. Water moved underneath me, but it was like I was on a treadmill. I wasn't getting anywhere.

Fear took over. No one knew where I was. No one was even looking. No one would come for me, not in time. I was alone, scared, sinking.

All manner of terrifying creatures and what they could do to me flashed through my brain. My leg brushed against something. My hand felt scaly skin. Tricks. Or not. I didn't know. I stopped swimming, looked around, and expected to see the terrifying dorsal fin of a shark.

A wave hit me square in the face, filling my mouth with salt water. I gagged. My heartbeat quickened, and my whole body trembled. That's when the cold darkness introduced me to a painful reality.

I wouldn't make it.

Chapter Thirty-Four

DROWNING

THE MOON EASED into its descent, lowering itself toward the sea. I wondered which of us would sink first. The sky became darker, reflecting my waning hope.

"I can't tell you how many times I've replayed that day in my head over the years. It's been a light in some dark places in my life."

I remembered how warm the sun had felt on my skin that day and smiled. *"Face the shore,"* he'd said. He'd managed to get me paddling out past the break zone on his surfboard. I'd straddled it, waiting for further instructions. He'd maneuvered the board for me, treading water at my side.

"When you feel the swell underneath you, pop up, just like we practiced."

I'd given him a 'yeah-right' look. Sam's encouraging smile had told me I could do anything, and that I was there, in the water and doing okay—well, I'd believed him. That was the last time I felt truly brave.

In real time, I started swimming again, slowly, achingly.

"*Cup your hands,*" Dad's voice echoed. "*Put your muscle into it, Bean.*"

I moved faster.

"*Get ready,*" Sam had warned me, backing further away. I got into paddle position, as he'd shown me several times on the beach, and the wave came. I kicked up, balancing carefully, and for about three seconds, I did it. I surfed. Then I fell. The water wrapped me up, swallowing me. Sam's arm reached in to pull me out. When I surfaced, I was laughing.

"*That was really good,*" he'd said, smiling.

"*It was like flying,*" I'd told him. A dozen more attempts earned me more success—I got up to ten seconds, roughly. However long I stood atop the surfboard with the force of the wave under me, I felt powerful, like I could do anything.

Something about my life had shifted that day. The sharp sting of the near-drowning became dulled by Sam's smile and the joy of being with him. Nightmares kept plaguing me, but having one good memory of water almost balanced the other out.

Almost.

Time slipped on. My body raged. My legs Charley-horsed. Exhaustion. Pain. Frustration. I trod water, bobbing up and down, and laughed sarcastically.

"I'm so glad I learned how to swim."

The night is always darkest before the dawn. Was that just a saying or the truth? For once, I couldn't remember where the saying had originated, and it hurt to try.

Searing pain jolted through my head. I got sick again, and wretched into the water. Coughing and heaving, I cried out. Then I calmed down.

Breathe. Remember.

Without the sarcasm, I whispered, "I'm so glad I learned to surf."

Turning on my back, I let my body sink into itself atop the

water, floating, and eased into some kind of acceptance. I was so tired.

"*Belly button to the sky, Bean,*" Dad had told me. "*And relax.*"

I eased my floating into a slow backstroke, though each movement sent my body into torment. My mouth was dry— *Water, water everywhere, nor any drop to drink*—and my throat was raspy and sore.

Loved ones popped into my mind like I was sifting through an album. Arms moving back and forth, legs kicking gently, I grasped on to memories we shared. My body was cold, but I felt warmer.

My eyes fluttered. I widened them and rubbed them with my fingers. Should I even try to stay awake? I could drift away, give in, and sink. Go peacefully. No fighting. No struggling.

My peace I give to you… I have overcome the world.

Then there was Sam. *We're the same, me and you.* I felt the pain of tears, without the ability to make them.

We'd laid an extra-large beach blanket on the upper beach, where the sand was packed but not wet. Facing the ocean, we lay there on our stomachs well after our surfing adventures had ended. The sun was sinking. I leveled the sand in front of us, and with my finger wrote "*Thank you*" in letters as big as I could reach without getting up.

Sam had grinned. "*Again?*" he'd written.

"*Yes.*"

I'd added a smiling face.

I wished we'd been able to do it another day.

It's okay, I thought. *Grandpa will tell him I found the life vest. He'll know I knew the truth.* Sam knew my heart was his. That'd have to be enough.

I eked out a backstroke. My sides cramped. My calf muscles knotted. Up and down, my body moved as the waves took me. It wouldn't be long now.

Stars dotted the sky, a sea of eyes looking down on me.

"*When I look at the night sky and see the work of your fingers—the moon and the stars that you set in place—what are mere mortals that you should think about them, human beings that you should care for them?*" I whispered between splashes of water. "*Yet you made them only a little lower than you and crowned them with glory and honor. You gave them charge of everything you made, the flocks and the herds and all the wild animals, the birds in the sky, the fish in the sea—*"

I gulped a swallow of water.

"*And everything that swims in the ocean currents.*"

A wave toppled over me. I bobbed back up, a cork fallen into the bottle.

"*This is the way the world ends,*" I said. "*Not with a bang but a whimper.*"

I'd wasted time, could measure out my life in coffee spoons. Still, I'd been graced with pieces of heaven that flooded my mind now. I could hear them, see them, feel them.

Dad teaching me to swim, even though I hated the water; Mom reading me Shakespeare even when I was too young to understand it; talking books with Great Aunt Laura; laughing, learning, and even crying with students, for there were all of those glorious things. Sam's arms around me, his kiss.

My legs turned into rocks, hard and immovable. I let my feet sink again and found something hard. A monstrous wave rolled me up and took me under. In my underwater delirium, I wondered if that had been a hallucination, too.

Chapter Thirty-Five

SCHOOLING

THE OCEAN DIDN'T want me. At least, that's what I say sometimes when asked how I survived, and it feels too personal a question. That's how it felt, anyway. After six hours of dodging unconsciousness and drifting, the ocean spit me up on her shores like she was throwing back an unsatisfactory catch. Once on the beach, I passed out, slipping in and out while the sun came up, the early morning fishermen found me, and the EMTs rushed me to the hospital.

The concussion, dehydration, exposure, and exhaustion caught up with me, putting my heart at risk and almost sending me into shock, but they slowly, achingly dragged me back. The aftermath of my night at sea blurred; I slept through most of it.

Now I stared up at a sea of faces I thought I'd never see again. Whispering through forced smiles, the Duffy family circled my bed like schooling fish. The irony struck me. Predators instigate fish families to swim together tight enough to form bands thousands strong. Left alone to fend for themselves in the great sea, they're targets. Together, they're safe. Seeing them all there, I finally felt safe, too.

My eyes fluttered. I pulled myself up, the movement driving pain through my head. I blinked, face to face, taking them all in with a weak smile.

"Is Sam here?" My words came out in a raspy clump.

The Duffys parted. Sam smiled from the chair at my bedside. He leaned up, taking my hand.

"He hasn't left your side since the beach," Raina said. "Don't you remember?"

I squinted. Everything jumbled together. My hospital gown and blankets tucked in around me were all clean and dry, though I wasn't sure how that happened. I ran my fingers through my hair, almost expecting it to be damp, but it wasn't.

"How do you feel, honey?" Grandma Betty asked.

I cleared my throat. "Like I got in a fight with the ocean, and the ocean won."

Sam laughed. "You put up a good fight, though. The ocean looks horrible today."

I smirked. Sam stood, handing me the water on the table. I sat up higher on the bed. My muscles were weak, like jelly. I took a long sip of water.

"Do you remember what happened?" Rachel asked. "Who did this to you?"

Clark leaned closer. "Yeah, did you get a look at him?"

I shook my head, making it hurt again.

"Geeze, you've gotta remember something," Clara said, waving her pink fingernails in the air.

Mamma Rose changed the subject. She handed Clara a bottle of Jergens from her purse, and without hesitation, Clara started dousing my legs and arms with it.

"Your skin's as pickled as a dill." Thankfully, she didn't mention the ligature marks on my wrists and ankles.

Raina took a space on my other side and fiddled with my nails. She pulled a file out of her purse and started smoothing the rough edges. Amazingly, as if she couldn't help herself, Candy moved to my other side and braided my hair down my left shoulder.

"You sure are lucky your daddy taught you to swim," Grandpa Charlie said. "He told me you fought him tooth and nail."

"I had good reason," I said. "I hate the water."

Clara squirted more lotion into her hands. "They're comin'. Should be here soon."

I sighed. "That'll be fun."

"Is there anything you need?" Aunt Charlotte asked.

"Clothes. My keys. I don't know where my purse is. Willie!" I sat up, my head searing.

"Take it easy. Willie's with us," Grandma Betty said. "I'll go by your place."

"The purse is in her Jeep, and I sort of broke your door down. Sorry." I cast Sam a confused look. He shrugged. "Henry Bellows told me that a marauder took you. I had to do something."

"I'll take care of the door." Damon typed something into his phone.

"If you guys see Henry there, don't be afraid," I said. "He can stay while I'm away. He's harmless."

Clara put the lotion away. "Who's Henry?"

"Henry's a homeless man that Delilah's been helping," Sam answered for me.

"Sweet." Clark scribbled into his notepad. "I can see that Woman of the Year trophy slipping right out of your fingers, Clara."

"This isn't the time for teasing." Charlotte punched Clark playfully in the arm. "We need to focus on Delilah and gettin' her better."

Candy finished braiding. I laid back against my pillow, careful not to put too much pressure on my gash. My head throbbed and pulsed like no headache I'd ever had before, even after grading hundreds of essays under florescent lights.

"I'll bring everything in the mornin'," Grandma Betty said. "Clothes, shoes, make-up, hairbrush. Anything else you might need?"

"No." I looked over at Sam, "You need anything?" Still wearing his dark blue uniform, gun and all, I wondered if he was technically working or just hadn't been home.

He smiled. "I've got everything I need, thanks."

"Delilah? Delilah?" The crowd of Duffys dispersed, letting my mother reach the bed. She smiled, teared up, and embraced me a little too roughly.

"Hi, Mom," I said weakly. "Dad."

"I knew comin' here to this god-forsaken island was a bad idea," Mom said. "Why can't you ever listen to me? Look at you. Oh, my baby!" She buried her head in my chest, and I touched her neatly cropped hair.

"It's okay," I said. "I'm fine."

She sat up, eyed me up and down. "Where's that nurse? Are you in pain? Have you had any pain medications?" Before I could answer, she swept across the room and out the door looking for my nurse.

Dad leaned down and gave me a warm and gentle hug. "She's like a tornado. Been cryin' and frettin' the whole way here." He sat on the edge of my bed and rubbed my arm. "What can I do, Bean?"

I leaned up and embraced him tightly. Tears filled my eyes, like my emotions were finally catching up to what I'd been through.

"We should all go," Mamma Rose whispered to the others. "Let them catch up." The surrounding room emptied.

My mother burst back into the room, frustration on her face. "That is the surliest nurse I've ever encountered. She's bringing your dinner, but I told her she better have fresh fruit on that plate.

I told her about your stomach problems, Delilah. She'll see to it. And she's bringing you some pain meds along shortly, too. She said the dehydration and the constant swimming—who's this?"

"Mom, Dad, this is Sam Teague."

Sam hustled over and shook their hands.

"My daughter's been through a terrible ordeal. She needs her mother and rest. If you're here to watch over her, then you can watch from the hall—"

"No, Mom. He's staying. Sam's *with* me. He's, um, well, he's my…" Maybe it was the head injury, but I didn't know what to call him.

Sam chuckled at me. "I'm her boyfriend."

My parents looked at me, confused, and then ogled Sam as if they couldn't figure him out. Granted, I hadn't introduced them to many boyfriends over the years, but I hardly expected it to stun them into silence.

"Oh, great," Dad finally said, shaking Sam's hand a second time. "A police officer. Well done, Bean."

Mom's face pinched. "Geeze Louise! A boyfriend? Well, we must talk about this."

"Mary, maybe the nurse needs to give you a pill." Dad chuckled. Fortunately for all of us, she saved that talk for another day.

While my mother irritated the nurses and soon after my doctor with an onslaught of questions and requests, my father interrogated Sam like a thirsty reporter digging up material for a book. It was all a bit much, but for once, I didn't mind. When the questions dried up, and I complained of being tired, my parents left, promising to be there bright and early the next morning.

I ate little of the hospital meal, battling bouts of nausea thanks to my head. But the room was quiet with just Sam and me. He dimmed the lights. I turned on my side, so I could face him.

"Sam? Why do you hate hospitals?" I closed my eyes, fighting dizziness.

"Um, that's a long story—"

"I need a story."

"And that's the one you want, huh?"

I opened my eyes. "If you don't want to tell me—"

"It's okay." He pulled his chair closer to me. "I hate hospitals because my parents liked to hospital hop. They'd hit up emergency rooms for painkillers. They'd go in with false names and made-up ailments."

Sam took my hand in his and rubbed my fingers. His touch relaxed me. I closed my eyes again.

"They made it an art form, scamming hospitals. I spent half my childhood in ER waiting rooms. A couple of times, they got busted by streetwise doctors. The hospitals would try to hold them until the police came to arrest them, but they usually got away. One time—they must've known they were about to be caught because they slipped out an emergency exit. Forgot me, though."

My eyes shot open.

"Spent all night in that damn waiting room, watching people come and go, trying to avoid the nurses. Finally, at lunchtime the next day, my dad snuck into the ER wearing dark glasses and a baseball hat and got me."

"They must've felt so bad."

"I'm sure they must have." I could tell by his face that if they had, they hadn't shown it.

"I'm so sorry."

Sam shook his head. "Eh, that life is over. I'm a better man for it—I think." He squeezed my fingers.

"Thanks for staying with me."

He smiled. "Love you more than I hate the hospital."

My wide grin pushed against the pillow. "I found the life vest, Sam."

"You did?" He chuckled, blushing. "Tell the truth. Was it

cheesy or romantic? I kept going back and forth about it."

I laughed. "You're asking the girl who just spent a night in the ocean if she thinks a life vest was a good gift? Really?"

"Guess the timing tips the balance in my favor."

"I loved it, Sam. Seriously."

Sam nodded. "Course, you won't need it now. You've got me."

I grinned tiredly. "I'm glad you said that. Come over here and hold me all night?"

Sam stood up, removing all his cop garb. Down to pants and a t-shirt, he wedged in beside me, chuckling. "It's not exactly how I'd imagined our first night together, but it's perfect, anyway. You're changing my mind about hospitals." He tugged me closer. I rested my head on his shoulder. With his heart thumping beneath my ear, I drifted to sleep.

Chapter Thirty-Six

WATERSPOUTS

SCHOOLING FISH CAN sometimes be yanked out of their tight, protective spin cycles by another rotating phenomenon—waterspouts. These sea-tornadoes twist whatever's nearby into their grasp and stretch skyward, forcing a unique family drama for the fish.

One peaceful night with Sam aside, everything spun up over my attempted murder continued the next day. I received a parade of visitors before being released late Friday afternoon.

Detective Lewis stopped by to irritate me again. The only positive outcome of our discussion was that he seemed to admit I was no longer a suspect. Uncle Clark visited and snapped a few photographs that I didn't appreciate. What I appreciated, however, was that both agreed my past wasn't interesting anymore. My survival at sea trumped any sketchy past, so in a strange way, my horrifying experience had done me a favor.

Not that it mattered. The side effect of nearly being murdered was that everyone believed I'd give up my Beach Read dreams, including me, maybe. Nearly dying *is* a powerful motivator for backing off.

Even so, I couldn't wrap my aching head around what seemed like good, common sense.

Rain splattered the windows of Dad's Explorer as we drove to Grandma Betty's house. I sat in the backseat with Sam, curled up against him.

"We'll stay a few days," my mother said, "to let you rest and recover. I can pack up your things, take care of the apartment and the store."

Dad nodded. "I can rent a U-Haul, if we need it, or I can drive the Jeep home."

"Well, Uncle Joe won't care," Mom went on. "Candy told me he was only interested in driving up the selling price. He thought you'd make the property more interesting, Delilah. You surely did that. No doubt Clara will pay out the ears for that place now."

I breathed out heavily. Sam held me a little tighter. He whispered, "It's okay."

"Maybe they're right," I whispered back.

Willie jumped up on his hind legs and danced with me when I walked in the door. His face bore a great big smile and his tail swung like windshield wipers.

"Get down, Willie!" Mom's sternness didn't faze us. I held him as long as my strength allowed. He licked my face, making me laugh.

Duffy drama continued through dinner. Clara and Charlotte tried, unsuccessfully, not to gloat. Clark shifted back and forth between light chatter and probing questions. My parents made arrangements for shutting down my fresh start. I only sat there, fighting off a headache.

Once everyone'd gone, Sam and I ventured out to the back deck. The great beast glittered underneath the moon's delicate fingertips. The ocean winds whipped through me, pulling at my hair, sliding over my wound. I shivered. Fear curled and knotted in me. Sam wrapped his arms around me and eased my anxious thoughts without even realizing it.

"Do you think I should go back home?" I asked after listening to the sound of the surf too long. It didn't relax me the way it used to.

Sam breathed out heavily. "I don't know. I want you to be safe. How do you feel about it?"

"Pissed off, mostly."

Sam sighed. "I can relate."

"I don't want fear driving my choices, but I don't know what else to do, either. Letting Beach Read go'd be best for everyone."

Sam shrugged. "Or maybe it's too soon to decide. Despite what your mother says, you don't have to do anything until you're ready."

"I *do* have a head injury." I smirked lightly. "How come you're so normal?"

"What do you mean?"

"You've been fighting wars all your life, and not just the ones you signed up for. Your terrors have made you a better man, while my few have left me frozen, running home to Mommy. What's your secret?"

"I don't know. Whatever happens, you push through it. You move, and you sleep, and you work, and slowly the numbness wears off and you laugh and you love. It gets better. You need time, Delilah. Time and a different perspective."

"What perspective?"

He brushed the hair off my shoulders. "You had no control over what happened. You don't have control now, either. That's what's pissing you off. Take control back. Go home if you need to. Stay if you want to. Make other options, I don't know. It has to be your choice, though. It's just like with the boat. You'll feel better when you're driving."

I smiled lightly and leaned my head against his shoulder. "You're here."

"Don't worry about me. I can be wherever you are."

Grandma Betty fixed a breakfast casserole along with orange juice, coffee, and fresh fruit, at my mother's insistence. The rain'd kicked back up overnight and now pelted the deck. Willie whimpered by the sliding glass door. He didn't like the rain. I called him over to my feet at the breakfast table and fed him a small piece of ham.

"Delilah, don't feed that dog from the table," Mom said.

I sighed and patted Willie's head.

"So, what's the plan, Mary?" Grandma Betty asked.

"I plan to head to the store and start packing. What're we going to do with all those books? Surely there's a Goodwill or Salvation—"

"It's okay, Mom. I'm not leaving. No one has to do anything."

Mom huffed. "That's not funny, Delilah. Of course, you're leaving."

"No, I'm staying. I talked to Joe. He's happy to go on with our plans for Beach Read. I'm not ready to give up yet."

Mom threw her napkin on the table and stood up, wagging her finger at me. "Delilah, that's enough. You're coming home. That's final. No more discussion."

"We never discussed it, Mom, but that's okay. I wasn't entirely sure I wanted to stay, but I can't run away again. If I do, I'll never feel right."

Dad laughed, shaking his head. "That's my girl. Tough as nails."

"Wait a minute!" Mom said. "Have you forgotten that someone is trying to kill you?"

"No," I said with a roll of my eyes.

"Then, where's your brain? The smartest thing to do is get the heck out of Dodge before he tries to fix his mistake."

"He'd be an idiot to try again," Sam said.

Mom's hands went to her hips as she glared at Sam. "Mr. Tough Guy, huh? Couldn't save her the first time, could you?"

"Mom, that's not fair!"

"He's probably the reason you want to stay so bad." Turning back to Sam with her accusatory eyes, my mother said, "This is your fault!"

Sam turned to me. "I didn't tell her what to do, but I'm proud of her decision. It's her choice, which is exactly the way it should be."

"Geeze, Louise!" Mom rolled her eyes. "You've known this joker for what? Two minutes? And already you're—"

"It's been a little longer than two minutes," I said, smirking at Sam.

Our smiles didn't please my mother. She pushed her chair out behind her. "Staying would be a huge mistake! This whole town is just one big cesspool of criminals. You're nearly murdered. Mamma Rose is robbed. Why would anyone want to live here?"

My eyes shot back to Sam. "Mamma Rose was robbed? When?"

"The same night you went missing."

"Why didn't you tell—"

"I wanted you to focus on getting better. It wasn't important."

"Of course, it's important. You can't coddle me." I jumped up from the table and stomped down the hall toward my temporary bedroom.

Sam followed. "I wasn't coddling. I would've told you soon. It's not like you could've done anything."

I stopped suddenly, sending Sam slamming into my back. "What the—"

"Ah." My gash throbbed, and I rubbed the bandage softly. "That hurt."

"Sorry," Sam said, reaching for me. "Are you okay?"

I pointed to a picture on the wall—a hand-drawn pencil and

charcoal image of Grandma Betty and Grandpa Charlie's house, beachside. "Raina drew this. I've seen it a million times, but I've never really looked at it before. Look, this is her signature. Three dots in the bottom right-hand corner."

"Weird. A triangle?"

"No, rain—drops of rain for Raina," I told him. "We need to talk to her."

Chapter Thirty-Seven
SECRETS

ENTERING THE PIGGLY Wiggly, we didn't find Raina working the register. A bagger informed us she was on her break and directed us to the back room. We hurried through the dairy aisle, past swinging double doors, and into the stockroom. Raina spotted us through a glass window and met us under a tower of dog food.

"What're you guys doing here?" Her face was pale, and she wouldn't look me in the eye. Instead of answering her question, I pulled the sand dollar out of my pocket and held it up to her.

Her mouth dropped open and tears burst from her eyes. "I'm sorry. I've kept the secret for so long that sometimes it seems like a dream."

She pulled us behind another row of tall stock shelves, so her coworkers wouldn't see her crying. Sam handed her a handkerchief.

"You were right," she said to me, "I knew him. We worked together here at the Piggly Wiggly until he got fired because of me."

"How d'you get him fired?" Sam asked.

"You guys don't understand what it's like being the smart one." She whispered it as if it were a bad word. "Mamma's been micromanagin' my life. I got this job thinkin' I'd get some freedom out of it, but she puts all my checks directly into savings. If I want to buy something, I have to ask her, and many times she tells me I don't need it. So, I did something terrible."

She rolled her eyes up to heaven as if making a confession.

I tilted my head at her. "What d'you do?"

"I, um, took some money out of the register."

Sam and I looked at each other, eyes wide and mouths gaping.

"I know!" Raina hid her face in her hands. Then she shook her head and tried to explain. "I needed art supplies. Reverend Bill had asked me to do a mural in the nursery, but Mom wouldn't give me the money. So, I took three twenties out of the drawer. Oh, please don't arrest me, Officer Teague!" She started crying again.

Sam and I cast each other disbelieving looks before I asked, "So, how did Darryl get involved?"

Raina wiped her eyes. "He saved me. That night, the office manager counted my till and realized the money was missing. She called me up to the front office where everyone was clocking out. She confronted me. I denied it, of course."

I nodded. "Of course."

"Well, she was really upset," Raina went on, "and she said she was goin' to check the cameras. I didn't even know they had cameras! I 'bout had a heart attack! My life was over. I could kiss college and church and everything goodbye." She wiped her tears on her sleeve. "Then, Darryl walked over. Handed her three twenties out of his wallet, said he'd done it, and quit."

I smiled. "Wow."

"I know, right? He saved me, for no reason at all. I know it might sound funny, but 'cept for Jesus, I'd never known anyone to make such a selfless sacrifice, 'specially not for me. I, well, I stalked 'em a little. I had to know him better. We started seeing each other in secret."

"Why the secrecy?" Sam asked.

"My family would've freaked out if they'd learned I was datin' Darryl."

My eyes narrowed. "Why? They didn't freak out about Candy dating Damon, not like she thought they would."

Raina huffed. "Damon didn't work in a strip club or have a momma that enjoys playing with dolls too much."

I shrugged. "That's true."

"Darryl wanted to keep it a secret, most of all. His family wouldn't understand. His own brother moved in on his last girlfriend, the stripper, giving her all kinds of presents and stuff. So, we kept it quiet, met in secret places. I thought he was afraid to be seen with me, but I didn't care too much. It was very romantic."

"Was Darryl involved in any criminal activity that you know of?" Sam asked.

Raina shook her head. "He had a nest egg, and was trying to get out of a business arrangement he was in, but he never explained any of that to me."

"He never told you what the business was?" I asked.

"No, but he made decent money at it, I think. Delilah, he was going to marry me, gave me a ring and everything."

Sam turned to me, and said, "So the Duffy family picture in his room was really a picture of Raina."

"Yes, he was protecting her with the rest of us."

Raina dabbed her eyes again. "He really was a good man, no matter what everyone says. I was only with him six months, but I felt like I'd loved him my whole life. I can't believe he's gone." She crumbled into my arms.

Sam and I left Raina in the hands of her sister, who came immediately after I called. Leaving one sibling relationship, I thought deeply about another.

Sam smiled, opening the car door for me. "You've got that thoughtful look."

"Angel told me that Darryl had given her all those gifts, not Ronnie."

"Maybe Darryl lied to Raina. Ex-girlfriends are a touchy subject."

"Yes, but he'd lie about having a relationship with a stripper in the first place, wouldn't he? Benny also said it was Ronnie who gave Angel the presents, not Darryl. Is that enough to get a new search warrant? Search Ronnie's portion of the house?"

"No way. There's nothing illegal about giving gifts."

"What if they're stolen?"

"Still, it's all hearsay—"

"What if Angel told the truth and turned over the goods?"

Sam's eyes squinted. "That'd be enough."

"Wanna go see a stripper?"

He chuckled. "Wow, you're like the coolest girlfriend ever."

Angel Jenner rented a blue and white trailer in a place called The Estates. Trailers lined the roadside like trees, barely enough room between them to breathe. The dirt road through the middle had been roughed up by the rains, and the bumping caused my head to hurt as we made our way there. Sam went slowly, avoiding unwatched children who occasionally darted out without looking.

We pulled behind a red Honda Civic hatchback with its trunk open. Angel stuffed bags and suitcases into the car.

She rolled her eyes at me as we walked up to her. "You again? I ain't got time to talk."

"Leaving, Angel?" Sam leaned against her car.

She flicked her long blond hair and gave him a sarcastic smile. "That's none of your business, now is it?"

I put my hands out submissively. "We won't stop you, but we need your help."

"I ain't got nothing to say."

"Darryl Chambers is dead. I almost died." I pointed to the bandage still on my head.

A brief look of sympathy drifted over her heavily made-up face. She breathed out. "See what askin' questions and stickin' your nose in stuff gets ya?"

"You're right. It's a dangerous world, for *both* of us."

Sam stepped closer. "If you talk to us about Ronnie, we can end this once and for all."

Angel rolled her hazel eyes and glanced around at the other trailers, as if looking for prying eyes. "Okay, okay."

I smiled at Sam, and then said, "Ronnie's the one who gave you those presents, right?"

"Yep, I was with Darryl at the time, and he was real sweet. But, Ronnie started givin' me things. A girl like me's gotta go where the gettin's good, you know? Can't be a stripper forever. Leaving Darryl for Ronnie was a mistake and a half!"

"Why's that?" Sam said.

"Ronnie's a nutbag! Sure, he gave me gifts, but they cost me! Boy has some weird appetites." Angel cringed and folded her arms over her chest. "He's rough and possessive, like I was somethin' he owned, and he could use me any way he pleased."

My eyebrows crinkled together. I thought of Jonathan Dekker, and how easy it was to get caught up in the wrong relationship. I squeezed her arm softly. The touch surprised her, but a smile eased up over her mouth. Behind the make-up, I could see she was hurting, and scared.

"So, did you know his gifts were stolen?" Sam asked, and she nodded. "Do you still have them?"

Angel turned and dug into the bags in the back of her car, handing over items to us without looking. An angel pin. A white mink coat. A foot spa. A string of pearls. By the time she'd finished, our arms were full.

"I don't want 'em no more, anyway. Everything about that boy gave me the creeps."

    I knew how she felt.

Chapter Thirty-Eight

POST-STORM

ONCE ANGEL'S ITEMS were verified stolen, things moved quickly. They issued search warrants. An arrest warrant followed. I expected to feel relieved, but I didn't.

Like the calm before a storm, a peace settles afterwards. Soft waves topple like falling feathers. The sand is cool to the touch, packed down and easy to tread on. The ocean rests placidly, waiting for the next uproar. The hushed aftermath is typically short-lived, but intoxicating, easy to get lost in.

"Tomorrow, we'll go shopping," my mother said. We all no longer fit at Grandma Betty's long table. With the addition of Sam and my parents, they moved the kids to their own table in the kitchen. Sadly, 'kids' included Rachel and Raina, though I think Raina was happy to be set apart. Neisha and Nikita gladly moved to what they deemed 'the girls' room' and dinner suddenly became adults only.

"Shopping?" I asked.

Mom nodded. "If you insist on staying here, you'll need a few things for that sparse place of yours, unless you intend on living like that bum friend of yours for however long." I smiled, grateful that she'd come around.

"Six weeks," Clara said. "That's all she's got before Joe pulls the plug on Beach Read forever."

Mom pointed her fork at Clara. "A lot can happen in six weeks, Clara."

Not wanting to talk business, especially my short deadline, I said, "His name is Henry, Mom. He may be homeless, but he's no bum."

Sam's phone rang. He excused himself from the table.

"What's the difference?" Charlotte asked me.

"He doesn't have a home, Charlotte, making him homeless. But, he's not a bum. He doesn't avoid work or sponge off others."

"Oh," she said, face still confused.

"Besides, he spouts poetry," I told the table.

"Like a rapper?" Clark asked.

I smiled. "No, like a poet. Anything from Shakespeare to nursery rhymes. He's amazing."

Sam appeared in the hall, motioning for me to follow him. I left the table.

"It's Lewis. He has some news." He pulled me into the family room where we could be alone and put Lewis on speaker.

"Go ahead, Detective Lewis."

Lewis cleared his throat like he was giving a press conference. "We've arrested and interviewed Ronald Chambers. He confessed to his brother's murder and your attempted murder, Ms. Duffy."

"Wow, just like that?"

"I happen to be a very skilled interrogator, Ms. Duffy," Lewis replied. "After several hours of experienced police questioning, he spilled like a bag of beans."

I wasn't convinced. "What did he say, exactly?"

"Concerning you, Ms. Duffy, he claims that he finished the

Rose Duffy house early, drove by the church and saw you leaving from Bingo. He raced back to the store and waited for you to arrive. He knocked you out, put you in the back of his truck, and took you to the marina. Chambers borrowed a friend's boat, a fellow by the name of Mel Sanders—we're checking on him now. Well, you know the rest. He drove the boat out past the point, far enough into the ocean for someone who couldn't swim, dumped you in, and raced back before anyone discovered the loot in his truck."

"Did he mention the details, like the duffle bag?" Sam asked.

It sounded like Lewis shuffled through some papers. "Yes, said he used an old gym bag that Darryl carried his football gear in. Satisfied?"

Sam and I looked at each other and shrugged.

"Why?" I asked. "Why'd he do it?"

Lewis breathed out heavily. "He killed his brother because he screwed him. Ronald thought he could force Darryl to continue with their business, but Darryl refused. You, Ms. Duffy, pissed him off. Imagine that. He found out you'd been asking questions, following him around, and he worried that you'd get to the truth."

"So, what now?" Sam asked. "Arraignment or bail?"

"We have seventy-two hours before we officially need to charge him. We'll use it," Lewis said, "especially since it's a weekend and all. Once we seize all his stolen assets, I don't see how he'll post bail, not that the judge will grant it. He'll sit."

"Excellent," Sam said.

"And Teague, I know you have enough built-up leave to take a sabbatical, but you really need to come back to work."

"I'll think about it." Sam grinned and ended the call. He wrapped his hands around me. "That's good news, right?"

"Yes," I said. "Very good."

Sam eyed me skeptically. "You're not sure?"

"It's nothing. I'm sure it's nothing."

"What?"

I bit my bottom lip. "Why would Ronnie think I couldn't swim?"

"You've told people about your fear of the water."

"Not him."

"I don't know." Sam's eyebrows pushed together thoughtfully. "He could've guessed."

"Most people know how to swim. He used a gun on Darryl. Why use the ocean on me?"

Sam flipped his phone back open and redialed Lewis.

Lewis huffed. "What is it? I do have some work to do here."

"Did Ronnie say how he knew that Delilah couldn't swim?"

"Didn't ask. Is it important?"

"Could be."

"Okay, I'll find out," Lewis said. "Anything else?"

Sam cocked his head. "Is Ronnie right or left-handed?"

"Holy Toledo, do you want his shoe size and measurements, too? I think he's left-handed. Pretty sure."

"Delilah's assailant was left-handed. Be very sure."

"I am. He's left-handed. He's the guy. Now leave me alone."

Chapter Thirty-Nine

NEAR-LIFE

"**F**EELING ANY BETTER?" Sam drove my Jeep while I soaked up the warm summer breezes. After dinner and all the commotion over the arrest, my head'd started throbbing again. Since walks on the beach were off the itinerary for multiple reasons, Sam'd suggested a drive.

Three days had passed since my night in the sea. Overall, I'd done well. My muscles had gone from gelatin, to aching, to sore and weak. The bruises on my ankles and wrists had darkened, but felt better. The nausea had passed, but headaches still plagued me.

"Is this helping?"

I nodded. "Know someplace quiet and shaded?"

Sam drove to Tipee Island State Park. The path wound through an open area for picnicking, bike trails and footpaths, a playground and duck pond, until Sam pulled onto a side road in the opposite direction to the sign that read "BEACH". The one lane road became bumpier and overgrown with unruly shrubs and trees.

Soon, the path opened to a small clearing in the thick forest, where Sam parked.

Sam took my hand. "You'll love this."

He led me down a trail into the shady trees where the forest soon opened into a miniature estuary. Somewhere beyond the maritime forest, the ocean had spilled into this small deposit which was shaded almost all the way across by extended trees—live oaks, red cedars, and wax myrtles surrounded by loblolly pines—interweaving and joining branches with each other, creating a brilliant ceiling fifty feet across the pool. The sunlight speckled through the canopy, if only to warm the waters of the peaceful lagoon. Lily pads rested, cattails wavered, and marsh grasses swayed. Egrets and herons fluttered in their mega-birdbath. A fish jumped, sending ripples out like a sound wave. Sam led me to a cedar bench.

"It's beautiful," I said.

"Knew you'd like it." He held my hand as the birds played.

I rested my head on his shoulder. "You're going back to work tomorrow?"

"If you're ready."

I sighed. "I can't monopolize you forever. Besides, Ronnie's in jail."

"Feel safe again?"

"I guess so. Do you feel good about it?"

"Well, statistically, only ten to twelve percent of the world is left-handed, so we've probably got the right guy."

I smirked. "That's a weird thing to know."

"Well, I'm left-handed."

"Gosh, I didn't realize. There's a lot I don't know about you, I guess." I hoped that he would seize the opportunity to elaborate on some of those things, but he shrugged.

"I feel confident about Ronnie. Besides, you're you."

"What's that mean?" I asked, sitting up and looking at him.

"Delilah, I'm here because you want me to be and I'm thrilled, but you don't need me." He brushed his fingers on my cheek. "You're the toughest person I've ever met."

I cut him my best you've-got-to-be-kidding look.

"I mean it. You amaze me."

My face flushed, and then I smiled.

"So, then you aren't too mad about the stealing evidence from a crime scene thing that I did?"

"Don't care."

"And the whole thing where I thought you were lying to me?"

He shook his head. "You know the truth now."

"What about when you get a domestic disturbance call and realize I'm beating the crap out of Candy?" I suggested. "Will you be angry then?"

He laughed. "I might be slow to stop that one, but, angry? No. Delilah, at this point, I don't think you could make me mad, even if you set out to. Though there's one thing you could do that would really disappoint me."

"What's that?"

A warm, but playful smile reached across his face. "Put a stop to this kiss."

"Wouldn't dream of it," I whispered.

I grinned as he leaned in and decided not to disappoint him. As I melted into him, I remembered that these were the lips I thought I'd never kiss again, and felt a surge of joy, like firecrackers of bliss exploding inside me. For the first time since my near-death, I felt near-life, and I got lost in it.

Concussion is a tricky business. Some people get knocked out, only to come to and rejoin whatever activity that knocked them out in the first place. My grade five concussion had left no permanent damage, but I had moments of uneasiness that reminded me how weak I truly was. Dizziness and confusion made me feel a little drunk. Screens were hard for my eyes, and although great meals were being prepared for me, I didn't have much of an appetite. Consequently, I made Wednesday Beach Read's *For Real Grand Opening,* giving me another three days of rest. I even took out an advertisement in Clark's paper to make it official.

The great support that I'd hoped for but didn't get at the beginning kicked in to a fantastic frenzy. My parents took charge of my apartment, getting me bedside tables, an area rug for warmth, a cushy white couch for lounging, curtains, a few potted plants, and other decorative touches that would've taken me ages to do on my own. Dad handled the new stove and fridge by trekking to Shawsburg, interrogating the Lowe's salesman, and then installing them himself. He had his toolbox in the car for 'times like these.'

Clark gifted me with five incredible beach pictures. Though my relationship with the sea was on shaky ground, the pictures generated more warmth than fear. In return, I forgave him for the dreadful hospital picture of me in Saturday's paper under the headline *Delilah Duffy Defies Death at Sea; The Book Isn't Closed on Beach Read.*

Grandma Betty set up my Beach Read technology department—the computer, all-in-one printer, and software. She created an inventory. Together, we learned how to operate the credit card machine and cash register, creating different sales scenarios for practice.

Henry Bellows appeared back at the store on Monday. After a marauder had snatched me, Henry combed the island in pursuit. Though he didn't find me, he was pleased to report that he found an umbrella and a new beach towel.

With the hubbub over, Henry jumped into his experimental role at Beach Read. Damon brought Neisha and Nikita to the store for a private pre-opening performance. With the girls and Willie cuddled up on the beanbags and large, colorful pillows Mom had scored at The Cotton Exchange, Henry settled onto the barstool by the window and read a pirate picture book from which he often digressed, much to the girls' delight. I'd found my niche—a real storyteller.

Mike Ancellotti visited the shop Monday, while Grandma Betty and I were busy with computer work. We did the usual roundabout concerning my ordeal.

"I always knew those Chambers boys were bad news," he told me. "I'm sorry that you had to be an innocent victim in all that."

I took a deep breath. "I don't feel like a victim." As I said those words, my head retaliated with sharp pains to my right temple. "I'm really doing much better. Let's go out on the sidewalk and talk. I could use some air." He held the door open for me as we went out into the stifling July heat. I leaned against the brick wall of Beach Read. Suddenly feeling awkward, I muttered something like, "Um, I'd like to talk—"

Mike showed off his disarming, sexy smile that surely had him spoiled at the hands of women.

"Don't worry, Delilah. I know you're seeing Teague. Far be it from me to get into a pissing match with *RoboCop*." I chuckled at the reference. "He's like ex-green beret. He'd probably snipe me from a rooftop to get me out of the picture."

"I'd like us to be friends, and I think we could be good ones, if there are no misunderstandings."

"Works for me. I figure, if we can join forces, maybe we can put the squeeze on your aunts, and then we can be the business powerhouses of the block."

"A lofty, but awesome idea."

Mike promised to cater the grand opening with some light refreshments, which was completely his idea, and I was happy to accept. When I returned inside, without Mike, Grandma Betty gave me the stink eye.

"I hope you're not doing anything that might upset Officer Teague," she said. I eased myself into a beanbag, rubbing my head.

"No worries."

I'd mounted mistakes, but with my voyage at sea came a rebirth of sorts. I'd done some good, too, and maybe my mistakes, however monumental, were necessary hurdles to get where I belonged. Making peace with the water may not happen, but my mistake-making I could live with. Until I realized I'd made a deadly one.

Chapter Forty

SHOALS

OFF THE COAST of North Carolina, the Gulf Stream collides with the Labrador Current from the North, creating the Diamond Shoals—shallow sandbars surrounded by rough waters. Sailors happily moving along on the stream's currents forget about the dangers at the Shoals and get caught in its traps. While a blessing for its speed, The Gulf Stream has been a curse to sailors who get too comfortable there, contributing hundreds of vessels to the Graveyard of the Atlantic.

Tuesday afternoon, Willie and I ventured out for the first time alone. With the store opening tomorrow, I needed to do things independently, having gone for so many days without. Still, Sam practically interrogated me about my plans before he headed for work, and for once, I wasn't stubborn about telling him.

Top to Bottom: A Hat and Shoe Boutique is a rose crammed between two thorns by appearances. To its left sits Mystic Delights, a hippie store displaying hookahs and tie-dye t-shirts. To the right, of course, is my rustic work-in-progress Beach Read.

Top to Bottom's store front, twice the size of mine, had professionally styled windows with mannequins and fabric backdrops, mostly in pink. Long flower boxes adorn the front windows, spilling over with pink, purple, and white daisies, tulips, and carnations. When inside, a light perfume filled your senses. Pink covered most surfaces from the carpet to the walls. And though I've never been a pink-fan myself, Victoria's Secret excluded, the color choices work, and create a soft, warm atmosphere that said, *"Come in. Relax. Stay awhile. We're all friends here."* Hat trees formed an odd forest on the left side of the room. On the right, the shoe department was littered with cushy pink chairs, side tables, and even a coffee and water bar.

Clara stood at the long glass counter, reading glasses perched on her nose, and face buried in paperwork. I stepped toward her.

"As I live and breathe." She barely looked up from her work, "Delilah Duffy! I bet you need a hat for that unsightly new haircut—"

"I'm not here for a hat."

"Came to gloat then?"

Truthfully, gloating would've felt fantastic. Once Great Uncle Joe learned about my aunts' devious attempts to thwart Beach Read's opening, he went ballistic. He extended my profit deadline, tore up the aunts' offer, and promised them that if they tried anything else and I failed to make it work, he'd sell to Via and let Beach Read become an extension of the strip club. I had a feeling Aunt Clara would behave from now on.

"No, didn't come for that either. I need to see Candy."

Clara's eyebrows scrunched together. "She's in the back with Charlotte. What'cha need her for?"

I didn't answer, but gave her an irritated look. She called for Candy, and both Charlotte and Candy emerged from the backroom. The three glared impatiently at me, hands on hips. Whatever care and affection I'd received after almost dying had dissipated.

Candy huffed. "What do you want? You already cost me my job. Here to rub it in?"

"I need to know why."

"Why what?" Candy sauntered over to the coffee bar. She poured herself a cup of water and dropped a lemon wedge in it.

"Why you deliberately sabotaged my relationship with Sam," I said, bothered that I had to explain. "Why did you lie to us?"

Clara moved out from behind the counter. "Wait, what's this about?"

"This isn't about the store?" Charlotte asked.

I shook my head. "No, this isn't business. It's personal. Course, it's all personal to me, but nothing is more personal than him."

Candy winced. "You know, I'm workin' here now. Thanks to you, a dozen years of hard work at Beach Realty are down the drain." She snapped her fingers. "Just like that."

"That was Uncle Joe's doing, not mine," I told her. "Stop avoiding the subject and tell me why."

"I'm confused." Clara stepped between us. "What exactly are you claimin' she lied about?"

I stared at Candy's hardened face. "After Sam and I shared the most perfect day together, Candy told him I'd left and couldn't see him, and told me he wasn't interested in me—"

"Was that the summer you became so distraught?" Charlotte asked, blue eyes wide.

"I had a broken heart, thought the boy I loved didn't love me back, and it crushed me. And Candy let me believe it."

"I'm still confused," Clara said. "You gals were inseparable back then. Candy, why would you—"

"Were you in love with him, too?" Charlotte gasped.

Candy grimaced. "Hell, no!" She moved around the counter and went about the business of straightening shoes on their perches. The three of us followed her.

271

"Then why?" Bothered by her delay, I raised my voice. "Why lie about it? Did you even have a reason or was it just plain, old-fashioned cruelty?"

Her eyes welled with tears. "Because of Damon!" She spat it out in one huge emotional burst, shocking both me and my aunts. "You weren't the only one in love that summer, 'cept I was too afraid to tell anyone, too afraid to bring him home to meet Mom and Dad, too afraid to tell my sisters, to tell you. I guess all that fear built up—"

"Because he's black?" Clara asked.

The three of us glanced at each other with dumbfounded faces.

Candy grunted. "I had friends who wouldn't even talk to me anymore after they found out I was seeing a black man, and if they reacted like that, well, I knew the shit would hit the fan when I told the family."

Clara rolled her eyes. "It wasn't that bad—"

"It was a nightmare! Daddy 'bout had a heart attack. Mamma kept sputtering some nonsense from the Bible about mixing yolks. Grandpa practically disowned me." Tears fell, but she brushed them away.

Clara, Charlotte and I shared a knowing look. Candy's flair for dramatics often led her to exaggerate. What wasn't a big deal, Candy turned into one.

"What did that have to do with Sam and me?"

"You think it was easy bein' shackled to you all summer?" Candy took a deep breath. "I could barely get away to see 'em. You tagged along everywhere I went, when I wasn't working, and made things impossible for me—"

"Ah, this is bullshit!" My hands went to my hips. "All you ever had to do was tell me. I would've understood."

"No one understood! All you could think about was yourself. Sam Teague this and Sam Teague that. Only reason I set up that date for you was to get you off my back. I was so sick of hearing about him." Candy scooted across the room again, using up her nervous energy. "You drove me crazy. I thought things would get better after your date, that you'd get him out of your system. First dates never turn out so good—"

"It was the best day of my life."

She laughed sarcastically. "Yeah, that's what he said, too. Can you imagine how angry I was when I saw Sam Teague comin' up *MY* driveway and walkin' up *MY* porch and comin' into *MY* house? My Damon couldn't do that, but here was your boyfriend callin' on you like a lovesick puppy. You! Sixteen years old! And me, twenty-two years old and hiding around corners like I was doing something wrong."

"You were jealous—"

"I was angry. My relationship with Damon was complicated—stressful—and you made it worse!"

She moved into the hat tree forest, tilting the brims and adjusting the way they hung from their perches. I followed, steaming.

"That wasn't my fault! How could you take it out on me?"

"You deserved it. You're nothin' but a coddled little princess—"

"Coddled? You know my mother. How can you say coddled?"

"Always gettin' your way, and when you were here, I had to coddle you, too. Got sick of it!"

"So, I was the bug under your shoe?" I circled around hat racks to keep up with her. Clara and Charlotte stayed close behind. "You broke my heart!" Anger pulsed through me. I jumped in front of her and knocked the hat rack over to get her attention. Clara and Charlotte gasped. "And you still kept up the lie, even now. Why?"

"Well, he'd be a real good reason to stay, wouldn't he?" she said coldly. "Like everyone else 'round here, I wanted you gone."

Clara sucked in air. "I created a monster."

"Daddy told me you found the life vest." Candy leaned down and picked up the fallen hat rack. "I couldn't believe Sam Teague had the nerve to ask me to give it to you, like I'm some kinda delivery person. I looked at 'em like he was nuts on top of looney."

My eyes squinted and pinched together. Something rock hard formed in my stomach. The more she spoke, the larger it grew.

"Knew I shoulda thrown that damn thing away."

Punching her in the face wasn't my plan. Honestly. Only she was in the middle of saying, "We all said you were a fool to come back here. What's it gonna take for you to learn—" when I snapped and my fist rammed against her cheek. Her head swung back, her earrings jingling as she went. She toppled to the pink carpet, taking the hat rack she'd just fixed down with her, a squeaky cry belting from her lips.

I leaned over her stunned face. "You stole thirteen years of love from me while you had Damon and got married and had two beautiful babies. Thirteen years, Candy! How could you do that, you bitch? If you don't feel a shit-storm of guilt for that, then you're a heartless she-devil!"

I exited through the hats, knocking down rack trees as I went. I'd survived the shoals.

At least, that's what I thought.

Chapter Forty-One

BREAKERS

A BREAKER IS a crashing wave that collapses onto the shore in a fit of foam and spray, then pushes up the beach until devoid of energy. It's also the name of the poorer section of town—The Breakers—where ramshackle cottages are practically shoved up against each other, rounded up by the dense marshes.

Mavis Chambers lived in a small one-story yellow cottage with black shutters. Two pickup trucks, one blue and one green, sat in the gravel driveway along with a dark green golf cart. A wooden sign on the door said 'Welcome'. Willie and I knocked.

Mavis answered wearing a black dress with purple flowers, slippers on her feet, and a warm smile that immediately made me feel more comfortable about popping in.

"I hope I'm not bothering you," I said.

Her face brightened. "Ms. Duffy, how nice for you to visit."

"You've been on my mind. Maybe you could show me your doll room, if you aren't busy? I don't collect them, but it sounds very interesting."

She nodded, a grin coiling up on her left cheek. "Surely, but no dogs." She held her finger up to exercise her firmness. "I don't allow pets in my house."

I should've remembered that fact. Flashes of two little boys chasing baby snakes in the backyard skimmed across my mind.

"No problem. I'll leave Willie in the Jeep."

I pulled Willie back to the driveway. He jumped in the front seat, and I gave him a reassuring pat. "Won't be long."

Walking into Mavis' living room, I could understand the no-pet rule. Victorian furniture competed with floral wallpaper and brass lamps and fixtures. Every surface had a lacy covering, and from the curtains to the throw pillows, everything had ruffles.

"What a lovely home," I told her. I followed Mavis down a hallway to the right. A few closed doors stretched the length of the hall. Two of the doors had indentions where locks had been removed.

She hesitated, seeing that I'd noticed the missing locks. "My boys rented their rooms from me. They insisted on keeping their rooms locked for privacy. The police smashed the locks off."

"I'm sorry. You've been through a terrible ordeal." I didn't know what else to say. The boys using padlocks on the outside of their doors struck me funny. Sure, they were thieves, but were they really so worried about their mom snooping in their rooms? I glanced back at Mavis. Maybe.

Mavis pivoted to the left, into what should've been the dining room, as it shouldered the kitchen. I hesitated in the hall long enough to notice another anomaly. No family pictures graced the walls. No sports trophies in a curio cabinet. I shuddered and followed her.

The Doll Room held floor to ceiling shelves. Spaced evenly apart, the dolls lined the walls, their eyes black and lifeless. They reminded me of the snakes, all lined up with eyes like death.

"Beautiful, aren't they?" She circled around the room like a child playing in a fountain.

"Wonderful. How many do you have?" Many of them looked old, with their glass eyes and dated clothing. Surely, they were expensive, for every detail on them had been perfected, down to each hand-stitched button or painted freckle. In front of each one, a little card had been placed with the doll's name and a date.

"Oh, these are only a few of my collection, the ones who have behaved. The rest are in the basement. I have hundreds of doll children. I'm like the little old lady who lived in a shoe." She chuckled with a quick snort.

I smiled. A steady nervousness swelled in my stomach.

"Let me fix you some tea. You look a little pale." She pointed to the tiny two-person table in the middle of the Doll Room. A lace doily graced its middle.

"Oh, please don't go to any trouble. I can't stay—"

"It's no trouble." Her thin lips pushed up her cheeks in a wide smile. "Water's already hot."

She disappeared into the kitchen. A headache was coming on. I sat down. Why was I here? It's true—she'd been on my mind. I felt sorry for her, and indirectly responsible for what'd happened, at least, to Ronnie. I worried what losing two sons would do to her already fragile psyche. Given that she'd been so friendly, I'd thought we might bond.

"*A doll in the doll-maker's house looks at the cradle and bawls: 'That is an insult to us'.*" The words from Yeats' poem struck me now as the glass eyes stared down at me. I shivered. Coming here may've been a mistake. My head throbbed.

Mavis carried a lovely China tea service, complete with dainty cups, saucers, linen napkins, and a small plate of ladyfingers. She set the tray down carefully, poured, and handed me a delicate teacup.

"Drink up, Ms. Duffy," she said sweetly, "before it gets cold."

I sipped, as ordered. I imagined that I was Alice in Wonderland.

Curiosity often leads to trouble.

My eyes darted from doll to doll. Singly, they were pleasant, beautiful even. But, taken together, they were overwhelming. Like too many chocolates can make you sick, I felt strangely ill-at-ease in the Doll Room.

"You are looking much better than that dreadful picture in the paper." A gentle smile eased up on the left side of her mouth as her eyes drifted over me. My right hand instinctively shielded the marks on my wrists. I shoved them both under the table. My uneasiness grew.

Mavis set her teacup down and tossed me a girlish grin. "Let's invite Paisley Lynn to join us, shall we?"

My mouth dropped, but nothing came out. I shielded my surprise with a quick smile. I'd come across a few odd ducks in my day, but Mavis—she jumped to the front of the crazy line. Nuts on top of looney, like Candy had said earlier.

Mavis stood and grabbed a doll from the second shelf. She placed her carefully on the edge of the table, between us, and then returned to her own seat with a satisfied smile. I sipped my tea, unsure. Half of me expected—or maybe just hoped—this was all a ruse. Could she be joking? Attempting some tea-party silliness? I remembered Mavis calling her dolls her inanimate family, but she couldn't possibly think—

"Paisley Lynn joined our family a few weeks ago, and she's been so wonderful since all this mess about the boys."

"How's that?" I tried to ignore the doll now almost right in my face. It had pink and purple paisley pants, as one might have guessed, a fluffy white blouse, and two brown braids draped on its shoulders.

Mavis smiled. "Oh, you know. She's been a real shoulder to lean on. The other night, we stayed up for hours talking."

I wanted to crack a joke about how Paisley Lynn must be a terrific listener, but I could tell by Mavis' expression that this was nothing to joke about.

"Um, it's a real blessing to have someone to talk to. I know I—"

Mavis held up her finger and shushed me. She leaned into Paisley Lynn, listening. "Oh, my." Mavis leaned back into her seat. She shot her doll a disapproving look.

"What's wrong?" I asked, but feared the answer. My head pounded.

"Paisley Lynn doesn't like you very much." Mavis took another sip of tea. "She is very particular about her friends, perhaps too particular."

"Oh, well, I'm sorry to hear that."

"On the other hand, she was right about Madame Posey. Madame Posey was nothing but a... a... BACKSTABBING BITCH!" Every word out of Mavis' mouth had been controlled, soft and sweet like birdsong, until she roared like the devil. I pushed back in my chair, heart racing, head jolting with pain.

"You know, I'm not feeling all that well—"

"It would be rude to leave before finishing your tea." Her normal voice had returned, but her warning chilled me. I settled back into my seat, taking my cup back in my fingers, now shaking.

I breathed out. "You're right. I'm sorry." I looked at the doll. "Forgive me."

Mavis smiled and leaned toward the doll again. "Oh, Paisley Lynn, pish posh. I'm sure Ms. Duffy didn't mean to take your brothers away. Right, Ms. Duffy?"

My phone and keys were in my pockets. Willie and my Jeep were just outside the door. All I had to do was get around this table and Mavis. Still, I didn't move. Mavis smiled widely, seeming to revel in my distress.

My voice shook. "Right."

"Your first name—Delilah." Mavis' eyes lit up. "Did you know that there was a Delilah in the Bible? She was a Philistine whore who brought a great man to his death. Isn't that funny?"

My head thundered. "How… how is that funny?"

Placid, her face looked just like one of her dolls. "Well, you did the same thing, didn't you? How did your mother know that name would suit you so well? Must be your nature."

I set my teacup down. "I… I—"

"My boys understood their places. I understood their natures, like your own mother, perhaps. I trained them up in the way they should go. That is, of course, until you—"

"Me?" My thoughts flooded as everything came together, combining with head-splitting fear. *Yes, I have a Corrine. Mint condition. She's a peach! Corrine Masterson*, I thought. How could I have been so blind?

"Darryl and his dithers." She shook her head as one would over a funny anecdote. "He has shown devotion to three things in his life, when there has only been room for one." She held up delicate fingers to emphasize the numbers. "Boys should be dedicated to their mothers. Not football. Not whores. He was mine in the beginning, and mine at the end."

My head pulsated. *I'm finally ready to trade the Rose. You'll love her. She's lovely. All original parts. And I have another doll I want to show you, too. This one's very special.* Mamma Rose and me. Filled with wild desperation, much like I felt out at sea, I needed to get out of there—fast.

"We knew he was involved with someone. Didn't we, Paisley Lynn? But, unlike that club whore, he dug deep and spewed out some kind of affection for you. How on earth did he manage that?" She smiled, leaning into the doll again. I seized the opportunity, jumped up, and pushed the table over against her, sending the entire tea service and Paisley Lynn crashing to the floor.

I skirted around the mess and Mavis. But she was faster than I expected, snatching up at me. She grabbed a huge wad of my hair and yanked me back. I screamed. Pain cascaded across my head.

"I'm not done with you yet, you bitch!" She pulled, hard.

I elbowed her in the nose. She let go. I skedaddled through the doll room and into the kitchen. In my hurry, I knocked into some dolls perched on the end of the shelf. They tumbled off and dropped to the floor. Mavis cried out, going to the dolls' aid. I fled to the kitchen and into the first door I came to.

Darkness. Shit! I felt a bolt at the top of the door and swiftly slid it across. I heard Mavis storm into the kitchen.

BANG! BANG! BANG!

"Come out, Ms. Duffy!"

I took a step away from the door and nearly fell. Stairs.

BANG! BANG! BANG!

"Can't hide in there forever!"

My heart thundered in my chest. My hands slid over the walls, searching for a light.

Mavis' voice changed into a raging scream. "I can't wait to slit your throat, you whore! No mistakes this time. I'll enjoy your hot blood dripping on my hands."

I pulled my phone out of my pocket. Its soft light lit up the top of a set of wooden stairs. Basement. Frustrated and fearful, tears flooded my eyes.

"Sam?" my voice trembled.

BANG! BANG! BANG!

A scream involuntarily leapt out of me. The vibrations of her pounding rippled through the door, the wall, and the floorboards.

"Delilah, what's wrong?"

"Sam, I'm in trouble." I moved down a step to get away from the banging, and then another. "I'm locked in—"

The call dropped. Shaking, I held it up to my face. I'd lost the signal. Maybe on the top step, I could retrieve it again.

BANG! BANG! BANG!

"There's nowhere to go, sweetie," Mavis cooed, pounding door with something hard. The bangs rattled me, sending me further down the steps. *Do not go gentle into that good night.* I took another step down and another. No window. No light. No escape.

Look for weapons, I thought.

Footsteps, loud ones. They moved across the kitchen.

"Take care of the vehicle and the mutt," Mavis told someone. "Quickly."

"Ms. Duffy, olly-olly-oxen-free!" she sang to me. "You came all the way to Tipee for Darryl. Let me send you along to meet him."

Tears raced down my cheeks as I reached the bottom. I felt along concrete walls. No light switches. My head banged into something hanging. I screamed. The snakes from the store awnings popped into my mind, though I knew it couldn't be snakes. There was fabric. Hand shaking, I felt for the object, hoping it was a cord of a light.

It was a doll.

I held my phone up and prompted the screen. In the blackness, a half dozen porcelain dolls hung from nooses. I stepped back, mouth gaping. My heart seized. The walls closed in, like swells encircling me, ready to swallow me up.

Breathe. Think.

BANG! BANG! BANG! Pounds erupted on the door again.

I quickened my search and found the string of a light. Hanging dolls decorated the room. Broken dolls littered the tables. One doll's head was in a vise. Someone had smashed others against the concrete wall. I scurried around the room, looking for something that would help me.

I spied another door and rushed to it. Locks braced the outside, but it was undone. I pulled it open to find a small cubby of a room. A chair, blanket, and bucket filled a corner. A bottle of bleach and a sponge sat on the floor. Along the wall, lines had been marked and crossed out by fives. I fell back. Horrific ideas circulated in my head of what evil could've happened here.

Two boys chasing snakes in the backyard, trying to make pets out of anything. Two boys, maybe one at a time, locked in this room. I felt sick, and sad, and desperate.

"We're coming for you!" Mavis shouted. I grabbed the bucket and bottle of bleach and fled to the stairs.

Get ready...

"He was always such a fool. If only he could've been like his brother, loyal and responsible. I devoted myself to them. They had to do the same for me, for all of us. We were growing. New ones were arriving every day. Why'd he mess it all up? Oh, well. I'm glad you stopped by so we could have this little chat. I planned on calling on you soon, and this saves me so much trouble."

I stood, ready, at the top of the stairs and unlocked one lock silently.

She giggled like a child. "Come out, Ms. Duffy. It's our turn to play."

I gripped the bucket, filled with bleach, quietly turned the knob and swung the door open. "I go first!" A liter of bleach splashed into Mavis' surprised face, sending her shrieking and flailing. I pushed by her and raced toward the front door.

Chapter Forty-Two

SIRENS

BOLTED OUTSIDE, right into the gigantic arms of Lenny Jackson, the Mr. Clean prevention specialist from Via's. He hooked my waist, lifting me off the ground and preventing my escape.

"No use fightin' me. I could snap your neck like a twig."

I believed him. He bent my arm behind me, sending sharp pains up my shoulder and back. Mavis' screams and coughs echoed outside. The bleach smell emanated off my hands and irritated my eyes.

"Ah, what's that smell?" Lenny asked. "What the hell is goin' on?"

"M… Mavis needs your help." My voice cracked as my mouth went dry.

"Nice try." He bent my arm a little more. I screamed.

"Let me go! How could you do this?"

He leaned in to my ear, smiling devilishly. "Best gig I ever had, 'cept that Mavis ain't let me be the one to toss you in the drink.

She wanted to do that herself."

I cringed. My shoulders sagged under his force. Lenny pulled me toward the door.

"Bet she wants to do it right this time."

The pain shooting up my arms and back swirled with the throbbing in my head, making me dizzy. I couldn't think but didn't try long.

Sirens are named after the Sirens of Greek mythology, and they can create sound even under water, like their namesakes. This is really the only thing the two have in common, seeing as how mythological Sirens led sailors to their demise, whereas their modern counterparts mean, at least to the most desperate of people like me, that help's coming.

Sirens. I heard them like church bells.

Lenny peeked his head in the door to see Mavis, but kept his body outside, unsure what to do. He clearly didn't know if the sirens were meant for us, even as they sang closer. Lenny pulled me tighter to him.

"Mavis? You okay?" he called through the door. Nothing.

"She's burning," I told him. "I threw a gallon of bleach in her face. She'll die if you don't help her."

Lenny's face went bright red. His eyes glared.

"You vicious bitch!"

He twisted my arm back further. SNAP! I screamed.

Two Dodge Chargers raced around the corner and gunned it to the end of the block. Lenny Jackson froze. Four officers descended on the lawn, guns drawn, and yelling commands. But I only saw him. With my eyes clouding with tears, I focused on him, telling me to be calm and patient.

Lenny pulled me closer, grabbing both my arms in one hand, so I could be his shield. His other hand reached for my neck and held it like one would steady a fishing pole. The horror dug into me, causing my heart to hammer my chest, tears to scurry out of my eyes, and every piece of me to hurt, as if revolting.

The officers ordered him to let me go. A frantic discussion ensued. The only ones who were quiet were me and Sam. The more Lenny spoke, the tighter he squeezed. My head, arm and shoulder seared with pain. I could barely stand.

Sam's eyes fluctuated calmly between Lenny and me, his black gun raised and ready, left finger twitching. How long would this go on? The more seconds that passed by, the more the situation escalated, like the timer on a bomb drawing nearer to the end of the countdown. Lenny pulled me toward the door.

"Back off!" he yelled in my ear. "We're going inside."

"Hold it, Jackson! Don't move!" Williams shouted back.

Sam leaned slightly, whispered to his partner. It looked like *"I got him."* Fear surged in me like a tsunami. Sam's eyes squinted.

Two shots. Quicker than a breath. The first screamed by my right ear and buried itself into Lenny's shoulder. He released my neck. The second breezed by my left leg, capping his left knee. Down he went, like a house of cards falling over in a brisk wind. Lenny was on the ground writhing in pain before the echo of the shots stopped sounding. I toppled next, three parts shock, pain, and relief.

Shouting ensued. The officers approached. Guns aimed.

But an explosion stopped the advancement, busting the front door into pieces and sending the officers back against the lawn. A shotgun had been fired. I screamed and covered my head with the arm I could move. Sam ducked, rushed to me, gun ready.

"It's Mavis! She's the killer!"

Sam grabbed my side and pulled me up, watching the doorway for movement. He dragged me away from the house to the driveway. Officer Williams yelled for Mavis to drop her weapon and exit the house.

A shotgun cocked. Sam pushed me back. He raised his gun toward the smashed door. A barrel appeared.

"She can't see," I called out. "I threw bleach in her—"

A shot rang out. Then another.

Mavis dropped with a thud before her feet crossed over the threshold. Officers rushed upon her, and Lenny still curled up in pain.

Mavis was dead.

Even the ocean has its diabolical females. Unlike the male of the species, the female black sea devil possesses two menacing features: the bioluminescent lure mounted to her head to entice prey and a mouthful of depressible, glassy fangs to destroy her victims. A she-devil.

In the days, months, years to come, I'd be haunted by the devil in Mavis Chambers, and be soul-sick at the way she destroyed her boys. For the moment, though, I crumbled under the weight of my agony. Sam holstered his gun and bent down to help me off the gravel driveway. I gripped his shoulders with my right arm, and he lifted me up. My left arm, immovable, pulsed in agony. The joint swelled.

"It'll be okay." He led me over to his car, propping me up against the passenger door. He touched my face and brushed my wet cheek. "It's over. I know you're in pain—"

I shook my head and whispered, "She was terrible to them, Sam. The things in that house—"

I couldn't go on. Tears streamed down my face. "*I feel like I already know you.*" Darryl's words haunted me. Now, I knew him, too.

Chapter Forty-Three
WEIGHTLESS

THE WRIGHT BROTHERS first flew their airplane on the beaches of North Carolina, lifting off the ground for twelve glorious seconds, a little longer than I once surfed. For however hard it was or long it took to do either, those amazing seconds made everything worth it.

Beach Read opened Wednesday. One day after Mavis' death. Twenty-five days after my arrival in Tipee.

I was heavily drugged, with my broken elbow in a sling, but smiling anyway. My first customers were my parents, followed promptly by my grandparents, and then most other members of the Duffy clan, with obvious exceptions. The story times drew decent crowds, thanks to Clark's promotions in the paper.

Beach Read's Grand Opening sales weren't so grand and would've been downright dismal if not for the Duffy contributions, but it was a start. The store was open. I expected that from now on, everything would be smoother, even if I didn't reach my goals.

Of course, I'd made mistakes before.

Once the police had digested what I'd told them about Mavis Chambers and searched the entire house, they formed a new equation that added up into something sad and sinister. Mavis'd spearheaded the robberies from the very beginning. She planned the hits and coordinated the timings, like in her phone conversations at Bingo. Because Mavis was a collector and integrated herself so well in the church and community, she could pinpoint good targets and vulnerabilities. My water fears made for easy conversation at the bingo table and inspired Mavis' plans to do me in. She used my words against me.

Darryl and Ronnie couldn't disobey their mother without severe consequences. Mavis had punished them by locking them away. It's no wonder that Darryl learned to pick locks.

The boys had probably practiced some kind of thievery all their lives, but it wasn't until the last year that their activities had expanded into a business. With them and their mother working together with Lenny, they created an impressive team. Darryl was the brains behind each break-in, while Lenny and Ronnie fenced the goods. Ronnie auctioned collectible items online while Lenny traded and sold everyday items to vendors and customers in flea markets all over the coast.

When Darryl fell in love with Raina, everything changed. And unlike football, his mother couldn't break him away from her. Wisely, Darryl had kept his love's identity a secret, having only the family picture of the Duffys in his room as a clue for his snooping mother. The combination of me moving to town, Mavis spotting us together on my first day, and Darryl working on my store led her to conclude that it must be me. I'm glad that she made the mistake, especially after I learned about Raina. My terror at sea suddenly wasn't so terrible.

By the following week, life had settled into some sort of normalcy. I lived in my own apartment; Henry lived downstairs on my air mattress. We worked in Great Aunt Laura's bookstore. And the evil shadows that had consumed me crept back into their dark corners again, mostly.

On the roof, Sam had set up two lawn chairs and a small table in the corner with the best view. He'd placed a single yellow rose in a bud vase. An assortment of store-bought snacks and beer waited for us. After closing, we sat there, feet up, staring up at a night sky filled with bright stars.

Everything was perfect. And yet, as I sipped my beer and stared into the darkness, images from my nightmares bombarded me. It'd been happening a lot in the quiet moments lately.

"You don't seem like you're in a celebratory mood," Sam said.

I shrugged.

"What's wrong?"

"Haven't been sleeping well."

"Bad dreams?"

I chuckled sarcastically. "Silly me. I thought the tidal waves were bad. Now it's Mavis and Lenny and decomposing snakes and hanging dolls and, ugh. It's over, but it doesn't feel that way yet."

"You're still recovering. It'll get better with time. Anything I can do?"

A smile crossed my face, thinking of answers. He grinned back, as if reading my mind. Finally, I shook my head. "I'm really okay. The store's open. I'm still here. My arm only hurts when I move. I've got you. Hell, I'm not even mad at Candy anymore."

Sam gave me a skeptical look. "Really? Knocking her out was that cathartic?"

I shrugged. "That was fun, but no. And, I'm not entirely over it, especially when I go crazy with the what-ifs."

Sam stood up and moved in front of me, leaning against the ledge. He sighed heavily. "What-ifs'll do that to you."

"It's hard not to be angry at what we've missed." I smiled at him again. "But, I'm so grateful for the second chance that it's hard to stay that way. I'm ready to make up for lost time. It's like something inside of me has clicked into place, and it won't go back again. And strangely, this thing between us, I don't know... It's new, but it isn't. You've been with me this whole time, even when you weren't."

"That's how I feel, too." Then a light chuckle escaped him. "You're right. We're the weird new, old couple." He reached out to me, and I took his hand. He pulled me up, drawing me close. "Maybe we weren't ready then. We're both better people for all we've been through. That has to count for something, right?"

"Yes, as long as nothing gets in our way this time around." I smiled hopefully. His fingers slid along my cheek. A tiny crease formed between his eyebrows, and his eyes danced over my face. He opened his mouth to say something, but then hesitated. I tilted my head.

"Nothing's easy," he whispered. "The things in life that are worth fighting for—well, there's always a fight, isn't there? And this—this thing you do to me, seems like there'd have to be an epic war to earn it. Good thing we're both fighters."

The pangs of worry I spied in his eyes migrated over to my own. "What is it?"

He took a deep breath and shook his head. "Nothing." He kissed one cheek and then the other. With a much different tone, he said, "When you're better, we'll do all the normal-couple things. No more hospitals and hostage situations—"

"Are you sure?" I laughed. "Your negotiating tactics were very impressive."

He cocked his head at me, locking his fingers around my waist. "I've never been so confident, pulling that trigger. Course, that doesn't mean I want to do that again."

I nodded. "I never doubted you, but you're right. I don't want that to happen again, either."

"Let's keep it simple. You put on a sexy dress. We'll go out to dinner, movies, even the theater, if you want."

"The theater?"

"Yes, how about some Shakespeare?"

I gave him a skeptical stare. "You don't seem like the type who'd enjoy that."

"I could become a fan, especially with the right teacher."

"Okay, but no tragedies for a while. Only comedies."

"Fine by me. Whatever we do, it'll be nice to just be us. Get all this behind us."

I winced. "That may take some time. Clark said that the story's spreading across the state, hitting all the major newspapers in the next few days."

"It was bound to happen, and it's a good story, Delilah."

"Clark was very gracious, but I'm anxious for the murder and mayhem to be behind me."

Sam kissed my forehead. An ocean breeze swept up over the building and met us on our perch, cooling us off.

I caught his gaze. "So, tell me what you meant before you distracted me with promises of dates and Shakespeare?" He cast me a confused glance. "I'm here for you, too. Something's bothering you. I can feel it. You say that there must be some epic war to earn what we feel right now. We've already been through it, Sam."

He smiled. "I'm sure you're right."

"Sam, whatever it is—"

"It's funny—strange, funny, I mean. It'll take some getting used to—"

"What?"

"You can read me just as well as one of your books, Delilah Duffy, and it's unnerving—"

"Only when you don't want to be read."

"No, I want you to know all of me, just maybe not tonight." He tucked a strand of hair behind my ear and brushed my cheek with his finger. "There's plenty of time for catching up."

I leaned in closer, so that my lips almost touched his. "When I have two arms again, and it better be soon, there's *other* catching up I'd like to do."

Sam's fingers tightened against my back. "There's nothing I want more than to spend all night, every night, wrapped up in you."

Smiling, I kissed him, and lingered weightless much longer than twelve seconds.

Epilogue

TREASURE

RACHEL PACED THE rooster bedroom in Grandma Betty's beachside cottage, looking more nervous than she needed to be. Raina, who should've been the nervous one, sat on the bed, dazed.

"Do it like you're taking off a Band-Aid," I told her, hand on her shoulder. "Just yank it off, really fast." I made a whipping noise for emphasis. It came out pretty well—a fizzing whistle.

Rachel fidgeted over to the window. "Officer Teague's here with his aunt."

I perked up. "Really?"

Rachel nodded. "Mamma Rose invited them. I heard her talking about it earlier."

An easy smile crossed my face. All of this would go better with him here—at least for me.

Raina took a deep breath. "Should I wait—"

"No!" Rachel and I said in unison.

"There's safety in numbers. Get it over with and you'll feel so much better—"

"Like when you take off the Band-Aid," Rachel said. "That was a good one. Go with that."

I gave Raina my best reassuring smile and brushed her cheek. "You can do this."

She nodded weakly. "Okay."

I eyed her skeptically. "Okay? Do you want to pray or recite a Psalm or something?"

"No, I've been sayin' 'em all day. God's tired of it." She took a deep breath. "Let's go."

The girls rushed off to the dining room. I greeted Sam and Aunt Beverly at the door. After a hug, Beverly held up a basket of fresh-baked bread, and she delivered it to the kitchen. Sam gave me a short kiss. I couldn't wait for my arm heal, so I could wrap them both around him again.

"You look beautiful," he told me. I smiled. "Feeling okay?"

"Nervous, but decent otherwise. Head's great. Arm's average."

"Why nervous?"

"You'll see." He followed me down the hall toward the crowd.

"It won't involve police or ambulances, will it?"

"Gosh, I hope not, but you never know with this family."

We took our places at the table. Grandma Betty had added a table to the end to accommodate our whole family and draped both with sky blue tablecloths. The center bore a vase with bright white daisies, cut low, so we could all still see each other. Her red chicken dining ware stood out well against the pale background. She laid out two piping hot platters of seafood lasagna, Beverly's bread, red and white wine, and enough salad to please a few families of rabbits.

Clark kick-started conversation. "So, Teague, did the police locate Darryl's money?"

Sam shook his head. "The money's a rumor. Whatever they profited, they spent right away, mostly on expensive collectible dolls and computer equipment."

"Well, if I've learned anything about Darryl Chambers," I said, giving Raina a nod, "it's that he was not only very intelligent but also resourceful. If there's a stash, I'm sure he put it somewhere clever. I bet it's got a lock to it."

Rachel nudged her sister, but nothing came out of Raina's mouth. Instead, Raina fiddled with the pendant of her necklace.

"There ain't no money," Candy said. I cringed at the double negative, and at the sound of her voice, too. "Can't believe what a boy like that said 'bout anythin'."

My eyes narrowed at her. "Darryl was actually a good person with a lot of potential. He would've joined the army, and he worked hard for Damon—"

"Sure did. Best worker I had. Could fix anything."

"He was turning his life around," I went on. "He had plans for the future, good ones."

I paused to let someone (Raina) chime in, but there was silence.

Clara smirked. "You sound like a commercial for 'em, Delilah. I'm sure if he were still alive, you woulda hired 'em and let 'em live on your roof, too."

Charlotte stifled a giggle. "How are things workin' out with ol' Henry?"

"He's running the store right now. He's wonderful." I didn't mention that he'd been laundering his underclothes in the bathroom sink and hanging them to dry across my office, or the far-out gaze that sometimes drifted over his face that I literally had to snap him out of. I considered these things mere eccentricities. "My employee is better than some of yours, Clara."

Candy didn't look up from her meal.

"How've sales been, Delilah?" Clara asked.

I gave her a one-shouldered shrug. "Fine."

"Oh, come now. Be honest. We're family. I hoped that after the horrid ordeal you'd been through, you'd at least have a decent opening week, if only to give you a much-needed ego boost."

"How generous of you. I don't need sales to make me feel good."

Clara grinned like a devious banshee. "So defensive, Delilah, dear! The whole town knows you're tankin'. But you get our votes for diligence and determination, that's for sure. You're like the little engine that could, chugging up the hill—*I think I can, I think I can.*"

She and Charlotte laughed. Sam's hand squeezed my knee, telling me to be calm. I ignored it.

I took a sharp breath. "I'm sure you didn't read the book, but that train makes it."

"That's why it's called fiction."

"You are such a—" Sam covered up my word by clearing his throat. Cursing in front of my grandparents wasn't a bright idea, if I could help it. "You're right, Clara. The bookstore might not make it. But at least I can take some pleasure in the fact that you won't get it. Right?"

Clara shook her pretty head, smiling. "Never know what might happen. I may not buy it from Uncle Joe right now, but he'll calm down and see reason. It ain't over yet, sweetheart."

"Holy crap, I love this family." Clark pulled his notebook out of his pocket.

"You may hate me for taking over Beach Read, but you'll see. My presence hasn't hurt as much as it's helped. You're just too blind to see it. Once the secrets—"

"Secrets?" Clark perked up. "What secrets?"

I gave Raina another look, but she stayed quiet. "Mavis Chambers targeted me because she thought Darryl and I were together. She was wrong, but only by a few branches of the family tree."

"Holy shit!" Clark said, earning a scowl from Grandma Betty, which he ignored. "All you other gals are too old, except—"

"Raina, pull the Band-Aid," Rachel said.

Raina stood up, nearly knocking her chair back behind her.

"I'm pregnant!" she yelled. Then, as she dashed out of the room, "And nauseous!"

The announcing-then-running strategy was a smart one. Her coy smile gone, Clara jumped up and followed. The rest of the table sat paralyzed, staring at me.

"You know," Clark said after too many seconds of tense silence, "if Chambers amassed a treasure—other than the one he's left with Raina, of course—and he couldn't keep it at home and it isn't in a bank, there's only one place it could be."

All eyes turned to him, mouths hanging open.

Clark smirked. "Perhaps Chambers didn't just come back that night to install a light."

I shifted in my chair and huffed. "Don't say it and don't you dare print it."

Clark laughed. "Beach Read: Books, Gifts and *More*. Right?"

THANKS FOR READING
Sea-Devil: A Delilah Duffy Mystery.

If you've enjoyed Delilah's adventures, please leave a review!
Your feedback matters to me & anyone looking for a good mystery.
Thank you!

To learn more about me & my books, visit www.jessicasherry.com
& check out my blog, Coffeebrained, for writing ideas, motivation,
& positivity. Grab a cup of coffee first—it's better for everyone
that way. Tea is also acceptable.

Thanks for supporting me & my writing dreams.

Murder, mayhem, sassy relatives…

For a teaser & sample chapter of Book Two, Luna-Sea, stick
around. Delilah's mystery series continues on the next page.

Happy Beach Reading!

Luna-Sea: A Delilah Duffy Mystery
Book Two

Chapter One

TURTLES & SHARKS

MY FEET TEETERED on the wooden planks of the boardwalk overlooking the great Atlantic, dipping into the sand like toes into cold water. My heart pumped wildly, stomach churned like the waves. Willie, my golden retriever, sat beside me, waiting. Daylight hung on stubbornly, spewing its last hues across the mighty ocean, warming my skin and giving everything an orange glow. It was all so typical of a Carolina beach—gorgeous, peaceful, breathtaking. Still, I couldn't move any closer.

Willie whined, as if saying, *"Come on, Delilah. You can do it. It's only the beach."*

In my defense, Willie hadn't been a firsthand witness to *all* my recent traumas. After our move to Tipee Island at the end of June, I'd been embattled in a fight to save my business—my late-great-aunt's bookstore—solve a murder, and stay alive, while keeping the past where it belonged, far behind me. Meanwhile, a mob of nosey-nelly "concerned" citizens and store owners came after me with torches and pitchforks, convinced the earth had opened up, and hell had coughed me out to ruin their perfect little town. Well, I'm kidding about the pitchforks, but the we-don't-want-you-here climate had felt just as tangible. I'd muddled through, but only barely.

A month had passed since the grand re-opening of Beach Read Books, Gifts, and More, and not much had changed. I was still fighting to save my business while battling the demons stirred to life in all the chaos.

Every sunset is a fingerprint. My eyes danced across the seascape and I breathed in the salty air. I came here for this—beauty, everywhere you look—and now, I could no longer enjoy it. Or let Willie enjoy it, either.

On the pier above us, the usual fishermen had taken up their posts. On the boardwalk, Valerie Kent, our resident triathlete, blew by on her ten-speed. Ahead, on the beach, Nathan Hainey and his club circled the beach like vultures, holding out their metal detectors. Near Jubilee Park, I spied Ira Keane, easel up and paintbrush in hand.

Normal islanders doing normal island things, and me wondering if I'll ever be a normal islander. Unable to take another step, normalcy seemed unlikely.

The Atlantic Ocean is the world's second largest. It's named for Atlas, the Titan from Greek mythology. The name Atlas means to endure. Most people believe that Atlas, after going against the Olympians in their epic battle and losing, was forced to hold up the earth for eternity. Actually, his punishment was to hold up the heavens. Judging from the view before me, Atlas grew tired. The heavens spilled out all around.

Willie pulled on the leash, beckoning me to come out and play. He moved into the sand and jumped around. I smiled, taking a step toward him. My palms sweat while the rest of me erupted with sharp chills. My heart thudded. Was that a palpitation? I'm too young for those, right? The water, though alight with soft orange strands, darkened before my eyes. The ocean wind kicked up and blustered through my long, brown hair.

The last time I'd touched the beach was when my almost-lifeless body washed up on its shore. The weight of my near-death bore down on my shoulders. I knew how Atlas felt.

I pulled back, giving Willie's leash a gentle tug. "Sorry, Willie. Maybe next time."

Weeks ago, I'd survived a night in the ocean. *My mistake was not going further out to sea, you bitch!* Mavis Chambers' wicked voice echoed in my ears. Her attempt to murder me by sea wasn't the first time I'd almost died by drowning. When I was six, I fell into a friend's tarp-covered swimming pool. The blue tarp suctioned to my body like being swallowed by a snake. My friend's father pulled me out and brought me back to life. Strangely, my first experience had saved me from the second. My fear of water had forced my father's insistence that I learn to swim—lessons that saved my life many years later.

Here, standing on the edge of the beach, my memories waved over my reality. My eyes burned. My throat tightened. My breaths became shallow. Panic pulled me back into those dark places, like I'd never left.

Willie whimpered as we turned away from the sea.

We crossed Atlantic Avenue and headed up Starfish Drive. Middle August meant the tourist trade—the bread and butter of the island community—was drying up. Empty parking spaces, a speckled beach, a lightly occupied Tipee Island Fishing Pier—these were all testaments to the near end of a difficult summer. Still, while most businesses lavished in long sales receipts and large bank balances, I'd nothing to show for the summer, except survival. Nothing at all.

Beach Read Books, Gifts, and More was a dismal failure.

I picked up my pace. I slipped passed Top to Bottom: A Hat

and Shoe Boutique, my aunts' store next door, and jumped at the sight of Great Uncle Joe standing in Beach Read's doorway. His black Hummer loomed crookedly in the parking spot at the front door, and Great Uncle Joe's expression was as dark and overwhelming as his vehicle.

Great Uncle Joe owns Beach Read, along with many businesses up and down the East Coast. Several months ago, when I had trouble at my last job, he offered me the chance to reopen the store. *See if you can do somethin' with it*, he'd told me, as if the store was a child he'd gotten frustrated with and ignored. Truth is, he hadn't touched the place in over ten years. Beach Read had been Great Aunt Laura's dream, closing only because she got sick. Beach Read and Laura Duffy died together, and my resurrection of the business had been zombie-like. It's not nearly the same as it was.

Great Uncle Joe had dished out a good deal of money for the store's revival, and he still waited for a return on his investment. While consoling myself with the fact that he had a lot of money to dish out, here, there, and anywhere he pleased, I felt guilty that it'd been nothing but a money pit for nearly three months with no signs of recovery.

"Let's talk." He opened up the passenger door of the Hummer. He nodded toward the window of Top to Bottom, where Aunts Clara and Charlotte eyeballed us. Little would interest Clara Duffy-Saintly more than eavesdropping on a conversation between Uncle Joe and me. She'd probably give up her own children to get her hands on the property. I huffed. Willie jumped into the truck with zero coaxing, giving Uncle Joe a belly laugh.

As I waited for Uncle Joe to drive off, I noticed that Atlas had resumed his duties. The heavens now properly contained left only a black sky, dotted intermittently with stars and a nearly full moon.

"What's this all about?" Nervous stomach acids popped as the engine roared.

"Time to talk 'bout turnin' turtle."

When the people of Tipee speak, I often say, "Huh?" Most locals, like my Duffy family, have a buttery, slow Southern accent, sometimes put on thick when they're frazzled or excited. Others, the native islanders who can trace their family lines back to the first settlers, speak something I call Backwoods British, a dialect that would make Eliza Doolittle—pre-Professor Higgins—sound like the Queen of England.

I don't have an accent. Between my father's Southern twang and my mother's curt and crisp Maryland pronunciation, I inherited what I call Normal American English. Mamma Rose predicted I'd be a TV news reporter for that reason. Aunt Clara always brushed off this idea, saying I was "too pale and freckly for TV."

They often pair Southern dialects with colorful clichés and idioms; these I'm learning as I go. "Turn turtle" is a nautical term meaning *to capsize*; when a turtle turns over, it's left helpless. Great Uncle Joe was telling me to give up.

He cruised down Starfish and met up with Atlantic Avenue, stopping for pedestrians out for evening strolls or on their way to dinner.

"You promised I'd have through October," I said.

Great Uncle Joe adjusted his bucket hat back, so the brim wouldn't darken his eyes. "I keep my promises, Bean."

"Then why—"

"Delilah, listen here. When it comes to Beach Read, you've been thinkin' with your heart, not your head. It's a special place, no doubt. But, you gotta look at the numbers and realize what's as plain as the nose on your face. You can't make a real life outta this. You can't, honey. You'd never make enough, even if all was right in the world and everythin' was goin' your way—which it ain't."

Tears crested my eyes, running tracks through my sweat. A flush of embarrassment rushed over me—crying in Great Uncle Joe's Hummer like a child with a boo-boo. I stared out the passenger side window.

He cruised down Coral Avenue, circling the block like a stalker. "I know all about your late car payment, and your apartment with no TV, how you've been givin' every extra dollar you've got to your buddy, Henry, and tuckin' hospital bills into a shoe box don't make 'em vanish, Bean."

I shook my head. Great Uncle Joe had asked Grandma Betty to help with the books. I should've known that included snooping. I pictured her rummaging through the office, around the counter, finding my overdue bills and notices. Anger mixed with my embarrassment.

"We may not like what numbers say, but they don't lie, Bean." Uncle Joe breathed out heavily. "Don't sink any more of your money into this. There's a time to press on and there's a time to turn turtle. Your turn's way overdue."

I sucked in my tears and shook my head. "I have until the end of October."

"Yep. It's your decision, Bean. I'm only offerin' my advice. But there's somethin' else."

"What?"

"Ya see, my old friend Baylor came callin' with a bottle of Wild Turkey yammerin' about this great new organization here in Tipee. I got lawyers on speed dial, but since it was Baylor, well, I just signed up for it."

"For what?"

"It's called TIBA. The Tipee Island Business Association. You know how ritzy communities got them homeowners associations?"

I nodded, though I'd never been a part of one.

"Well, this is kinda like that 'cept for businesses. It's all about makin' sure the businesses meet standards."

"I don't understand. What's this got to do with me?"

"Well, Beach Read now falls under the leadership of TIBA," he said, "and the leadership of TIBA is—"

"Clara." I sighed.

"Clara."

My temples throbbed. I put the window down, letting the warm breezes hit my face. The panic I'd felt earlier near the water rose again.

Joe cleared his throat. "Not sure what that'll mean yet, but she's up to somethin' considerin' she used my good friend Baylor and the devil's nectar to pry that signature outta me."

He parked in front of Beach Read, crooked again, and waited for Willie and me to get out. I couldn't move right away. Maybe I hoped he'd give me some kind of encouragement, like Great Aunt Laura would've done.

Instead, he scratched his head. "I hear you're goin' to that party at The Peacock Inn tomorrow night."

I'd forgotten all about the party my cousin Rachel had suckered me into. "Right. I'm Rachel's wingman."

Great Uncle Joe laughed. "It'll be good for ya to get out, have some fun. But let me tell you what I tell anyone 'bout to jump in the deep. Watch out for sharks." He chuckled heartily.

I watched him drive away, my unease growing. Sharks? What did he mean? It was just a party, right?

Clara waved from her store window, smiling deviously—a stark reminder that nothing around here was as it seemed.

Strange things are happening at Beach Read Books, and not just within the pages.

THE DOORS TO Delilah Duffy's seaside bookstore are open, but will they stay that way? Still fighting to save her business and recover from her most recent crime-solving adventures, Delilah's new start might have a quick end. A fancy party at the luxurious Peacock Inn should be a pleasant distraction. When the party takes an eerie turn, this amateur detective discovers another mystery - or so she thinks. No one believes her. With her nightmares, anxiety, and panic intensifying, she's not sure, either. She searches for answers, determined to find the truth. With her island life at risk, is she becoming a lunatic or facing one?

Want to read more? Check out

Luna-Sea: A Delilah Duffy Mystery Book Two